Behind the Wire

Andrea Myers

Good Morning Publishing

To Grandpa:
You believed I could do it, so I did.

To Tori and Connor:
You are my greatest accomplishment, joy, and reason for everything that I do.
My favorite title, above all else, is Mom.

Chapter One

Lincoln, Nebraska

September 1941

Where Have All the Men Gone? — Margaret Murphy, the
Daily Nebraskan

*Our welcome back parties should be joyous occasions. In-
stead, they're a continuous series of "Where is he?" So many
of our brothers in Scarlet and Cream have been drafted for a
war we aren't even fighting. Enrollment for the University has
dropped for the first time since 1935. Uncle Sam's demands have
taken a toll. Boys that have not been called into service have
taken the jobs of men who have been drafted and are reluctant
to leave those jobs for a semester at college that may be cut short
by deployment.*

*How many do you know that didn't come back last week?
How many of them can we not live without? Not because they
look good on our arms. But because they are to stand beside us
as we all learn to be engineers, writers, and economists.*

*This situation is dire. We do not deny that national security
is important. However, one must ask. Is learning to shoot guns
and build bombs more important than learning architecture*

to design buildings, more important than learning medicine to become a doctor, or more important than learning history to help understand and shape the world's politics and laws? We do not believe so. This war, if there is to be one, will be a war of wits where the best strategic mind wins. Modern warfare will require nerves of steel - not brute physical strength - and the more educated we can keep our men (and women), the better off we will be as a society.

The consequence of warfare is greater than just not enough men at our dances. We stand to lose an entire generation of men to battle. We, as the women of Nebraska University, will be called upon to help rebuild the post-war world. We must encourage our brothers to stay in school until the last futile moment, always hoping that this war doesn't come to fruition.

We must also fight against the social pressure to couple up and settle down with those that are heading off into the service. The atmosphere of war smells of a romance that is highly intoxicating. Let us not drink from the carafe that threatens to destroy our generation.

It was a short piece but would be a controversial one. Most of her classmates were ignorant by choice to the probability of war. The paper, which generally focused on sports and socializing, didn't want the mood to be anything less than jovial. *"We're a lighthearted rag where you can read about the best parties and the who's who of NU."*

Things were changing in the fall of 1941. Last year's editor had been called to service and was in Fort Sill doing daily training exercises. Many other writers had suffered the same fate. Left behind was a staff of mostly women. There was dissension in the newsroom. They'd fought on whether to even mention the disappearance of the men. Those remaining behind didn't want the reminder of their possible untimely demise; the women with sweethearts in the service didn't want to be reminded either; the journalism students fought for the integrity to tell the story as it was really happening.

In the end, Margaret's faction won the fight, and would be writing weekly columns about the war effort and how it was affecting university life.

Margaret Murphy fought for the staff writer position of the *Daily Nebraskan*, the student newspaper for Nebraska University, and she was proud that, as a sophomore, she had multiple bylines in the first edition of the new school year.

She had come back to her second year at university determined to not fall prey to the push from her mother to focus on finding someone to marry. She'd even called off seeing her steady high school boyfriend, Bob Hale, just to spite her mother. It seemed that the only column her mother cared about in the paper was the "Shucks" column on the society page that chronicled the coupling-up frenzy on campus. To keep her mother on her toes, she planned to be listed with a different date at any notable event. This week's column would feature the following:

"No longer going steady are Pi Phi Margaret Murphy and Alpha Sig Bob Hale. She has decided her heart is elsewhere. Could it be that it went to the game yesterday? She does have an eye for those football players."

Knowing that line would cause her mother distress she'd fed it, verbatim, to the editor.

She tucked the paper under her arm as she set off across campus to meet up with her childhood best friends, June and Bea, for their shared economics class.

Chapter Two

"**D**o you really believe that war is inevitable?" Bea was the sensitive one of the trio. Always had been.

Margaret and June answered simultaneously, Margaret in the affirmative and June in the negative.

"Well, we're no help at all, are we?" June was the jokester of the group, and her default response was to make sure that Bea was never sad. She was often in opposition with Margaret. They were on the debate squad throughout high school and could have a raucous take-down of each other's opinions for an hour straight then lock arms and be the closest of friends the next moment.

Margaret was grateful for these two women. They'd been friends since the early days of walking to elementary school together, the close geography of their houses within a four-block radius cementing their friendship. An only child, Margaret was thankful that she saw her friends as siblings. The three shared everything, including a room at the Pi Phi house.

Today was Margaret's nineteenth birthday, and they were prepping to go to a "Back to School" dance that evening. Margaret reached over and grabbed Bea's hairbrush. Bea's hair, long, blonde and with just a touch of a wave was always very easily pulled together.

"In my opinion, we are likely destined for war. It seems like there is no way for Roosevelt to save face if we don't join in with Britain. Germany is tearing through Europe. Our limitations on Hitler after the last war were too weak."

Margaret was mostly parroting the thoughts of her father. Frederick Murphy was the president of the bank in Gering and he enjoyed talking to Margaret about news and politics. He would make a point to call her weekly from the bank away from the constant supervision, and interjections from, her mother.

"There's no threat of conflict on our soil. Didn't we learn our lesson in the last war when Wilson sent over a hundred thousand Americans to their death?"

June was parroting the thoughts of her mother. Her father was a veteran of The Great War and had died when she was quite young. She reached her hand out for the brush and Margaret passed it down even though she hadn't fully tamed her thick hair that couldn't quite decide between dusty brown and auburn depending on the light.

Bea shot each of them a glare in the mirror.

"Oh, I should have known better than to kick you two off. This is not a good birthday conversation. How about we change the subject? Who is picking you up this evening? I know I'm going with Ted. I've always gone with Ted. I suppose I'll always go with Ted now that we're getting married."

"Do I hear some hesitation in your voice?" June teased. "You know, we could just go to these things without men."

June was always quick to analyze other people's relationships though she wasn't all that interested in dating and had never had a long-term relationship herself. She was watching herself in the mirror and threw the hairbrush down, giving up on doing much of anything.

"No. No hesitation," Bea said. "I just live vicariously through you girls."

"I'm going with my old prom date, 'Stand-by Andrew'." June was more focused on school than dances.

"I'm going with Joe Rebus," Margaret said. "I figure going with an older football player is the best way to get my name in the 'Shucks' column to appease Rebecca."

Rebecca was Margaret's very overbearing mother and Margaret always referred to her by her first name when telling stories.

"Now Margaret," June took on the affected voice that Rebecca used when scolding her daughter. "You do know that Joseph Rebus is a bit of a playboy. One might worry about what he would do to your reputation."

Margaret joined in on the fun, "Rebecca, darling, it's all for show. Joe is just a stand-in this week to keep you on your toes."

The girls all laughed. Rebecca was always an easy target for humor even though they were all, Margaret included, a little bit scared of her.

Chapter Three

Coeds in their new sweater sets and boys in their suit pants filled the Union Ballroom. Every song sounded like Glenn Miller had gone just a little bit country western, and what the band lacked in talent, they made up for in volume. Margaret hoped that her smile was genuine enough to make her date think she was having a good time. It was always easier if he, whoever he was, thought she was enjoying herself.

"Are you ready for the game tomorrow?" Margaret shouted over the screeching music.

It was homecoming weekend, and almost everyone from her sorority was expected to be on the arm of one of the starting players. Joe was handsome as he was dumb, she knew they'd look good in photos but have nothing to talk about. It would serve to provide fodder for next week's 'Shucks' column.

"Want to go somewhere quieter?" Joe asked in response, shaking a pack of cigarettes.

"Sure, let me just grab June."

June's date had abandoned her for his buddies from high school the moment they walked in the door and Margaret could see that her friend was standing alone looking quite annoyed at the whole experience. Their best friend, Bea, was treating every song with her fiancé as a slow dance and was not planning on spending any time with her girlfriends that night.

Joe put his hand at the small of Margaret's back and instead steered her towards the door.

"We can come right back and get her. Let's get some air."

As one of the starting players for the football team, Joe was a good foot taller than Margaret. Her cousin, Sam, was the quarterback and Joe was one of his wide receivers. It seemed harmless to go outside for a smoke.

She let him light her cigarette as they sat on a bench outside the student union.

"Do you think we're going to war?"

Margaret realized this was the same question she'd been asking everyone these last few weeks. It gave her an idea for a column.

"War, war, war. All everybody wants to talk about is war. The guys on the team are talking about enlisting which would really screw up our season. Even your do-gooder cousin thinks it's the right thing to do." He continued his tirade while Margaret took refuge in her imagination.

It was a crisp autumn night and the smell of the turning leaves mixed with cigarette smoke made her miss home with the big front porch overlooking all their towering cottonwood trees. She missed the scent of her dad's cigars. She'd rather talk about anything with June than be here for one minute longer. She was getting ready to tell Joe she wanted to go back inside when he leaned over and kissed her. The kiss was an impatient attack and was not one that Margaret expected. Or wanted.

"Hey now," Margaret pushed him back.

"Hey now, yourself," Joe replied, and began pawing at her sweater. His grinning face showed that he was incapable of understanding that she did not consider his kisses a compliment.

"Joe, no, I'm not..."

Margaret attempted to push him away. She couldn't yell while his mouth was suctioned over hers. Her fists were pointless as she tried to escape his grasp. She was no prude but preferred to be in control of the good night kissing.

Suddenly, Joe's face was no longer suffocating her. Instead, it was being pummeled into the concrete by her cousin, Sam.

"Get your hands off of her."

"Hey man, we were just getting some air," Joe said, trying to push himself up from the ground. "It's all in good fun, right?"

"Fun?"

Margaret took one look at Joe's face, squared up her high-heeled foot, and kicked him in the nose.

"C'mon Sam, let's get June and get out of here."

"Are you sure you're okay?" Sam asked. "I promised your parents I wouldn't let anything happen to you, yet here you are with Rebus of all people!"

"Don't tell my folks!"

"I won't, but Megs," his pet name for her since she was born, "You can't be trusting cads like that. Girls who are seen with him get a reputation."

Margaret stopped walking and whipped around to face Sam. "How is that even fair? Why is it that women get the reputation for the actions of idiot boys?"

"Those idiot boys are twice your size, little cousin, and it's hard to stop them once they get their mind set on..." Sam hesitated. "Well, you know."

"Sam, we don't need to talk about any of that. I can take care of myself. You saw that kick, right?"

Margaret tried to turn the conversation into a more light-hearted tone.

"Maybe I could help you kick those extra points tomorrow in the game."

Sam was as kind as he was overprotective. He was two years her senior and was the reason her parents acquiesced to her going to Lincoln in the first place. They'd grown up across the street from each other, in houses that their grandfather had built for their fathers. He was her constant chaperone from the first day she walked to kindergarten under his watchful eye. They were family first, and friends second. She knew his loyalty was to her parents to protect her, and she needed him to not make a bigger deal out of this than it was.

"Fine, you can take care of yourself. It sure didn't look like that to me." She'd hurt his feelings. Margaret immediately went back into their sibling-like scuffle mode.

"Oh please, don't tell me that I need to lump you in with the Men of the Fragile Ego Fraternity, the Pi Kappa Alpha Males. You, of all people, should know that I'm completely capable of doing what I want."

"Whatever you say, Margaret."

He'd stopped walking with her. Their Scotch-Irish tempers were flaring.

She grabbed the handle to the ballroom and stormed inside to grab June, leaving Sam outside on the sidewalk.

June was dancing with someone, so Margaret stood on the sideline seething and planning her next column. She turned quickly when someone tapped her shoulder, fully expecting to have words with Sam, or Joe, or whatever unsuspecting victim would dare to bother her in the middle of her mental gymnastics.

"Can I help you?"

"Bob Hale's the name, and dancing with pretty ladies is my game."

Though she'd just ended it with Bob, it was quite amicable. They simply had both decided that there were so many fish in the sea in Lincoln, and they weren't ready to settle down. At least that was what they chose to tell their friends. They were on friendly terms, but tonight was not the night for banter.

"Bob, please leave me alone. I'm not in the mood."

"But wouldn't you like to take a quick spin across the dance floor? We always did make a good dance team."

"What I would like is to see you break your neck as you walk away." Her temper, always at the surface, fueled her sharp tongue and was ready for Bob's retort. Their breakup had obviously not ended amicably enough to quash their temperamental responses to each other.

There was a break in the music, and June rushed over from dancing, providing a welcome distraction as she asked, "So, is it old home week? Go Bulldogs!" June could see that the two of them were squaring off for a battle.

"Bob, I simply must steal Margaret away. Girl stuff and all, wonderful to see you."

They turned and walked away, leaving Bob staring after them.

Leaving the dance, they walked across campus, silently smoking their cigarettes, and enjoying the quiet breeze through the oak trees that were just starting to change colors. June turned to Margaret.

"Okay, out with it. I've known you too long to know that you're not just mad about Bob being annoying. Bob has been annoying since we were in kindergarten, and he will be annoying until the day he dies."

"Do you really think we'll go to war?" Margaret knew June wasn't going to let her off the hook that easily but she'd try anyway.

"Masterful deflection. What's really going on?"

"No, it's all part of it," Margaret replied. "We're all on edge. There are too many unknowns. We cannot focus on what's right in front of us. We're not kind, at least I know I'm not, to the people around us. This war is turning us into the worst version of ourselves."

"Did something happen with Joe?" June was glad that Margaret was walking home safely with her instead of that jerk.

"Let's talk about something else."

Margaret was not a warm and fuzzy person, nor could she be pushed to share her feelings. If she needed to hide her emotions in discussions of the war, so be it. Luckily, June knew when to let it go.

"Alright, the war it is then!" June laughed.

They continued through campus to the sorority house enjoying the camaraderie that only a lifelong friendship can provide. Talking of everything and nothing provided a soothing balm to the events of the evening.

Temper Tantrums — Margaret Murphy, the Daily Nebraskan

Please indulge this writer as there's no real news from the potential war front, but the war on campus demands addressing. If women are known to be the fairer, gentler, weaker sex, then can someone please tell this writer why the temper tantrums of boys are still tolerated long into (what should be) manhood? Without exception, the boys that are left on campus today seem to be acting out. Is it because most of the strong fellows have taken their leave? Is there no motivation to be better humans?

The petulant child stamps his foot when he doesn't get his way and is promptly scolded by his mother. The petulant underclassman stamps his foot, and it seems no one is there to set him straight. The boys that have been left behind are using the leverage of a possible war to manipulate and cajole women into acting against their will. The inability of these boys to accept a 'no' answer to any of their questions or whims is maddening. Love does not happen as a result of control. It's not right that women's reputations are on the line for the behavior of these weak men.

Boys, would you like some advice on how to get a date on Saturday nights? Remember that the women who sit next to you in class and cheer for you on the football field are your equals. We have thoughts and opinions that would be of interest to talk about at one of those many social events that the university is throwing to distract us all from world affairs. We are more than just someone to grope at a drive-in or a dance. Let's celebrate homecoming weekend with some more respect and maturity.

As it is, this writer is fine, thanks to the fact that she has a mean right kick. We'll teach you what happens when you stamp your feet. Right ladies?

When the phone rang at the Pi Phi house early in the afternoon Margaret should have looked at the time. It was shortly after three o'clock which meant that mail had just been delivered to her parents with a copy of the paper and her mother had taken five minutes to read last week's column.

"Margaret, the phone is for you!" Darla shouted from her perch during the house receptionist shift. Margaret, assuming it was a date for the evening or her editor with some questions about her next column, ran down the stairs.

"Margaret Murphy speaking."

"Well, at least you remember how to properly answer a phone."

"Hello, Mother. I see you read the paper. Everything is fine."

"I think it's time for you to come home. Obviously, it's not safe for you there. You're doing nothing but ruining your father's reputation with this writing and carrying on. We're coming out this weekend on the train to discuss this in person."

She had known this column would upset her very conservative mother. She also knew it would be pointless to argue with her on the phone, so she let the diatribe continue with no response except to interject "Okay, Mother" and "You're probably right, Mother" into the conversation at appropriate intervals. It would be easier to convince her father to see her point of view in person after all, so she almost welcomed the visit.

Chapter Four

Margaret joined many of her classmates in dutifully waiting at the train platform for their parents to visit. Rebecca Murphy was always volatile, and Margaret wasn't sure if she'd come off the train swinging or if it would take a while for her to cook up and serve her disdain for her daughter. Margaret was hopeful that her father would help soften the mood with his humor.

Her mother had telegraphed to inform her that her father had called for a car service to bring her to the platform, and she was expected to be dressed and ready for dinner at the Cornhusker that evening. Frederick worked to make sure his only child didn't suffer too greatly at the hands of her mother so she held out hope that the evening wouldn't be too terrible. As the bank president, he hardly had time for dinner at home let alone a train ride across the state.

The train pulled into the station. Margaret's anxiety heightened. She'd worn her most conservative outfit, made sure her hair and makeup were done just so, and stood ramrod straight. Her mother might be ready to criticize her, but it wouldn't be because of her appearance. She'd learned to remove the ammunition from the crazy person's reach so she could not reload her weapon as easily.

If she dared to complain to any of her fellow classmates about the circumstances she knew they would take one look at the polished car with a driver standing by, and the outfit that was far too formal for a train station, and consider her a spoiled rich girl. Which she was. Somehow that frustrated her even more, though she knew all of these nerves were just because of the visit.

Rebecca Murphy smiled as she descended the steps from the train. This was going to be worse than Margaret anticipated.

"Maggie, honey, I have someone you just need to meet!"

Margaret had been so focused on her mother's uncharacteristic facial expression she'd neglected to see the woman her mother had been talking to as they disembarked. Struggling to contain her surprise at the Maggie moniker, she reached out her hand.

"Hello, I'm Margaret."

The slight woman reached out her gloved hand. "Violet Davey. It's such a pleasure to meet you, Margaret. Your mother has been raving about you all the way from North Platte."

Raving was a word Margaret used to describe her mother often—stark raving mad, a raving lunatic—but never with a positive spin. Margaret knew what was expected of her in situations like this, due to the extensive etiquette training as a child, so this type of forced politeness came as second nature.

"It's very nice to meet you. I hope your travels were pleasant."

"Mrs. Davey has just been traveling back from visiting her sister in North Platte, and we were lucky enough to share a table in the dining car. Her son is a senior here at the University. Do you know Thomas Davey?"

So that was it. It had taken mere seconds for her mother to reveal her intentions. She'd found the mother of an eligible bachelor. If Margaret wouldn't do it on her own, her mother would do it for her. The Davey name was familiar, but she couldn't place it.

"What is he studying?" Margaret asked, knowing that each class had a few thousand students and, since he was older, it was unlikely they'd have connected.

"He's wrapping up his final year as pre-med. He'll be taking over the pharmacy."

The Davey sounded familiar because it was the name of the drugstore in the lobby of the Cornhusker Hotel. The hotel's brochure boasted that they "were the only five-star hotel between the Mississippi and the Mountains." It was where her parents stayed when they came to visit and the pharmacy housed a candy shop Margaret visited frequently when she came back east as a child.

Not only had her mother sought out a mother of a single, college-age man, but she'd also managed to find someone that came from money. The Murphy family wasn't wealthy compared to Henry Ford, but her father's connections in the banking world helped them survive the depression, and compared to many of their western Nebraska neighbors, they were well off. The Davey family had connections to old ranching money and had a string of drug stores throughout the Midwest.

"I'm so sorry, his name seems very familiar, but I don't believe we've had a chance to meet. I'm in the journalism school, so we don't see a lot of the pre-med students."

"Journalism is a hobby of Maggie's. Always has her nose in a book or is banging away on her typewriter." Rebecca said. "She's actually studying business so that she can help her father at the bank."

At the mention of her father, Margaret looked around to see where Frederick was and why he hadn't joined them on the platform.

"Oh, your father won't be coming dear. He's much too busy at work to make it and I encouraged him to stay home. It will just be you and I for dinner. Violet, would you care to join us? Maybe we could introduce these brilliant children of ours?"

Checkmate, Rebecca. Margaret could always manipulate Frederick and he always took Margaret's side. Much easier if he was out of the picture.

"That would be lovely," Violet replied. "Let's plan for seven o'clock at the Terrace. It was a pleasure to meet you both."

"It was a pleasure to meet you as well Mrs. Davey, I look forward to this evening."

Margaret hoped only enthusiasm came through from her feigned response.

"Oh, call me Vi, sweetie."

At that, a porter came over with her bags and Margaret was sure Violet gave a wink as she turned to walk away. Rebecca's motives were not well hidden, and it was entertaining to everyone except Margaret.

"That was clever, Mother."

"Oh, hush with your smart mouth. You're lucky I didn't just put you back on the train tonight and send you home."

The porter who had been standing silently behind them with Rebecca's suitcase turned and led them to the waiting car.

"Is that what you're planning on wearing this evening?" Rebecca looked Margaret up and down, examining her appearance for any missteps. "I suppose that will do, though I'm sure you have more flattering things in your wardrobe for your figure."

"Let's just go, Mother. It will be fine, you'll get to hold court soon enough, let's not exhaust our conversation now."

Margaret slid into the back seat of the car and slammed the door.

"You will not be calling her Vi."

Her mother slammed her own door in response.

Margaret and Rebecca arrived at the Terrace Restaurant in the lobby of the Cornhusker Hotel promptly at seven. Rebecca just happened to have another outfit for Margaret with her on the train. It was as if her mother's brain had nothing to do but conjure up imaginary scenarios for her daughter and, no matter the situation knew that her daughter wouldn't be appropriately outfitted. If love could be shown through wardrobe options then Margaret was a well-loved child.

"Rebecca and Margaret Murphy. We are meeting Mrs. Violet Davey," Rebecca said to the maître d'. She took any opportunity to name-drop.

"Right this way," he replied, leading the way through a dining room that was part first-class train car, part Old-West saloon. With plush carpeting, rich leather, and amber lights encased in frosted glass; it was definitely the nicest restaurant in the state. Back home they only had the country club and The Gaslight Lounge. Margaret liked to infuriate her mother by reminding her that they were small-town upper class, not big-city upper class. As they went further into the restaurant Margaret's eyes adjusted to the dim light and made out Mrs. Davey—Vi—who rose and waved as they approached.

Next to her stood a tall boy, on the cusp of having the broad shoulders of manhood, with close-cropped blond hair and dark brown eyes. He was very nearly handsome, though his eyes seemed a little too big for his face, and you could tell that his hair would be unruly if it grew even the slightest bit. He reached his hand out to her mother first.

"Good evening Mrs. Murphy. I'm Thomas. Thank you so much for keeping my mother company on the train. I do so wish I could have met you at the station, but I was volunteering at the student medical center and could not get away." Thomas knew how to play the game, nearly as well as Margaret. Make the mother feel like the center of attention.

"And you must be Maggie?"

"Margaret."

Thomas chuckled. "I actually already know who you are. You're the little spitfire that has all the girls up in arms about the future. Your columns are a riot. It is such a pleasure to meet an esteemed writer such as yourself." He grinned down at her as he reached out his hand.

Margaret wanted to turn and leave. Her columns were not a riot. She was not here to amuse people like Thomas Davey. She was prepared to launch into one of her tirades when she noticed her mother's firm expression. If she wanted to stay at school and not get back on the train with her mother tomorrow, she needed to play a different game.

"I'm so glad you enjoy them. They're just a little hobby of mine." Turning on the charm, Margaret lowered her voice, turned her eyes up to meet his, and grinned so that her dimple showed. The old standby worked again as Thomas came around the table to pull back the chair for her mother and herself, never once taking his eyes off her.

Chapter Five

Weeks passed, and it was clear her mother's plan had both backfired and been executed to perfection. Margaret stayed at school and distracted her mother with Thomas as a steady beau. Dinner with the mothers resulted in numerous walks to the soda shop and a standing date to all the fraternity functions. Soon, Thomas was an ever-present person sitting on the porch of the Pi Phi house and could be heard crooning love songs as he approached her on campus. Thomas had fallen hard. Margaret had merely stumbled into a convenient situation.

It seemed that he was always there; when Margaret left the newspaper office, when she stepped out of class, when she went to a University Women's meeting with June and Bea.

"Can't you just have one evening out without him?" June asked. She was worried she was going to lose Margaret to a relationship like they'd lost Bea.

"Oh, he's harmless," Margaret replied. "And you know that he tells his mother everything, who in turn writes Rebecca, who then leaves me alone."

June and Bea didn't know the details about the unpleasant interaction with Joe and didn't know that Margaret was using

Thomas for the safety of having a steady boyfriend. The harassment from other men had stopped completely.

"I like Thomas," Bea countered. "You guys look good together and he's obviously smart. He's a pharmacist!"

Bea, ever the romantic, wanted everyone to be in love like she was.

"His dad's a pharmacist. He's just a milquetoast with limited conversational skills," June couldn't hide her feelings.

Margaret appreciated that about her best friend.

"Milquetoast is good with bacon and eggs," Bea said.

Margaret laughed. "Good one, Bea."

"Puns are my area of expertise," replied June. "Since when are you the funny one?"

Bea laughed, "Love is my arena, June. And I think our girl here might just fall in love if she gives that lanky pharmacist a chance."

Margaret shut her accounting notes and pulled out her portable typewriter to start working on this week's column. "Guys, I'm not falling in love. I have my studies, I have the paper, I have you two. It's just easier to have him around than to try to keep finding dates for events. It's efficient!"

June rolled her eyes, "Yes, efficiency is the gateway to love. Batting off all the suitors. That's what all those Cary Grant movies are about." She slipped into her best Cary Grant impersonation. "I suppose you'd still be attractive to any man of spirit, though. There's something engaging about it, this goddess business. There's something more challenging to the male than the, uh, more obvious charms." She'd turned up her shirt collar and was strutting about the room pretending to be the movie star they all loved.

At this point, the three of them were laughing so loudly that the house mother rapped on the door. "Quiet down now, it's study hours."

They all continued laughing quietly as they got back to their books and their writing.

Chapter Six

M argaret's editorial columns had moved away from the quite so cynical tone. She didn't want to trigger her mother into keeping her home after Christmas break, so her columns had become nearly as vanilla as Thomas. She wasn't getting the front page anymore, but it was worth it to fly under the radar from Rebecca's wrath for a little while. She figured her mother would appreciate a puff piece about Friday's Military Ball.

A Sharp-Dressed Man — Margaret Murphy, the Daily Nebraskan

Keep those uniforms clean, boys, and we'll be happy to keep you with coeds on your arms! With the Military Ball just around the corner, this writer has joined with the rest of the Scarlet and Cream to celebrate our troops and the war we hope never comes. With each dance more suits and tuxedos have been replaced by the sharp pleats and well-fitted coats of a military man. And this writer, for one, is not complaining!

Roosevelt and Hitler may finally agree on something. If war comes, it will be a "shooting war" (as if there is another kind). But with Christmas bells jingling in a matter of days and Europe thousands of miles away, it seems impossible that we are being

asked to do anything except put on a show that, here in America,
life is still grand. That show will be in full force when 5,000
students and their dates descend on the ballroom on December
5th. Let's kick up our heels and kick war thoughts to the curb for
one night.

Parents can put away their worries and expect photos by our
ever-talented journalism staff to appear here next week as part
of our end-of-semester holiday edition of the Daily Nebraskan.

What Margaret's mother didn't know is that she was also part
of the small group of editors that had met late into the night
to craft, their response to the America First Committee. This
anti-war committee was pressuring colleges around the nation
to help promote their agenda. Her name wasn't on a byline, so
she couldn't get into trouble with either Rebecca or Thomas
for expressing what was sure to be an unpopular opinion with
people that would blindly follow Roosevelt into battle.

Our Thoughtful Response is...No Thank You — the Editorial
Staff of the Daily Nebraskan
The national office of the America First Committee has sent
out a request to 12 college newspaper editors to cooperate in
a poll of students on their respective campuses on the issue:
"Should America declare war and engage in total participation
in the present European war, or should America not?" The Uni-
versity of Nebraska was selected as one of the 12 schools to be
polled through the Daily Nebraskan because, to quote the letter,
it "represents a particular section of the nation, where a college

poll will have definite significance in presenting a true picture of undergraduate opinion on this peace-war problem."

The Daily Nebraskan is not complying with the request of the America First Committee, not simply because this newspaper wishes to have nothing to do with that group, but also because we think a poll of this sort can have no value in deciding the fate of the United States in this war. According to the AFC letter, "College editors have a responsibility to their own generation. It is up to them to present to our leaders the true picture of undergraduate opinion, whether it be for war or for peace for America." We do not accept that responsibility.

War is a difficult endeavor and one that cannot be reduced to mere ink on a page. There is no right answer when it comes to war. Neither option is ideal. We are a school of diverse beliefs rooted in the midwestern values of patriotism. We are a conundrum, and we cannot sum up our opinions on war with the results of a survey of those who have been left behind to observe.
1

The fight had gone on late into the evening, ending in a draw between the Interventionists and Isolationists. Margaret admired the Editor in Chief, Mary O'Connor, for making a final decision and saying that the paper wouldn't participate in the fear-mongering for either side in the college paper. It seemed unlikely that the U.S. would commit to anything more than financial support to Europe and some grand posturing in the Pacific, but Margaret agreed with Mary that as journalists they needed to be careful not to spin the opinions or fears and simply work to report what was real and the truth.

Chapter Seven

December 5, 1941, Lincoln Nebraska

The entire Pi Phi house was blanketed in satin and hairspray. Someone had brought their phonograph into the hallway and the sounds of Benny Goodman blended with the cacophony of feminine voices. Another couple of girls were wailing because their dates called and canceled at the last minute. Two girls were fighting because they had discovered that the same boy had agreed to accompany them both. Every girl was elbowing for a moment in front of the mirror.

"Hand me that silver clip."

Margaret needed something to pull back her unruly mane. She'd planned to go to the stylist and get it done, but she'd spent too much time in the *Daily*'s office working on next week's articles and in her free time she was studying for finals. She would rather have some untidy hair than let her readers, or her professors, down.

"Megs, let me fix it," Bea said.

Bea had a talent for hair that Margaret couldn't manage. With just a couple of quick brushes, a twist, and a few stabs of bobby pins, Margaret was transformed from a little girl playing dress-up into someone who looked more sophisticated than her nineteen years.

"Pi Phi Women!" The housemistress shouted up the stairs. "The men are due to arrive in a few moments and it's time to wrap up the primping. Remember, I expect you all to be home by the extended curfew. For tonight only it is one a.m. Those uniforms might want to keep you out till dawn and convince you that they might be gone tomorrow. Always remember, a Pi Phi woman is..."

"Stronger in sisterhood! Modest and kind!"

The women were expected to shout in unison in response to their house mother's chant. June rolled her eyes and spoke in a snooty east coast accent.

"Longing for Mrs.-hood. Earnest and blind. Could they at least pretend that most of the parents didn't send women to college to find a man?"

Feminism and the possibility of war be damned, Margaret knew she and Thomas would look fantastic when they entered that ballroom. Her mother, thrilled that her daughter was falling in line, gave her an unlimited budget for a dress at Gold and Company. She'd found a gown in the exact shade of her eyes—blue in some light, grey in others, almost purple depending on the distance. The square neck was accented with tiny silver beadwork, and the thick satin hung down to just above her ankle and showed off the silver shoes she'd also cajoled her mother into buying.

Each sorority house hosted a dinner before the dance. The men all lined up single file at the door and asked for their date by name, and the freshman page would call up to the waiting woman who would then descend the grand staircase and then pose for a photo with her date by the front door. It was a laborious process. Girls were all trying to sneak peeks around the corner to see whose date was next. Thomas had arrived with June's date, Milt, and Bea's date, Ted. Margaret had convinced Sam to ask one of her other sorority sisters so that they could round out their table of eight and she'd finally be able to get Sam's opinion on Thomas.

If she had to be with anyone, it might as well be with someone Sam could tolerate. They'd put their differences aside after the homecoming dance, but he was still a little frosty. If Sam liked Thomas maybe Margaret could see herself liking Thomas a little more.

The entire evening was full of ceremonial rigamarole. Formal dinner, speeches from the sorority officers, pretending like they were all grownups and not college students playing dress-up. The conversation was supposed to be lighthearted, but news kept circling back into the volatile international waters of the Pacific or across the Atlantic.

"I just don't understand why you enlisted in that program instead of waiting to be drafted. Your family has money, right?" Thomas was pushing Sam to defend his decision of joining the Army's air force training program.

"It's the right thing to do." Sam was stoic in his response. "My family might be better off than some, but we're not big city folk, and I've been flying crop dusters every summer since I was sixteen. It's the best thing I can do to defend our country if it comes to that. And you're wearing the same uniform I am, just without the wings, so what's your problem?"

"Problem? I have no problem. Enlisting keeps me out of the draft, and the generous gift to our state senator's campaign keeps me out of harm's way. You know your family could do the same." Thomas replied.

Thomas was showing a more fiery side to him than Margaret had ever seen.

Tensions were running too high for a sorority formal. They'd been bickering for almost twenty minutes. She wanted Milt or Ted to butt in and break up the argument, but they hadn't been drafted yet, nor had they enlisted, so they sat quietly in their tuxedos and watched the showdown. Thomas was showing a more argumentative side to him than Margaret had ever seen.

Sam gripped the edge of the table. "You think that's an honorable solution?" He glared at Margaret. "Megs? Is this the best you could do?"

Margaret couldn't bite her tongue any longer. "The best you could do is to not want to go to war. Every pilot is going to be called. I agree with Thomas. You could have found a way to avoid fighting for as long as possible."

Margaret wasn't a blind supporter of Roosevelt and no one wished for war, but this was out of character for her. Usually, she would join Sam's side of the debate.

June stood up. This caused the men, trained since birth, to stand without thinking. "Well, sorry to end this first battle of the next Great War." Everyone laughed politely, grateful for the distraction. "Let's all just grab our coats and go. We need to get to the coliseum so you two boys can walk in the parade."

Thomas drew Margaret aside before putting her coat around her shoulders.

"What's your cousin's problem? He seems to think that I'm not good enough for you."

Margaret stiffened. She was concerned that Sam would report back to her mother and derail her plans for Thomas. "He's just protective. You'd be the same with your sister, right? And, anyway, you were a little heavy-handed with the talk of buying your way out of serving."

Thomas's hand, which had been gently resting on Margaret's elbow slid down and encompassed her wrist with a bit too much pressure. "Heavy-handed? You're one to talk all dressed up in the most expensive dress you could buy, showing off in front of your friends."

Margaret looked down at her wrist and then glared up at Thomas. Over his shoulder, she saw Sam watching her as he helped his date put on her jacket. Thomas caught her glance.

Without a word, Thomas dropped her wrist and the cloud lifted from his face. He reached out his hand to Sam and said, "No hard feelings, right, old man? We're all on the same side."

Margaret held her breath. Sam saw the pleading look in Margaret's eyes and accepted the handshake.

She took Thomas's arm, threaded her other arm through Sam's and they all walked across campus together to line up for the grand march.

The men in uniform, and their dates, walked down a crimson-red carpet running through the center of the coliseum, pushed along by the beat of a military band playing the same six-minute march on repeat. By nine o'clock they were all ready for some dancing, so the carpets were rolled up, the bleachers emptied and pushed back, the curtains were drawn back on the stage and the orchestra kicked off the evening with a raucous cover of Benny Goodman's *"Sing, Sing, Sing"*.

Thomas and Margaret joined the rest of the crowd in dancing and pretended that their greatest concern was whether the next song would be a feisty number or would have them dancing cheek to cheek. The bickering was forgotten, and they were caught up in the frenetic romance of the moment.

Chapter Eight

December 7, 1941

    Huddled up with a cup of coffee Margaret thought about her supplementary article about the Military Ball. The pomp and circumstance of the whole affair had such an undercurrent of fear that she knew the puff piece already sent to the press just wasn't going to cut it. She'd found a quiet corner in the Daily's office where she could write in peace on a quiet Sunday. The late morning sun streamed through the window, warming the space in stark contrast to the bitter cold outside. This would be her last article to submit before Christmas break, and she figured she might make it home on the train before it arrived in her parent's mailbox. Now that she was seeing Thomas on a regular basis her mother might be less triggered by articles in the paper, but she didn't want to risk it.

Marching Two by Two — Margaret Murphy, the Daily Nebraskan

Pardon me, dear reader, for the correction to the story published on Monday about the beauty and magic of the Military Ball last Friday night. And please indulge me, as I admit that I wrote the piece before attending the aforementioned Ball. Yours

truly felt that if you'd been to one Military Ball, you'd been to them all and merely churned out her feelings from last year's soiree. But 1941 is not 1940. A lifetime has passed.

One can only imagine that the youth of our great nation at colleges from Ithaca to San Francisco are being puffed up and paraded about as we were last Friday. Our elected officials, our university brass, all propped up on the bleachers patting themselves on the back for putting on such an elegant show. Because nothing is wrong if they say nothing is wrong. Right? We should just dance and carry on as if we have not a care in the world.

I cannot be the only one who cringes to hear "Don't worry your pretty little head about it" one more time. I am worried and you should be too. I'm worried that the grownups in charge aren't really seeing the real men and women who will be affected by their decisions. I'm worried that they just see handsome men and beautiful women dressed up like dolls parading like puppets. I'm worried that the war will never be real to us but the fear of war will be ever-present.

We are making decisions for the rest of our lives based not on our educational goals or passions but because we've been told that we need to defend the idea of freedom and fight tyranny an ocean away. We are in a game of musical chairs with our lives and when the music stops, and the war begins, where we are and who we're with will be cemented in stone. We need to fight the distractions and stay true to what we want to achieve. We need to end the relationships that are safe, register for the classes we love, and carry on as if our worst nightmare may never come true.

The door flew open. Mary, the editor, came screaming through the door.

"Turn on the radio. Stop the presses. Grab a notebook. Oh my God. Margaret. It's really happening."

Margaret initially thought Mary was joking. There were no presses to stop. The Monday paper was already put to bed. Besides, Mary could be very dramatic. Margaret's passion for news had nothing on Mary's.

The crazed look in Mary's eyes as she worked to tune the radio stopped Margaret in her tracks.

The halting cadence of the radio announcer came through the static. "It is unknown the extent of the casualties at Pearl Harbor. Again, the details are very scarce, but what we do know is that sometime this morning a fleet of Japanese warplanes attacked our forces stationed in Hawaii..."

"It's real," Mary said. "We're really at war." She slumped into the chair at her desk.

Margaret pulled her correction piece out of her typewriter, crumpled it up, and threw it in the wastebasket. She would burn it if she could. How ridiculous of her to think that any-thing mattered from just two days ago. Every boy in uniform would surely disappear now that the U.S. was attacked. Sam, Thomas—hell, even the ones who weren't in uniform yet would surely get caught up in the tsunami of patriotism and rush to enlist.

"It's time to go to work," Margaret replied. "Everything is changing faster than we ever considered. We have a paper to write."

Mary, the consummate editor, had already picked up the phone and started calling in the rest of the staff and dividing out each reporter's responsibilities.

Chapter Nine

M argaret spent the rest of the day interviewing students across campus about their reaction to what would surely be a declaration of war by the United States. Students were huddled together near radios that simply repeated the same news over and over again. The nationalism and patriotism that flowed as a result of this deadly attack were, unfortunately, not shocking. The word "finally" was never said even though it was felt by all. Months and months had been spent watching tensions rise and so many men had deployed for basic training that there was very nearly a feeling of relief.

With those feelings, there were also the "did you hear about so-and-so" moments of people trying to infiltrate the tragedy by finding someone they knew that was stationed at Pearl Harbor.

"Do you know Jimmy Winebaker from Minatare? He's there."

"My cousin's fiancé is stationed there."

"Five boys from Ogallala are in the Pacific."

The rumors were incredible. Living in the middle of the country where there was such isolation from anything on the coasts, didn't prevent people from diving into their imaginations with possibilities.

BEHIND THE WIRE   41

"I heard that they've attacked San Francisco, but they're not telling us on the news so we'll stay calm."

"Did you know that the Japanese have infiltrated our media and are cutting off communication?"

This all seemed ridiculous to Margaret. She wanted facts. The fact was they had short radio announcement bursts about the attack. The fact was they were all scared. The fact was when she stopped and thought about all that as unknown and out of control, she could hardly breathe. It seemed impossible that U.S. soil had been attacked without warning.

Her feet and soul were heavy as she trudged back across campus to the Pi Phi house. She hadn't consumed anything since that cup of coffee earlier, and she needed to just sit down and think. The *Daily* staff was meeting before classes early the next morning to submit their articles for the paper, so she knew she'd be up half the night writing her piece. She was distracted and very nearly jumped out of her skin when Thomas yelled.

"Maggie! There you are! I have been worried sick. I called the house, I called the paper, and I've been looking for you all day. Why didn't you come to find me?"

Margaret realized she hadn't thought about him at all beyond that first realization he'd likely be leaving soon.

Instead, she replied, "I was interviewing people for my column. Did you want to give me your thoughts about America going to war?" She tried to diffuse the situation with a flirtatious smile, using the last bits of energy she had to avoid a fight.

It didn't work. Thomas glared. "You know my thoughts. I am staying stateside for as long as I can. This development today might jeopardize that plan, and I really wanted to spend the day with you. Couldn't you have skipped your precious news cycle for one day and been with me?"

"My precious news cycle? Do you think I just planned for a bombing of our homeland so that I could avoid you? Do you think this is just my hobby?" Her voice was starting to escalate, and she could see a few of her sorority sisters looking out the window from the front parlor. "You are not more important than me." Margaret pivoted and turned towards the front door.

Thomas grabbed her arm. She was prepped for another fight. He'd proven at the dance that he could not regulate his emotions when it came to the war.

"Do not grab me. You grabbed me at the dance, you grabbed me today, you will not do it again." It was likely that it was all centered on fear, but Margaret didn't like the physicality of his immaturity. When she saw tears in the eyes of a scared little boy inside of a nearly six-foot-tall man she softened a bit. He, and all of the other men on campus, had seemingly regressed back to the time when they could have a tantrum and get what they wanted.

Thomas dropped his head. "I was just so worried and you're the only person that I can talk to. My mother has been calling all day. It's just the worst day of my entire life. Why did they have to force us into this mess?"

Margaret knew she had a choice. She could continue the fight and point out the fact that the day was far worse for everyone in Hawaii or everyone that had family stationed there. That was useless. Instead, she sat down on the steps in the cold December air and let Thomas pontificate about how hard his life was going to be and how lonely she would be when he left.

After thirty minutes they were both starting to get cold, and she could hear dinner preparations happening in earnest so she gently detached from his grasp and promised to see him on Friday night for dinner with his family. They had a full week of finals ahead of them and could celebrate the end of their semester together. His outburst so appeased, she was free to finally go inside for dinner.

Chapter Ten

The Pi Phi house was morose. Two of the girl's fiancés were stationed in the Pacific. One at Pearl Harbor and another on an aircraft carrier somewhere at sea. Others had beaus who had enlisted but had not yet been called. Everyone knew someone who would go and the mood was heavy.

Margaret knew the cook, who they all called Miss Kay, would want to comfort these girls with a warm meal and was grateful for the individual chicken pot pies she made for each of them. They were all still children at heart and there was nothing better she could do to take care of them.

As the girls finished up their dinners, the conversation was silenced by an announcement from their house mother that the First Lady would be speaking shortly, and they would gather in the parlor to listen. Margaret, June, and Bea curled up together on a window seat, finding comfort in the physical closeness of dear friends, and listened as Eleanor Roosevelt addressed the nation.

"Good evening, ladies and gentlemen, I am speaking to you tonight at a very serious moment in our history. The Cabinet is convening and the leaders in Congress are meeting with the

President. The State Department and Army and Navy officials have been with the President all afternoon. In fact, the Japanese ambassador was talking to the president at the very time that Japan's airships were bombing our citizens in Hawaii and the Philippines and sinking one of our transports loaded with lumber on its way to Hawaii.

By tomorrow morning the members of Congress will have a full report and be ready for action.

In the meantime, we the people are already prepared for action. For months now the knowledge that something of this kind might happen has been hanging over our heads and yet it seemed impossible to believe, impossible to drop the everyday things of life and feel that there was only one thing which was important - preparation to meet an enemy no matter where he struck. That is all over now and there is no more uncertainty.

We know what we have to face and we know that we are ready to face it.

I should like to say just a word to the women in the country tonight. I have a boy at sea on a destroyer, for all I know he may be on his way to the Pacific. Two of my children are in coastal cities on the Pacific. Many of you all over the country have boys in the services who will now be called upon to go into action. You have friends and families in what has suddenly become a danger zone. You cannot escape anxiety. You cannot escape a clutch of fear at your heart and yet I hope that the certainty of what we have to meet will make you rise above these fears.

We must go about our daily business more determined than ever to do the ordinary things as well as we can and when we find a way to do anything more in our communities to help others, to build morale, to give a feeling of security, we must do it. Whatever is asked of us I am sure we can accomplish it. We are the free and unconquerable people of the United States of America.

To the young people of the nation, I must speak a word tonight. You are going to have a great opportunity. There will be high moments in which your strength and your ability will be tested. I have faith in you. I feel as though I was standing upon a rock and that rock is my faith in my fellow citizens."[2]

By the end of Mrs. Roosevelt's address, Bea and many of her Pi Phi sisters were blubbering. Even stoic Margaret was choked up. The First Lady was right. This was a time of tragedy and great opportunity. She took her leave and went to write her article.

Our Test – Margaret Murphy, the Daily Nebraskan

With the brutal attack by the Japanese on our troops in the Pacific it became painfully apparent that the showmanship of men in uniform from last week was more of a going away dance as we prepare to go to war. A great many students have commented that "if we have to fight; we might as well just have as much fun as possible" and have chosen to double down on the gadding about and partying. Many comments were made along the lines of "What's the point of finals? My accounting class isn't going to help me in battle." Numerous students indicated that they would not be returning next semester as they would be enlisting or staying in their hometowns to help with the war effort.

It would be so easy to dive into the trenches of despair. But, as our First Lady so eloquently stated last night, "There will be high moments in which (our) strength and ability will be tested." This is the test we need to focus upon. A college education is even more important now than it was before. We must stay steady in our studies. We must find a way to focus even more diligently so that our minds will be trained to cope with the situation now, during the remainder of the war, and after the war. We must not let down our resolve. We must be strong. There has never been a situation so critical that strong people, with strong ideals, could not withstand. We must be the rock that stands steady in the storm.

The coming days will be filled with painful goodbyes as we wrap up our finals and head back to our hometowns for the break. Many of our men, and some of our women, will be absent when this column returns in January. But for now, we work to keep our morale up and work to celebrate Christmas at a time when it doesn't feel much like a celebration.

Our thoughts are with our armed service members in the Pacific as they recover from Sunday's brutal attack and with the families around the country that are mourning a loss too difficult to bear.

Chapter Eleven

The days after the attack on Pearl Harbor passed in a blur, and Margaret nearly forgot that she'd promised Thomas to have dinner with his family. He asked if she'd get dressed up and stay late for some dancing since there was going to be live music at the Cornhusker. With finals complete, there was no good excuse. Margaret chose the dress from the military ball, figuring his parents hadn't seen it. She was slated to head home to Gering in a couple of days, and Lord knows there was nowhere to wear anything this fancy back there. It shouldn't have been shocking that life had gone on as usual so rapidly after the attack, but it frustrated her greatly that she found herself so easily distracted by some sparkles and silk.

The Cornhusker Hotel was fully decorated for Christmas with greenery peppered with large white bulbs. There were extra candles on each table and, if you stopped thinking for a minute, you'd forget that America was at war. The small band in the corner featured a woman singing Christmas songs in a crooning alto voice.

Thomas had borrowed one of his parent's cars to retrieve her, and Margaret stood in the lobby enjoying the music while waiting for him to park. It had just started to snow outside, and downtown Lincoln was beautiful. She was going to miss this place for the next few weeks. She wasn't looking forward to heading home for Christmas, but she knew that there was no way she could suggest staying in Lincoln for the winter break. She'd been offered an internship at the *Lincoln Star* writing for their collegiate section, but turned it down, knowing the fight with her mother just wasn't worth it. With Sam heading to active duty instead of finishing his degree, she knew she'd be hard-pressed to come back to Lincoln after break without him.

"There's my beautiful little Magpie!"

The sound of her father's voice shocked her out of her reverie.

Surprises were not Margaret's favorite things. This week had been exhausting already, and she was taken aback by his presence.

"Daddy? What are you doing here?" She looked around for her mother and saw her coming through the revolving doors with Violet, Thomas, and his father, Dr. Tom. Tailing behind them were her aunt, uncle, and Sam. Thomas was grinning from ear to ear at Margaret's surprised face.

"Surprise!" Thomas exclaimed. "You seemed so down this week about the whole bombing thing, and I called your folks to see if they would come out so we could have a Christmas celebration with all of us."

"Well, that's quite the dress," Rebecca said. "It truly does suit you."

Margaret didn't trust the compliment. It seemed that her mother was holding back. Her father had his arm around Rebecca's waist and was looking at Margaret like she was a little girl.

He almost looked sad. Violet and Dr. Tom both were grinning as well. Her aunt and uncle were normally cheery but even they seemed amped up. Only Sam had a face that seemed to be sending her messages of warning as if by Morse code. It was all very overwhelming. Margaret chalked it up to a lack of sleep getting the rest of the paper together.

"Davey party? Right this way please." The nine of them followed the maître d'.

They moved to the favorite banquette in the back, the same as the first dinner with Thomas and Violet. So much had happened since that September evening. The war altered everyone's sense of the passage of time. It somehow felt like each day was a week but that months flew by in seconds. Margaret felt like now was as good a time as any to start setting the stage for the ensuing battle to return in January. Drinks and appetizers were promptly served, and Margaret decided to try and regain some control of the conversation.

"Mother, Daddy, how was your trip? You didn't need to come so far. I'm heading home in a couple of days for three whole weeks."

Rebecca glanced at Franklin. He shook his head slightly.

"Oh darling, Thomas shared that you were just beside yourself with worry and working yourself sick after the horrible news. We just had to come immediately." Rebecca was almost smiling as she said this, which felt very odd.

Violet interjected, "With all of the time you two are spending together, we thought we should all get together for a pre-holiday dinner."

Franklin picked up the glass of wine in front of him and took a healthy gulp. "I figured it was time for me to meet this Thomas your mother speaks so highly of."

This statement only thinly hid the fact that Margaret had only shared maybe a word or two about Thomas with her father on their weekly phone calls.

"Mr. Murphy, it has been such a pleasure to get to know you a bit," Thomas said.

"Get to know? You've spent two minutes together," Margaret said.

"Maggie, darling, there's something I'd like to tell you." Thomas grabbed a glass of wine. "I'd like to make a toast."

Margaret reached out to the crystal glass in front of her, taking a sizable gulp of the bitter red wine. The edges of everything were suddenly very bright. She felt like she was watching the world shatter. The sound of the restaurant seemed to become muffled, and the air was a bit suffocating.

"You all know how beautiful Margaret, my Maggie, is. I mean, just take a look at her. These last three months with her on my arm have been the best of my life. She's the reason for the smile on my face every day and she is who I will be fighting to return to when I come back from the war."

He pushed his chair back. He glanced at the band, who paused their music. The tables surrounding the Davey's banquette hushed. Thomas was dressed in his military uniform and the family was well-known, in Lincoln. Everyone was caught up in the moment.

Thomas dropped to one knee.

"No!" Margaret could have sworn she screamed out loud. Instead, she took a deep breath. Across the table, she could see that Sam's knuckles were white from gripping the edge of the table.

"Maggie, I wrote to your parents weeks ago and asked for us to get together this weekend. Of course, I didn't imagine there would be an attack. I've spent the afternoon getting to know your father and have asked him for permission to ask you a very important question. Margaret Murphy, would you do me the honor of becoming Mrs. Thomas Davey and marrying me?"

It might have been the sparkling candles, the smell of ever-green, the glass of wine, or it might have been the fact that Margaret thought her mother might be more agreeable to her continuing college if she was engaged, or maybe it was that he was leaving for war and wasn't it supposed to be romantic to be engaged during a war? Wouldn't every writer want to have a dramatic story like this? If she was engaged, she was sure to be able to come back to school after break. She was thinking strategically instead of romantically. Whatever the reason, the word that left her mouth was simply, "Yes."

With that one syllable, the restaurant erupted into applause, the band started playing, and nearly everyone at the table toasted their good fortune. She could have sworn she saw a flash of disappointment cross her father's face as he raised a glass to the young couple. Sam did not hide his disappointment well, and Margaret avoided his eyes.

It was late when Thomas dropped Margaret back at the Pi Phi house. He and Rebecca had conferred with her house mother and obtained a curfew extension behind her back. She snuck in quietly expecting everyone in the house to be asleep. Instead, Bea and June were sitting in the parlor waiting for her.

"So, did he ask?" June wasn't smiling as she asked the question. "Bea and I have a bet going, and she says you're engaged."

Bea, ever the romantic, was trying to hold in a smile and match June's stoic demeanor. "Well, did he?"

Throughout the evening Margaret had decided that she could find a way to be happy with Thomas. He wasn't a terrible man. His temper ran a little hot sometimes, he was rather whiny, but his mother was lovely. Her parents seemed happy enough, or at least her mother seemed elated. Margaret decided her life could be worse than being engaged to a relatively handsome future pharmacist in Lincoln. She could be marrying a farmer and have to live near her mother. Thomas would leave for the service, and she would stay in Lincoln to finish her degree. Bea's excitement was contagious even if June wasn't thrilled. She slowly took off her winter gloves and held out her finger to reveal a beautiful diamond ring.

"Does this answer your question?"

Chapter Twelve

Plans are just expectations that haven't yet seen adversity or reality. The plan was to go home to Gering for Christmas break and then head back to Lincoln for the end of her sophomore year. As each day passed in December and the new year began, it was becoming painfully obvious to Margaret that she was not going to be returning to her old life.

"But Mother!" Margaret hated how whiny she always sounded when she was in the middle of a fight. "You cannot make me quit school. I won't do it."

"And just how do you expect to pay for it? Your father and I will not be giving you a dime. It's not safe for you back there with Sam gone and Thomas leaving."

"But the paper needs me. And I need the paper. Daddy? Can't you tell her that she's being unreasonable?"

Franklin put down the newspaper he was hiding behind. He'd long since mastered the ability to ignore the escalating arguments between the two women in his life.

"Magpie, let's go for a drive."

"Don't you go taking her side, Franklin. I simply will not have it." Rebecca was frequently outvoted.

"Now Rebecca, we're just going for a drive to let cooler heads prevail. We'll be back shortly. No one's side is being taken here. Maggie, you're driving. Bring the dog."

She grabbed the keys to his Buick Roadmaster and stormed down the stairs and out the back door to the garage, jammed the keys into the ignition, and nearly flooded the engine while stomping her foot down on the gas as she waited for her father to join her in the car. Spike, her Brittany Spaniel, always happy to be included, was stationed in the back seat ready for an adventure.

Franklin took his time walking to the garage. She knew, as his only child, she was the most precious thing to him on this earth and that he did not want to let her down in any way. He always took her side. It would be different if they lived in Lincoln. She had gone so far as to bring up the idea of him leaving his job as the president of the bank and heading east just so she could continue her studies. He'd have no trouble leveraging his connections and getting a position at a bank out there. Thomas' father would see to it. That request was met with expected ridicule from her mother and a disappointed "no" from her father. Their life was in western Nebraska, cozied up on the corner of 14th and O, across the street from his brother and their family. His father had worked too hard to build a life for his family in Gering for her to encourage him to abandon it.

He pulled up the collar on his winter coat and crossed the lawn to the waiting car.

"Let's head to the lake."

It was a brisk December day, and the icy blue Nebraska sky was dotted with the frosty white clouds that indicated the potential for snow. The dirt road leading to Lake Minatare was empty, so Franklin encouraged Margaret to let off some steam as soon as they passed the sugar factory and were on open roads. Windshield time is what he called it. He'd taught her to drive when she was just fourteen, and she was proud to be driving just as fast and skillfully as any boy. She truly could look out for herself.

Margaret rounded the corner into the campsite overlooking the lake. Surrounded by towering cottonwood trees striped with the markings of just how high the water gets every summer, the white sand and bright blue water were blinding. The winter had not been as cold as years past and only the edges of the water were frozen, whipped into layers of ice by the ever-present Nebraska wind. She let Spike out and then slammed the door to the Buick and hiked down to the beach, almost laughing as Spike chased a group of birds quietly gathered at the edge of the water.

Her father was a stout man, shaped by his work behind a desk at the bank. He knew better than to follow Margaret down to the water without sturdier shoes. Instead, he leaned against the car and watched her as she picked up rocks and threw them out into the lake. She needed some time alone to process her thoughts.

She'd let her temper get in the way of preparation and had not brought a heavy enough coat, but her stubborn streak would not yield easily. She knew this was a fight she could not win. Many of her friends were not returning to university after the break. Bea had been called home. June's mother had moved in with her sister after she was widowed, and she supported June in staying in school until she could leave for the nursing corps. Parental fear of a lack of control was a power greater than the rise of fascism in Europe. And, since control could not be exercised over the boys taken by the draft, the young women were left behind to suffer with the doubling down of parental anxiety.

Did her mother not listen to Eleanore Roosevelt's address? Did she not understand that this was a time when she could learn to make a difference? She could finish her degree, maybe even find a job as a war correspondent, and report on the news from the western front as well as any Ernie Pyle or Nellie Bly. These were all arguments that had been shouted across the dinner table and shot down masterfully by Rebecca. If she wasn't to be trusted alone in Lincoln, Nebraska, there was no way on God's green earth she would be free to travel the globe as an unmarried woman. Prudence prevailed in all things with Rebecca.

She threw one last rock out onto the lake skipping it along the edge where the choppy ice met the dark blue water.

"Spike, let's go." She headed back up to the car. Her father took off his heavy winter overcoat and put it around her shoulders.

"Looks like you did some serious problem-solving out there." He approached her with a gentle voice, wanting her to drive the conversation.

"Dad, I just feel like if I stay here with you, I will be giving up on everything. I did everything she asked. I settled down with a respectable boy. I'm studying business and not majoring in journalism. Will it ever be enough?"

Franklin looked down at his daughter. "You will understand someday when you have children of your own. At a certain point, the outside world just becomes too filled with chaos to let your little ones out into the madness."

"I'm not a little kid anymore. You know that, right?"

"Magpie. You will always be my little one. And, because I was blessed with a daughter, I don't have to be forced into the heartbreak of sending you off to war. Just wait out this semester. Your mother might come around."

January 1942

A Goodbye, For Now — *Margaret Murphy, the* Daily Nebraskan
It is with a heart made heavy by the state of the world and, selfishly, by the state of her own affairs that this writer sends a sad adieu to her classmates and readers at good ol' NU. I have been summoned home to ride out the waves of our war from the quiet corner of 14th and O in Gering, nearly as far west as you can get from Lincoln without entering Wyoming. Life there will be devoid of late nights in the editorial office, quieted by the lack of dances, absent of the student rally cries at the football games. This should have been a column of quiet celebration as I, like many of my sisters, quickly coupled up and got engaged to my college sweetheart before they left for war. Instead, it feels as if it is a funeral announcement.

There is much to grieve at this time even if we have not yet experienced the loss of a loved one to war. We are grieving the loss of normalcy. We are grieving the loss of the vision for the future we had curated so carefully in our youth. We are grieving the loss of our youth.

Is there melodrama in these statements? Of course. Being called back to the safety of a small town during a war is nothing compared to being called to defend the very world from the rise of tyranny. I know I am not alone. Admissions are at a record low at universities across the nation as parents just like mine are holding on tight to that which they feel they can still control. We can simply hope that a new normal emerges after the shock of an attack on our homeland and that this writer comes back to join those who are still flying the scarlet and cream.

War is not forever. Fear is not forever. We will navigate this change with all the grace we can muster. It is this writer's hope that she will be returning in the fall of '42 to pick up where we left off. Until then, hold down the fort.

Chapter Thirteen

Camp Scottsbluff

June 1943

She did not yet have the resolve to put up with their Italian catcalls. Instead, Margaret sat in her car, her father's hand-me-down 1940 Buick Coupe. She knew the car was a luxury at the time and she knew the other girls talked about her because of it. Or maybe they talked because the catcalls were louder when she walked across the parking lot. She could already feel the eyes of the prisoners following her through their posts lounging behind the ten-foot-high barbed wire fences. Their stares and shouts were almost as offensive as the steaming dust she knew would swirl around her bare ankles the moment she stepped out of the car into the Nebraska heat and walked into the prisoner of war camp. How she longed for days of nylons to return. She damned the war, the soldiers, the Italian prisoners who leered at her, her parents, her fiancé. Margaret's foul mood matched that of the rest of the country. The war had gone on long enough and yet it felt like it was just getting started.

Margaret had evolved into quite a beauty by the summer of 1943 and there were very few American men around to see it.

Even Thomas was shocked at the change when she visited him at his stateside post. Always classically cute, she now had a more sophisticated look. Her hair had darkened from ash blonde to a more chestnut brown, her baby face had narrowed, and she'd stopped trying so hard. It was hardly fair. Selfishly she wanted to scream, "Couldn't the Japanese have just waited a few more years? Couldn't worthless Roosevelt just hurry up and defeat Hitler? Couldn't we just be a bit swifter on annihilating the enemy? Why must men make war take so damned long."

She knew she should consider herself lucky. Most of 1942 was spent in angry silence, volunteering for socially appropriate causes working part-time at the bank, constantly under Rebecca's watchful eye. She accepted this routine as her fate until the U.S. military sent a gift to western Nebraska and decided to build a new airfield under the supervision of the Army Corps of Engineers. Her father recognized Margaret's dejection during her time back at home and knew her part-time job at the bank was not exciting enough for her. He leveraged his connections to get her a job as an assistant to the captain who was overseeing the supplies for the base. In just forty-five days it went from a small town landing strip to a massive airfield with three runways surrounded by over one hundred buildings. Once the airfield was complete the military converted the old airport into the prisoner of war camp and her boss, Captain Arthur Chapman, was transferred, and became the camp's quartermaster and Margaret followed. For the first time in a while, she felt engaged in something with purpose.

As his assistant, one of her duties was to handle the accounting for supplies and products for the canteen where prisoners could buy various goods. Every prisoner was paid 10 cents a day in canteen coupons whether they worked or not. If they headed out to the fields, they made an additional 80 cents per day. All for doing work that American boys should have been home to do.

Margaret, at nearly 21 years old, was fairly confident that if Roosevelt would just listen to her, she could get this whole mess figured out in an afternoon. Her strong-willed nature and frank assessment of the president was a source of great mirth to her fiancé.

She'd just returned from a visit to New Orleans to see Thomas and was struggling mightily. Not because she missed him, but because she couldn't figure out why she didn't. She missed his mother (their ever-present chaperone) more. She'd been hopeful that having a fiancé in the service would provide some sort of drama to a relatively quiet war. The letter that arrived yesterday was not a step in the right direction. She'd brought it with her to work to share her thoughts on the whole matter with Bea as they drove in together. Bea, who worked as a secretary at the camp in a different department, had called in sick today, so she couldn't get her feedback. She'd likely tell Margaret she was simply overreacting. Thomas was a good guy; she should consider herself lucky. Lucky was one thing, bored was another, and Margaret found that she was bored by Thomas's love letters.

May 18, 1943 - New Orleans
Dearest honey:
Hi sweetheart. Are you recovering from your trip? I am getting
somewhat of a recovery, but it will probably take a couple of

more weeks. I miss you darling, and hope that you miss me too. It kind of spoils me to be with you and then all at once not be with you at all. It is just like smoking, you get in the habit and then all of a sudden have to give it up.

One thing that I am glad of is that you were down here when it was possible for me to spend so much time with you. I certainly could not have done it this month.

Starting tomorrow I am to take over the Mess Hall in Area 4. I will completely run the thing for three weeks. That means that I will have to be there from around 5:30 in the morning until 6:30 in the evening, seven days a week. Gee I couldn't have seen much of you that way at all could I.

What have you been doing since you have been home? Are you still as sleepy as you were when you were down here? I imagine that the cooler weather up there has made you snap out of it a little.

It is awfully still, damp and hot here tonight and I am stopping about every line to wipe off my brow. Guess that I will close and go over to take a shower. Be good honey, and write to me often I love you and wish that you were still here.

Yours, Thomas.

P.S. Hello again - This has been one hellava day. Just after I closed this letter to you the Colonel of the area came over and wanted to know about his officers who were supposed to be duty officers at the mess hall. None of them were around and he was really peeved about. Then just after he left a Major, Captain, and 1st Lt. came threw on inspection and were beefing about small things that weren't cleaned up. Every thing that they told me to do was utterly impractical and after he had chewed me for a half hour or so. Well to cut a long story short I blew up. You know me. I suppose I will be in the dog house but he apologized to me before he left and as far as I know he doesn't hold it against me. Why don't I learn to swallow my tongue when I get sore. I wish I knew.

He had compared spending time with her to craving a cigarette. Sure, she loved her cigarettes, but with the war going on there was such a shortage that she'd stopped—for the most part. Occasionally, an officer at the camp offered her one, and it would be rude to refuse him, right? Thomas didn't need to know any of that—so she couldn't fight with him about the comparison. She had told him she'd quit. Everything about what Thomas was doing sounded terribly boring. Even counting out bars of soap for prisoners sounded better.

Thomas had received a very favorable military placement due to his parent's influence. It seemed like his extended stay in New Orleans, and his commission as a mess cook, where he'd likely never see the front line of fighting, was more than just luck. The temper referenced in the letter was a more and more frequent guest in their correspondence and during their time together in New Orleans. It was for that reason that she hadn't shared that she was no longer working on the project at the airport and that she'd taken a job at the prisoner of war camp in Scottsbluff. He knew she was looking for other work as the airport project was wrapping up, but he thought she was going to go back to work at her father's bank.

She sighed, thinking of how little he knew and how that wasn't probably a good way to start a marriage. She folded the letter, put it in her handbag, and stepped out into the dust to start her day.

Chapter Fourteen

From the parking lot on the south edge of the camp, civilian workers entered through a tall wrought-iron gate staffed by a uniformed, armed, officer. There had been an attempt to make the gate less oppressive with some plants selected by a government hack back east. Likely every one of the camps across the country was given the same plants, with no regard to the climate in which they were planting them. Corrugated steel buildings grew in any climate; magnolia trees did not, therefore the trees on either side of the entrance were sickly. The hardened clay soil of western Nebraska was not conducive to the growth of anything desirous of moisture. The only decoration was a large "Days Without an Accident" sign that indicated that the Civilians had gone thirty-eight days without an accident and the Enlisted had only gone three.

This sign always gave Margaret a laugh. She thought of an article she could write for the local paper about the sign, the camp, and her thoughts on the whole thing. The title could be *"If Civilians Ran This War We Might Already Be Done."*

Just last week, two of the guards, if you can call twenty-year-old school-boys guards, burned their hands on the electric fence in a dare to see who could hold onto it the longest. How is it an accident when it's inspired by idiocy?

Margaret entered through the gate, as she did every day, and opened her handbag for inspection.

"Morning, miss." The newest guard blushed the color of a Nebraska sunset. He attempted to stand tall, hoping that this beautiful woman wouldn't notice that he needed a cane—or that he had angry red burns along the right side of his body.

Margaret gave her "Good morning, Soldier. How are you today?" standard reply to whoever was working the gate. Always with a smile that showed the small dimple on her cheek. It didn't matter who he was or where he'd served. He might last for several weeks, or even months. With the way that his hand was shaking as he opened her handbag and searched for contraband, she guessed that he was more injured—likely psychologically—than he was letting on.

"You're a beautiful morning—I mean have a beautiful morning—" stammered the young soldier. Margaret gave him a wink as she snapped her handbag shut and headed toward her desk.

There were over one hundred steel buildings of various shapes and sizes on the four-square-mile plot of land situated on the east edge of town—beyond where civilized people stopped paying attention to what was happening. If the weather was mild, it was a pleasant walk through the camp to the garrison area where the quartermaster's building was situated between the yard and the hospital. To the east were the officer's quarters and dining hall. To the west were three compounds, individually cordoned off with their own ten-foot barbed wire fences, each including twenty-eight prisoner barracks. Every prisoner was guaranteed forty square feet of space.

Her desk was situated at the end of the long main office hall. Captain Chapman, "Chap" for short, was injured when his plane went down at the battle at Midway. He, like most of the officers at the camp, arrived after a battle in the Pacific, mostly Pearl Harbor or Midway. Some of the enlisted men working at the camp were simply men who weren't fit to serve overseas, but who still wanted to be of service to their country. Some in the media referred to the guards as SCUs, "sick, crippled, and useless." Few of them had served in Germany, because to guard the same men who shot at you would be mental torture that no one should be forced to navigate. Margaret thought there was an article to be written on just how damaged some of these boys really were. Oh, how she missed writing.

Mary, her editor at the *Daily Nebraskan*, had enlisted in the press corps. Margaret couldn't even persuade her parents to let her stay in Lincoln, let alone head to Europe to cover the actual war effort.

"What's on the docket today, Chap?" Margaret asked as she reapplied her red lipstick before tucking her lunch bag and purse under her desk. As a civilian, she technically didn't have to refer to the officers by their rank. Behind closed doors, they were all familiars. It was only when superior officers from headquarters in D.C. came to huff and puff their way around the offices that even the civilians followed the chain of command.

"Word is that we're getting some Germans here soon," he said. "We need to get a count on supplies, so it's going to be a busy week. You know the drill."

Margaret and Chap's work together at the airfield had allowed them to develop an easy rhythm to their work days. He appreciated her intelligence, her efficiency, and her ability to direct him to the right local resources to get things done for the military. He tolerated her substandard stenography skills.

Though she would have preferred to be studying journalism at school, exposure to the large-scale business of construction and the masterful inefficiencies of government projects was intriguing and she was somewhat grateful to her parents for forcing her to major in business, though she would never let them know. The intro to accounting courses had proved useful more frequently these days. Journalism made it so she could type with a rapidity that made her lack of stenography skills less apparent. She'd decided that a business degree might not be so awful when she was free to return to school.

Chapter Fifteen

July 1943

Margaret knew that her job at the prisoner of war camp was embarrassing to her mother and that gave her a bit of a thrill. Rebecca hated all of those dirty Italians looking at her daughter. She berated Margaret and Franklin, endlessly trying to get her way. She'd even written to Thomas's mother to try to convince her to get her son to put an end to it. What she didn't know was that Thomas's mother sided with Margaret and didn't say a word to Thomas about the new job. When Margaret got home from work each day she had to steel herself for a new barrage of criticism on the one interesting thing she'd done since leaving school.

"Spike! C'mere my good boy, who's a good boy?"

Margaret came bounding up the back stairs as Spike barked an enthusiastic greeting, and then stopped short upon seeing her mother standing, as a sentry, at the kitchen window. Nelly, their housekeeper, was giving Margaret a slight headshake and communicated with her eyes that Rebecca was in one of her moods.

"Good evening, Mother."

"You're late," Rebecca said. "Why in the world do you stay so late at that terrible place? Why can't you just go to work with your father? Your hair is a mess. Go change for dinner." Rebecca turned on her heel. Just as she was about to walk into the dining room she spun back around. "Another letter from Thomas came. Not that you care about anyone but yourself. I have half a mind to write to his mother again and let her know what her future daughter-in-law is up to. You're lucky that your father is, as always, on your side." She threw the letter down on the kitchen table. With that, Rebecca pushed the large swinging door aggressively and stormed out.

Margaret grabbed the letter, scooped Spike up into her arms, and rolled her eyes. This temper tantrum was nothing new. If it wasn't this job, it would be her hair, her figure, her degree, or her father. As she often told her friends, "If she's not criticizing, she's not happy."

She was blessed with a bedroom that afforded her some privacy from the temperamental storm that was brewing in the house. She'd marched out the dimensions and determined it was the size of four prisoner cells, and when things were bad with Mother, she melodramatically acted as if she'd been sent to prison. Margaret curled up in the bay window and read Thomas's latest letter and draft a response as a peace offering to Mother.

June 28, 1943 - New Orleans
My darling:
Good evening sweet! Received a swell letter from you today and I got thinking an awful lot of how much I loved you. In fact you have been on my mind more than usual today. Honey, I

think you're wonderful. I also love you best in the whole world. Remember that when you see any of those boys coming through town.

Remember the fun we had in College? It was fun, wasn't it? All the picnics at South Bend and around. The good times dancing together at the Terrace. It would certainly be wonderful to relive those few wonderful hours we had together again.

How about the night you came back and it was a battle between the Arrow Shirt salesman and myself. It was such fun and I was in love with you every moment. OH, how you wanted me to stop fighting.

You know though, sweetheart, the moment I will never forget is when I met you at the train to see me after my graduation. Gee but you looked wonderful sitting there as the train pulled in. I think I have re-lived that moment over and over again. Also that Friday night at the Cornhusker when I asked if you would be mine. I was afraid to ask for fear you'd say "no".

I'm thankful that we don't have trouble with our future in-laws as do many people. I think that your Ma and Pa are swell and for my folks I know that they think your tops, one in a million. How right they are.

Wish that I could see you lovely but at present it isn't practical. I could get the leave but it is a long ways to go in only ten days. I would have to stay in Lincoln at least two days and from there it is a still longer trip to see you. Maybe my next post will be a little closer. At least it can't be much further. I don't relish coming home in the summer either. All in all I guess I won't be there until the wedding.

My roommate is quite a character. He has a beautiful red necktie hanging in the window. Where in the hell he got it I don't know. He also has a big portrait of a wolf with the fangs showing and who is drooling somewhat. Under that is printed "SURRE-ALISTIC PORTRAIT REPRESENTING THE SEX LIFE OF A SECOND LIEUTENANT". Then as you look about the place you will see pictures of all types of women. From the sublime to the surreal. From the naked to the fully clothed. Must say though that he has good taste.

On the next page you will find a little questionnaire. Send it back the next time you write.

Goodnight Mrs. Davey. How about a couple of kisses in your next letter.

Be good,

Thomas xxx

PS.

1 - Do you love me? 2 - Do you think of me? 3 - Are you happy? 4 - Do you miss me? 5 - How is Bea? 6 - Is there anything here in NOLA that I could get for you? 7 - How is your mother feeling? 8 - Is your Dad O.K.? 9 - Did you receive your postcards? 10 - Don't you think this is silly? 11 - Have you found a car yet? 12 - This is reserved for kisses. 13 - I need a little loving, do you? 14 - Any particular person? 15 - How is the bank? 16 - Would you like to see me? 17 - Aren't you glad this is over with?

His affection was smothering. The spelling and grammatical errors alone maddened her. Who messes up your and you're? Who tells his fiancé about lewd posters of women and his bunkmate's sex life? Margaret was not naïve to the needs of soldiers, even the prisoners were allowed a pinup girl or two, but if Thomas was trying to spark any sort of affection this wasn't the way to do it. They'd been engaged for nearly two years and those carefree college days of two years ago felt like a distant memory.

She sat down at her small desk in the corner of her room to draft a response. Starting with the numbered questions.

Dear Thomas,

1 - Do I love you? I'm not sure. I really like your mom. If I marry you then we can live in Lincoln and I can go back to school — as if you'd let your wife go back to school...

2 - Do I think of you? Only when I get your letters. Or when I head out with the girls to the Officer's Club and know how mad you'd be. Oh, and you'd better believe you'd be mad.

3 - Are you happy? Not right now. It's hot, work is busier than expected, and my mom is angry. We're at war. Who would be happy?

4 - Do I miss you? Nope.

5 - How is Bea? Well, she'd be livid with the response to this letter since she wants us to have a double wedding.

It was in thinking of Bea's response that Margaret stopped writing, crumpled up the piece of paper, and started over. They hadn't seen each other at work to discuss her response to the first letter, so she knew she couldn't send this one without Bea's advice. She knew June's advice would be to kick him to the curb but she'd ask for it anyway in her next letter.

Thomas wouldn't be furloughed for months, and she was sure, by then, something would happen to throw the wedding plans off. Maybe, much to his mother's dismay, he'd be called to Europe early, and the wedding would be called off indefinitely. She caught herself wishing something more dramatic would happen to derail these plans. It's hard to call off a wedding during a war. You'd hate to be the girl who broke the boy's heart right before he went off to battle.

Margaret decided to forego writing to Thomas tonight. Her head just wasn't in the right space. Instead, she pulled out a fresh piece of stationery and set out to update Sam and June on the goings-on at the camp, at home, and maybe even ask his advice on this whole Thomas situation. Maybe if her mother saw letters heading to the box, she'd think it was to Thomas.

Dearest Cousin -

How is my favorite fighter pilot? The Fourth of July party at the folks' house won't seem the same without you here to blow things up, but I take it you're doing plenty of that wherever you are. Mother and Daddy say hello. They are, as always, on my case about something or another, and I wish this war would just end so I could go back to Lincoln and pick up where we all left off. Don't you?

I envy you getting to see the world while I'm stuck back home. I don't know if you've heard the news, though. I'm working at the prisoner of war camp. You go capture them, and we'll make sure they do their time! This job drives Mother insane, more insane than she already is (!), and I love it. Right now, we have mostly

Italians. I'd heard from your mother that you might have had something to do with getting a few of those rascals to surrender.

Where are you off to next? I know you can't say. I wish you could.

It's so hot here. This summer has been brutal. One nice thing about working at the camp is the officers make sure that there are plenty of fans. And we're allowed to wear dresses and short sleeve shirts and all of our nylons have been sent to be used by your crew in their parachutes. No stinky uniforms for us! The POWs and the guards do enough of the stinking for us!

The mood here is pretty low. People genuinely thought the war would be over by now. The newsreels make it seem like we're winning, but the articles in the newspapers keep us unsure. How I miss writing for the paper! My editor, Mary, you remember her, is over in France as part of an international press corps. Jealous!

Oregon Trail Days are in a couple of weeks, and I know how you loved to go to the carnival and go on the fastest rides. I guess those will seem boring when you get home. Your mom says you're close to your hours and will be home soon.

Can't wait to see you!

Love - Your cousin - Megs

PS. Still engaged to Thomas. I know you don't like him. I'm not sure I do either. Shhh...don't tell Mother. You can take my side when you get back.

June would prefer a much more honest approach to her letter.

June,

You're about to get your wish. Thomas sent me a letter that was so juvenile it felt like those notes we used to hand boys in junior high. The ones that said do you like me? Circle yes or no.

I know you're swamped with school. I'll keep it short and sweet.

Should I end things with Thomas? Circle your response. Yes or No.

~M

P.S. Try and keep this secret from Bea.

Chapter Sixteen

August 1943

Margaret had just finished her morning tasks of cataloging the latest shipment of toiletries and was compiling a ledger of the items they would need to order if they did get the Germans rumored to be on their way. She was shaking her head at the inefficiency of the whole thing. The Germans could be here tomorrow for all they knew. She'd heard a story from one of the officers, which may or may not be true, that an entire trainload of Germans showed up in a town in Kansas before the bullets for the guard's guns did, and they managed to corral four thousand German soldiers with just the perception of strength as they marched them through town with unarmed rifles trained upon them. The posturing of war was ridiculous.

She raised her head as Chapman came in with Bea at his side. Bea was crying. Margaret assumed that some soldier, prisoner, or guard, had said something inappropriate to her sensitive friend and it would be up to Margaret to smooth things over. Bea worked in the personnel department of the camp and was always getting the brunt of the bad moods.

"Margaret," Chapman shut the door, "I have some news."

Margaret froze.

"It's Sam, isn't it."

Chapman nodded only slightly. "I'm so sorry Margaret. This war has taken too much from you."

Margaret was already standing, putting her things in her bag, and grabbing the keys to the car. She didn't wait for him to give her any more news.

Bea chased Margaret down the hallway as she headed to the car.

"Let me drive! You're in no shape!" Bea cried.

Margaret spun on her heel, "I'm in no shape? You can't even see through your tears. Get in if you want, but I'm driving."

The drive from the camp to home was about eleven miles, mostly on narrow dirt roads that were occasionally blocked by tractors or trucks hauling prisoners to their work assignments. It typically took twenty minutes to make it home. Today it took thirteen.

Bea was carsick by the time they screeched into the driveway. Margaret's aunt and uncle's house was right across the street from her own. Her grandfather had built matching homes for each of his sons and she and Sam had grown up like siblings running back and forth from house to house.

"Uncle Robert!" Margaret raced into their front living room. He stoically handed her a piece of paper.

12 AUGUST 1943

MR. AND MRS. ROBERT MURPHY

THE SECRETARY OF WAR DESIRES ME TO EXPRESS HIS DEEP REGRET THAT YOUR SON SAMUEL A. MURPHY HAS

BEEN REPORTED MISSING IN ACTION SINCE AUGUST 1
IN ROMANIA IF FURTHER DETAILS OR OTHER INFOR-
MATION ARE RECEIVED YOU WILL BE PROMPTLY NOTI-
FIED.

ULIO THE ADJUTANT GENERAL

She sunk down into a chair. "Missing."

Her mother, who was sitting on the settee with her hand on her aunt's back, said "Yes, and we're sure he's going to be found, and in perfect health, aren't we?"

Margaret didn't believe that for a moment. It had been six weeks since she wrote to Sam and he had not replied. For the last couple of weeks she'd been dreaming of him frequently, sometimes with fire surrounding him, other times he was trying to shout at her. She knew he was dead, but went along with the false hope that filled the room because there was nothing else to be done.

Margaret stayed home from work for several days after the notification of Sam's disappearance. She was simply too distracted. Chap understood. She combed the papers for details of every raid, visited the library for details about Romania and the surrounding area, watched the newsreels, and pestered her father for inside news from his connected friends. She wished she knew that he'd received her letter—she imagined that his thoughts were of his family. She blamed every mistake on the planners, the masterminds, the leaders of this horrible war. She genuinely thought she could figure out where he disappeared and where they should look for him on her own from the comfort of her wicker chair on the large, screened-in, front porch.

It was from this perch that she watched a dark government car pull up in front of the twin houses on O Street and two sharply uniformed men emerge.

They stepped out of the car and stopped, only briefly, to talk with each other before they adjusted their hats and stepped towards her aunt and uncle's home.

Margaret stood silently at attention, mirroring their posture and body language as they knocked on the front door.

Her aunt opened the door, and they removed their hats in unison.

She did not need to hear the words. She simply had to watch her aunt's face crumble. The only sound she heard was a moan that seemed to come from her uncle's soul as he joined his wife at the door as they learned of the death of their son.

The news was devastating. Sam was loved by all. The war just became more real for western Nebraska. The Germans had killed one of their own.

Chapter Seventeen

September 1943

Weeks later, still reeling from Sam's death, Margaret was hesitant to go with Bea and the girls to the train station for their weekly morale-boosting flirtations with soldiers as they headed across the country. Bea had stopped by to cajole her into attending, June had come back from school for the weekend to both celebrate Margaret's birthday and provide support in getting Margaret back amongst the living. They were all huddled in her bedroom.

"I'm not going," Margaret said, pulling a pillow down over her face.

"Megs." Bea struggled with what to say. "It's been almost a month. You need to get out of the house."

"I leave the house every day."

"To go to work."

"Exactly. I don't need to go see any new soldiers. They're all going to die anyway."

"Margaret! How can you say that!" June exclaimed. Bea joined in on the reprimands. Bea's fiancé, Ted, was in the service and was due to head out on a second tour. June had coupled up with their high school classmate, Milt, who was finishing medical school before deploying. Even with love interests they still enjoyed some harmless flirting now and again. It helped to distract them from the horrors of reality.

Margaret ignored them. She knew that death was a possibility in war, maybe even a probability. When she'd said goodbye to Thomas at the train station in New Orleans, she figured that someday he might head to Europe, but she figured that he'd be safe if that ever happened. He was a glorified mess cook. News from the Western Front was not good. Privately she wished it was Thomas, not Sam, that she was mourning.

Margaret emerged from under the pillow with a fierce glare in her piercing blue-grey eyes. She was taking no prisoners.

"Look," she paused to make sure she had their attention. "Sam was one of the best pilots they had in Europe. He was almost ready to come home. Uncle Robert said that he heard from one of Sam's fellow pilots that the whole raid was beyond screwed up. If Roosevelt and his damned military commanders can't start making better decisions and better headway in Europe and the Pacific, then our whole world is going to be overrun by Nazis and Japanese, and every boy that we love, or think we love, is going to be sent home in pieces or abandoned in mass graves in Europe. There's nothing we can do about it so stop asking me to meet more lemmings at the train station with you."

She slammed her head back on the pillow and turned her head to the wall. Her dog Spike, awoken by the commotion, began to whine.

Bea started to cry right along with him. Margaret's frank assessment of the stark realities of war was painful to hear.

"She didn't mean it," said June, trying to comfort Bea. "Our boys are going to be fine. Thomas, Ted, Milt. They're all going to come home in one piece, and we're going to get married. We're going to have babies, and our families are going to be inseparable until we're all old toothless women with white hair." She attempted to distract Bea by pulling her lips tight across her teeth and making funny faces while she talked. "Remember that day back in 1943 when Margaret wouldn't get out of bed?"

She hunched over and grabbed an umbrella from the bin next to Margaret's door to use as a cane. "Remember how she yelled so loud her dog started to howl?"

Her melodrama broke the mood.

"I'm sorry," Margaret said. "I shouldn't have said that." She may still feel it, but Bea was such a sensitive soul that she should have known better. This was a conversation better had with her dad, not her best friends. "Let's go. I'll stop being such a spoilsport." Margaret crawled off of the four-poster bed where she'd been cocooned and grabbed her hairbrush and attempted to smooth some of the unruly waves.

The walk to the train depot was a short one through town, and they made it just as the train was pulling in. Hundreds of soldiers—many who would not have been handsome out of uniform—stepped off the train to go through the canteen that the war effort volunteers had put together. Grabbing ham sandwiches and a soda, they also worked to grab a quick twirl or smile from a local girl. The stops were short but just long enough to exchange addresses for writing letters. Women were asked to help keep morale high as pen pals. Margaret felt she'd done her part writing to Sam, and she was responding to nearly every one of Thomas's letters even though it was becoming more and more obvious that their affair needed to come to an end.

With a false smile pasted on her perfectly lipstick-ed lips, she kept repeating the phrase "Go get 'em boys. You've got this!" or disingenuously asking "Where are you headed?" or "Where are you from?" all the while not listening to a single answer. These boys were too young to go to war. Some looked like they still belonged in high school. She gritted her teeth against her insincerity.

"Margaret?"

The sound of a familiar voice, somewhat deeper than she'd remembered, snapped her out of her thoughts.

"It's Charles. Charles Barton. From Long Beach." His voice trailed off, and the insecure boy she remembered from summer camp was standing before her. Though he didn't look like the Charles she'd summered with all those years ago. Just under six-feet tall, lean, with sandy blonde hair, he'd been an attractive boy but had grown into a man. She and Sam had spent several summers in Long Beach at a camp while their mothers rested by the water from their stressful lives as the wives of bankers and insurance salesmen.

"Charles! What in the world are you doing in Nebraska?" And what are you doing at war, she wanted to cry. He was always such a gentle soul, nose in a book, studious even at summer camp. They hadn't spoken since her last summer in Long Beach five years ago. They'd exchanged a few letters. He married his high school sweetheart, and the letters stopped.

"I just finished basic training and am headed back to San Diego to continue med school," he replied. And then, somewhat awkwardly, "I got divorced."

His first answer gave her some temporary relief. His second shocked her. Maybe he could be spared brutality by being a stateside doctor. She knew that was unlikely as they were speeding up the graduation rates for doctors to get them in the field as fast as possible. Now that he didn't have a wife and children waiting for him, he'd go even faster. He kept his eyes locked on her, feeling that something was off.

"How are you holding up?"

She couldn't respond at first, her voice caught in her throat.

"Sam died."

Charles didn't do the polite thing, he didn't do the proper thing, and he didn't ask any questions. He simply enveloped Margaret in an embrace. She knew there was no flirtation, no method to his familiarity, that he just saw pain and, being the healer he was by nature, wanted to fix it. Even so, she had to be very aware of appearances, and Margaret began to pull away. Charles simply held her at arm's length and looked down at her, and said, "I'm sorry. Tell me all about it." He walked with her over to a nearby bench, chastely holding her elbow as if leading her to church.

Her family and friends were all grieving Sam's death right alongside her and weren't great counsel. Charles only had a few minutes before his train, but in those fleeting moments, Margaret was able to share her frustrations, her fears, and her heartbreak with no judgment and no reaction except a sad understanding of the pain she was feeling. The conversation felt like going to confession. A confession that she never wanted to end, but the blast of the train whistle brought them out of their conversation and back to the cold reality that it was time to go.

When she kissed Charles on the cheek to say goodbye, she felt a tear touch her lips. Charles, quiet and sensitive, had absorbed her sadness. It was almost as if he had taken it away. As the soldiers boarded the train, she felt better than she had in months. Her head was clear. With clarity came power, and she knew what she had to do.

Chapter Eighteen

September 8, 1943
    Thomas -
    This should not come as a surprise. You know I'm not one to mince words and so I will not waste any time or ink getting to the point.
    I am calling off our engagement. It is not fair to you for me to pretend any longer that we are the same people now as we were when we met. You will make someone a wonderful husband someday. It will just not be me. I believe there is a depth of affection that is necessary to start a marriage that I simply do not have. It's quite likely that's a character flaw on my part, but I don't want to hobble our marriage and our future by starting our lives at such a deficit.
    I have written your parents and mailed the ring back to them for safekeeping for your future bride.
    I wish you health, safety, and all the best.
    Yours, Margaret

She emerged from her room with a stack of letters and a box. "I just ended my engagement with Thomas. I'm headed to the post office to return the ring to his parents for whoever does want to marry him. Because I do not."

Rebecca threw down the book she was reading. "Excuse me? You cannot call off your engagement without discussing it with us first. Right Franklin? Please interject here!"

Franklin had a bit of a grin on his face. "Looks like she's already sealed the envelopes, Rebecca. There's simply nothing we can do."

"You never did like that boy." Rebecca could not decide who to fight first and her head ping-ponged back and forth between her husband and daughter. "I cannot believe that you are stringing him along like this, especially during a war..."

Rebecca continued her diatribe, but Margaret had already leashed up Spike and headed out the door for the short walk to the post office.

Her mother would never understand if she shared the conversation with Charles. Rebecca wasn't focused on Margaret's happiness but rather on what looked good to her bridge group.

She knew she'd receive a very quick response to this letter and, because he was still stateside, a few short days later his response arrived a few days later .

September 12, 1943
Dear Margaret -
Received your letter this morning and I still wonder if it is true. I really can't make heads or tails out of what you are basing

your judgement upon but I have many times given up the idea of figuring out how you think.

I just talked to my folks over the phone and they are a little confused at everything too. Many things have happened in the last few days so I shouldn't be too surprised with your decision. When it rains it pours.

Maybe I had better tell you first what the other things were and you will understand what I meant.

Yesterday we had our first inspection and also found out that they were just ready to pull all of our medical officers. All hell has broken out in Europe and everything is pulling out of the state. It is possible that some of us will be transferred. I have all my personal equipment and supplies ready and can leave in 2 hours.

What I am trying to say to you is that if this were civilian life I would come to wherever you were to get our problems worked out but as the situation is I cannot get even off 3 or 4 days to fly to you.

I love you darling. I have since the first day and I believe that you love me too. We have been apart for a long time. We don't have too much in common at the moment because of that. If I'd been able to be stationed there I would have gotten to know your friends better and we could talk of something that both of us understood. On the other hand I believe, sincerely, that had we gotten married as per our original plan that you would have learned to know the friends that I have had for the past year. It makes a difference darling this being away and not being able to have fun together. Can you see it that way too?

My mother said that she wrote to you and said that the ring would be there if you ever wanted it. She is very right sweetheart - the ring will be there waiting for you. My mother knows that I love you very much and that if I thought you and I couldn't be so much in love that I would have mentioned that back at some time or other.

I have changed a lot darling since I have been in the Army. I realize it, my folks realize it and I think that you have seen it too. I think that it is for the better but maybe I am wrong. I will probably change a lot more before I get out of this mess too. Maybe that is the reason why I'm not writing that I can't live without you and such. I know better because anyone can live without anyone else and I have been doing just that thing now for the past nineteen or twenty months.

I am trying to give you what I think are facts and I want you to make up your own mind. I love you so much that it hurts to know you are so many miles away but if you don't think that you would be happy with me it is useless to try and change your mind.

I'm going to close now and tell you that I will love you forever. You know where you can get the ring. It would make me very happy for you to take it back but that is up to you. I probably won't write to you again for some time Margaret but the next time you hear from me I will be on my way.

As ever, Thomas.

When people asked why she called off the engagement, or if there was someone else, she knew she couldn't answer honestly. She would hide behind "We were so young." Or, "I'm not strong enough to bury a husband." The honest answer was that she cared for Thomas's mother more than she cared for Thomas. Thomas was not interesting. Thomas was a coward. Thomas hardly acknowledged Sam's death. None of the curated answers appeased her mother who spent nearly a week not speaking and broke her silence only to berate her.

"You do know that all of the eligible men have left the country?"

"What must his parents think of us!"

"Is there someone else?"

There was no one else. Her heartbreak at losing Sam made her wary of caring for anyone. She had her friends, though Bea definitely didn't fully understand her decision, and her work. That was enough for her now.

Thomas' mother, Vi, had written her a lengthy response, further solidifying the fact that she was going to be the thing she missed most about her pending marriage.

September 13, 1943

My Dear Margaret:

Your letter of Wednesday has just come, and after reading it we feel as though we have lost a very dear friend. Your decision to return Thomas' ring does come as a shock to us. We have, for so long, dreamed of the day you two would marry and we could have a lovely daughter in addition to a son. But let me say at once, that feeling as you do, it is a kind and courageous thing to do now. Now, before your lives become complicated with marriage and its attendant legal difficulties. I know how very, very, hard this has been for you to do, how hard to come to the decision and then to tell us and to tell him. Greatly as we regret this, we feel you are right in discontinuing your engagement to him. It is very easy for any person to make a decision or a promise, it takes a very fine person indeed to admit an error.

And believe us when we say we do regret it. We were pleased with Tom's choice of a girl, so very fond of you, and we have said innumerable times, that we couldn't have chosen anyone who would have suited us any more than you did. We will try our best to get used to the idea that you will not be one of the family some of these days.

We are feeling most awfully sorry for Thomas. We would like to be there with him at this time, for I know he needs someone to talk to, or not talk to, as he will. I only hope that he has felt that same uncertainty that you felt. If he does it will be much easier for him. But, unless you had a talk while he was with you in New Orleans, then he really will be feeling most awfully bad. Forgive us if we seem to think of him first, parents seem to be made that way.

I'm sorry too, that you feel you must return the gifts. I'm sure he would want you to keep them in remembrance of the grand times you have had together and in memory of your engagement. However, you must do as you think best.

We know you are losing a fine boy, but that's beside the point. There are many fine folks in the world, but we don't fall in love with them, and we feel as you do, that perhaps you did not have enough affection to use as a foundation for a successful marriage.

If there is any hope that you might reverse your decision, let us be the first to know. We will be so very happy to know of it.

Please write to us occasionally for we will be thinking of you.

In any case, we are still,

Affectionately, Violet Davey

Chapter Nineteen

October 1943

It seemed absurd to consider escaping into the prison preferable to staying home. Work was a place where she felt some semblance of control. She'd been given the additional responsibility to help process each prisoner and help ensure that Camp Scottsbluff was in compliance with orders from Washington. With Italy's surrender had come the ordeal of coordinating the transfer of all of the Italian prisoners. It wasn't as simple as sending them back to Sicily. The northern Italians need to go to Milan, the southern Italians to Rome, and the few American boys with Italian grandparents who just happened to be visiting Italy when the war started and were captured quickly after being conscripted still weren't sure whether they had to go back to Italy before they could come back to New York. They were to be organized according to their regions and would travel as groups to camps back east before being sent home.

Each prisoner needed to provide their home addresses and Margaret was growing tired of hearing the translator say, "Scusami, qual'è il tuo numero di identificazione? Il tuo indirizzo? Puo riempire questo modulo," as she handed each prisoner a clipboard and a pencil.

Flirtation is the same in any language, and the chatter from the boys as they filled out their paperwork was definitely not about their identification numbers or their home addresses. It took a sharp word from the camp translator for the men to come back to the task so Margaret could gather the information from this group and prepare for the next. This exercise would be repeated ad nauseum as the government perpetually changed the requirements for release.

It was taking an extraordinary amount of time, and the inefficiency helped fuel Margaret's rage, which seemed to be constantly bubbling under the surface. She slammed the door to Chapman's office.

"We're just keeping these boys here so there's someone to cook for the Officer's Club for the holidays!"

This was the first time Margaret was fired-up again after many months of sadness and no shortage of silence surrounding the end of her engagement. She had said nothing, simply removed the small engagement photo from her desk, and went about her business.

Chapman chuckled. "You're probably right. They make the best bread," he said, "But keep that opinion to yourself. The Geneva Convention just says they must be released promptly, but we both know how prompt Uncle Sam is."

As soon as he'd said the word Sam, Margaret's icy blue eyes sparked like the blue-hot flame on a gas stove as she turned to him.

"Uncle Sam is a chicken shit!"

She slammed her desk drawer. Margaret's sense of decorum and good upbringing had suffered, or at least relaxed, with the months at the prison surrounded primarily by soldiers. She'd isolated herself from the girls who worked in the typing pool and spent most of her time with the officers and Bea. June would understand her frustration but she was back in Lincoln wrapping up her nursing studies.

She was right about the delays. The government was slow playing the release of the Italian Prisoners as they mapped out the country's needs for labor to determine where they needed to start sending Germans. The logistics of the entire enterprise were overwhelming.

After the last Italians were sent down to Fort Carson in Colorado to get their travel orders to head home, Camp Scottsbluff would have a brief period of quiet before the Germans arrived. Fences were to be fortified, bunks needed to be secured, and procedures were discussed ad nauseum. The Italians never felt all that threatening. They were a jolly bunch of men, generally offensive only to the women in the camp, and were incredible cooks. They spent most of their time singing, playing soccer, and writing to their mothers. It was as if Mussolini's participation in the war was a lark, and they were just happy to escape the shooting by heading to America to wait it out. Everything Margaret had heard about the Germans was an entirely different story.

Chapter Twenty

December 1943

At the end of the semester, June enlisted in the Army Nurse Corps and was due to be deployed at the military's whim. She'd been home less than three days and already the girls had settled into their old pattern of rotating houses and staying up too late talking.

Their evening consisted of walking downtown to visit the light display and nativity scene set up in front of the courthouse. By the time they got back to June's house, they were freezing. They built a fire, turned on the Christmas tree bulbs, and since they were trying to be more sophisticated, made hot toddies instead of hot cocoa.

"Let's raise a glass to our newest graduate! May we be worthy of her intellect," Margaret kicked off the conversation.

The three all took sips of their drinks and worked to hide their reactions. Bea started choking, "This is just cough medicine."

"Hey, we're lucky to find some whiskey in the cabinets. It's the best I can do here. I think lemons might make it better. Does anyone know where to get a lemon in the middle of Nebraska in December?" June took a giant gulp to try and prove that it wasn't so bad, which caused the other two to laugh. June ended up spitting out the liquid as she attempted to stifle her own laughter which led to all of them having a complete fit of giggles which ended up with Bea crying. "Hey now," June reached out for Bea's hand. "What's this about? Don't cry over spilled toddy. I can make you something else to drink."

"It's not the drink, though it is awful, it's that I've missed you too much and now you're leaving." Bea reached for a tissue.

"Did you get my deployment papers by mistake? Where am I headed? Please tell me that I'm heading to New York and not getting assigned to the prison in Scottsbluff. I hear they employ some questionable characters."

Margaret joined in on the teasing, "I hear that there is this girl, her boss calls her Bumble Bee because she's so efficient. I think she's a secretary for some high-ranking mucky muck."

"He does not... Does he?" Bea was quite gullible.

"No, dear Bea, he does not, but we needed you to stop crying so we could hear about June's final days in Lincoln. June, tell us, are they still making those delightful fries at *The Lone Oak*?" Margaret attempted to change the subject.

"Umm, Margaret, one does not graduate in two and a half years by spending time off campus. I walked back and forth from sorority row to Bessey Hall and ate whatever Miss Kay put in front of me. I often missed my mouth as I was looking at a book and not at what I was eating."

"You must have had a nicer housemistress if you were able to eat at the table," Bea said.

"All of the rules have been relaxed on campus. We've outnumbered men, we're all wearing pants, it's delightful."

"Damn my mother for making me miss it all. Don't get me wrong, at least I have the freedom to work at the prison instead of, God forbid, accompanying my mom to her never-ending 'ladies who lunch' get-togethers."

"I actually really like working at the prison. The days go quickly. I'm good at the organization parts of the whole endeavor. Plus, we'll never be shot at..." Bea once again started to get choked up.

"Time for a story," June clapped her hands together. "We had to take a nine-hour course in Syphilology—which is the same length as the course in Professional Adjustments where we determine our specialty. The entire time we were in class I thought, 'There are people that would like to spend their entire day dealing with the rashy genitalia of promiscuous men—what better place to do that than the U.S. Army.' That was the moment I determined that I just wanted to focus on trauma and emergency front-line surgeries. No 'itchy scratchies' for me!"

"I did not expect our Christmas season to have the phrase 'rashy genitalia'. Can we all raise a glass to the brave nurses who have chosen that specialty!" Margaret lifted her hot, now lukewarm, toddy to the sky.

Bea interjected, "But first can we get some cocoa?"

Chapter Twenty-One

February 1944

Rebecca was waiting at her perch in the kitchen when Margaret walked in the door. The respite from her nagging was far too brief. Rebecca held out a letter and, surprisingly, it had not yet been opened.

"Who is writing to you from San Diego?" Her mother was still holding out hope that she would marry well and not end this war as a spinster. Her motives were so thinly veiled, Margaret laughed despite herself.

"The Navy, Mother. They have decided they need an assistant to the Quartermaster out in San Diego and I'm shipping out next week. There's just nothing you can do. Duty calls."

"You and your lip. I've half a mind to let you go."

Margaret rolled her eyes. She knew she was stuck for a while longer. She'd been saving her earnings from the camp and plotting her escape. There was no reason to further antagonize her mother, so she didn't take the bait. Instead, she took the letter and retreated to her room.

February 13, 1944 (US Naval Hospital, San Diego)
Dear Margaret,

Gathering up the happenings of the past few months and sending a story of them on to you will be a difficult job but I'm going to do my best. I'll begin by making excuses, a habit of mine, as you know, regarding correspondence.

I have thought of you so many many times and have wished often to hear from you. Knowing you as I do and your—I want for a more appropriate word than stubbornness— I should have known your letter would only arrive after I've sent mine. I do hope I will hear from you soon.

I have been busier than ever before in my life. My hours are long 8 to 5 and each third nite and two out of three Sundays I stand a watch at the hospital. Three watches are very busy and consequently, my two off nites are devoted primarily to recuperating. So far I have been out only a few nites. The Hotel Del twice and a few club functions a few of us do manage to get to the beach occasionally. The town is miserably crowded. It's a day's work getting to work on the streetcar and another getting home.

The hospital is huge, nearly 10,000 beds and growing constantly. We see every imaginable type of case from obscure disease to measles and from boils to horrific wounds and burns. They do some wonderful things here and I am more than pleased with my training.

I got a new camera a few weeks ago. It's an 8mm movie camera and a beauty but I don't have an exposure meter and I hate to waste film without one.

There is much more I'd like to write but I have to do some other catching up tonite. I've sure let things slip but this climate, I hope it's the climate, makes me lazy.

I'll write again as soon as I can, until then Good Nite.
As ever, Charles.
P.S. Happy Valentine's Day

After their meeting at the train station, Margaret wasn't sure that she'd hear from Charles again. His warm counsel at the train station was so comforting she'd found herself thinking of him often. She had wanted to write to him about the engagement, or lack thereof, but thought that might be a little presumptuous.

February 25, 1944 - Gering, Nebraska
Dear Charles,
I'm happy to hear that you're still stateside. Those of us back home often worry when we don't hear from our loved ones for months at a time. Though, I suppose my stubbornness could be partially to blame. Between my stubbornness and your hesitation, we might never have communicated!

For the first time in my life, western Nebraska is interesting. We finally shipped out our last Italian prisoner, and now we're moving on to the Germans. With the horror stories about the Nazis, I'm not quite sure what to expect.

Part of my job when the Italians were here was to help get supplies for the new prisoners. They smelled horrible so the first thing we give them is a shower kit with a bar of soap, a razor, and a new uniform with the letters PW painted in bright white letters so we could keep track of them. Between being clean and getting full bellies they almost seemed grateful.

People in town are angry that we're treating the prisoners well. The newsreels showing the conditions of how our boys are being treated never help. I wonder if this letter will make it through the censors. I'm not sure I'm allowed to discuss the camp. I imagine everyone is going to be really angry if we show the Germans a lick of kindness.

I head out this weekend for a trip to Omaha with Bea. We're having a sendoff for our friend June (she was at the train station with me) who is going to work in the nursing corps. Her mother is obviously more lenient than mine. Ah, well.

All my best - Margaret

Chapter Twenty-Two

March 1944

The Omaha Officer's Club smelled of cheap beer and the sweaty wool of nervous young men trying to dance. Surrounding a makeshift dance floor of barn wood—mostly clean of the hay and dust of its original purpose—were tables where people could set down the drinks procured from the bar in the corner. Bea and Margaret had traveled to Omaha for the weekend to visit June before she left for nurse's training in New York and, as an added benefit Bea's fiancé, Ted, happened to be in town at the same time. Bea's and Margaret's mothers shared the same puritanical belief that each girl would chaperone the other into behaving and allowed the getaway.

The band, *Doc and His Syncopated Surgeons*, had the club hopping. The trumpet player and clarinet player battled through raucous covers of the big hits of the day, keeping the crowd on their toes with foot-stomping swing tunes and heart-melting love songs. Though peppered with a bit of anxiety, the general mood was high.

"I just think this all feels a bit surreal. It almost feels like we're back at a college dance with everyone pretending the war isn't just getting worse!" Margaret was nearly shouting to be heard over the band.

"Oh, come on, Megs, the Germans will be here any day. We deserve a little distraction. Besides, you need to celebrate getting out of town for a couple of days!" Bea was tucked into the crook of Ted's arm. He was due to head out in the morning with a large convoy to the east coast and was enjoying a night of staring at his future bride.

"Nothing says heading off to fight Hitler like a jazzy beat." June snapped her fingers to the rhythm, grinning at a soldier across the room who took her snapping as an invitation to come over and lead her out to the dancefloor. Margaret laughed, shaking her head at her friend's antics.

She felt a tap on her right shoulder. Margaret turned from watching her two best friends to the familiar lopsided grin of Bob Hale.

"This old neck hasn't been broken yet, so maybe you'd like a dance or two with this old son of a gun before he puts his neck on the line against those Krauts."

It had been nearly two years since she saw him on campus. He'd changed nearly as much as she had, though in his case, he'd added a couple of inches and developed the broad shoulders of a man who had been through more rigorous training than just football practice.

"Well, if it isn't good ol' Bob Hale back to torment the women of the Western world." They settled comfortably into irreverent banter.

Bob took on a serious tone with a false northeastern accent. "I was sent back by Washington to find the second most beautiful woman in the west but looks like I'll have to make do with the first."

Margaret rolled her eyes, took his outstretched hand, and hit the dance floor. If you can't beat them, join them, she thought. Besides, *In the Mood* was playing, and it's almost sacrilegious to sit still through that song. Bob might be a bit of a jokester and the occasional cad, but he was an excellent dance partner, and Margaret, for all of her attempts at stoic refusal, began to realize the purpose of these Officer's Club dances. With each spin, the anxiety of the newsreels, the obituaries, and the trainloads of prisoners, fell further and further away.

"So, you're home for how long?" She used the relative quiet of a slower tune as an opportunity to catch up.

"Shipping out Monday but couldn't find a harbor in Omaha so I guess I'm gonna have to take the train." Margaret was grateful that Bob hadn't lost his sense of humor in basic training. "Heading east to New York and then the world is my oyster. Not sure where we land after that. You know me, trusting the good ol' U.S. Army to protect this beautiful head of mine." Margaret felt her breath catch in her throat.

Things were starting to get a little too serious. Bob began to sing melodramatically along to the music, whipping her quickly into a spin and a two-step that didn't match the beat at all, effectively breaking the mood that threatened to descend into melancholy. *"It's still the same old story, a fight for love and glory, a case of do or die, the world will always welcome lovers as time goes by."*

Margaret welcomed the laughter.

The next morning was spent wiping tears at the train depot.

"You promise that you'll be safe and come home to us?" Bea was biting her lip to keep it from wavering.

Ted had boarded with his company, and June was waiting for her group to be called.

June gently put her hands on each of Bea's cheeks and pulled her head up so they were eye-to-eye. "Dearest Bea, I would not leave you for all the world. Unless of course, that world was threatened by Hitler and there were bandages to be changed and wounds to be cleaned. Then, I would leave you. Oh, I guess that's what is happening. Sorry, I must go."

June's lighthearted approach to life was going to be missed. The threesome had divided the roles of the joker, the romantic, and the pragmatic. They balanced each other out and, though they were apart while June finished her degree, having one of them on a different continent felt like cutting off a limb.

"Girls, I feel a speech coming on." Margaret had tried to write down a few words the night before and pulled out a folded piece of paper from her pocket.

There is a love between girlfriends that is hard to explain. The whole world pushes and pushes for women to couple up with men and settle down. What we should be pushing is for women to find their people, their kinswomen, and hold on to them tightly once they are found and develop a deep, unyielding, connection. Holding on tightly though does not mean weighing the friends down but, instead, encouraging them wholeheartedly, without reservation, in pursuing their dreams. The love of a girlfriend means that you will always have a champion, a safe place to land, and a solid support system. To our dearest June, we send you off into the wild unknown with our love, our unconditional belief in you, and we will have a hole in our hearts until we know that you are safe.

Her voice had uncharacteristically cracked as she attempted to read the note out loud. She made it nearly to the end before she folded the note back up, and tucked it into the outer pocket of June's bag along with a picture of the three of them from a photo booth at the Pi Phi house. The three girls huddled into a hug for the remaining minutes until June's group was called.

Chapter Twenty-Three

M ay 1944
Country roads cross-hatched the farmland into neat boxes and gave a sense of order to the vast open space. Each stretch begged to be raced, faster than the last, with the shimmying gravel underneath the tires upping her adrenaline. Windows rolled down, she almost forgot the dry heat with each uptick of the speedometer. She left behind a cloud of grey-brown dust. The crunching demise of the grasshoppers on the windshield provided a rhythm section to the ride.

"Slow down! You're going to get us killed!" Bea still wasn't used to Margaret's aggressive driving but was happy to finally see what looked like the hint of a smile on her friend's face.

"Oh, hush. I'm not even going forty-five." The light blue 1940 Buick was a tank, and Margaret enjoyed pushing it to its limits. The adrenaline rush as the gravel spun behind her tires felt like the closest thing to joy in quite some time.

In the distance, a train moved across the horizon, east to west, and slowed as it approached the airfield and makeshift train station near the camp.

The Germans had arrived.

Newsreels continued to show the devastation that the Nazis were raining down upon Europe. Margaret had greedily consumed every bit of media about the war, much to her mother's chagrin. Each morning was spent drinking coffee and reading the *Omaha World-Herald* and the local *Star-Herald* while discussing Roosevelt's next move with her father. She had voraciously consumed every Pyle, Steinbeck, and Marguerite Higgins column she could find. She'd cajoled her father into a subscription to *Time* magazine, and she read every issue of *Stars and Stripes* that came to the prison. Jack Ellison, the editor of the *Gering Courier,* was a frequent dinner guest and her father let her sit in on their political conversations while they smoked their post-dinner cigars on their porch. Apart from the few nights Bea convinced her to go out, evenings were spent around the radio, strategizing with her dad on how the U.S. could win the war.

The race to get to the station would be followed by a race back to the gates of the prison. Bea held on for dear life. The wheels drifted as Margaret threw her car into park, and they rushed to the fence surrounding the train station.

Dozens of U.S. soldiers lined the side of the train with their rifles drawn. The first door opened, and a single man emerged. He was in dungarees and a blue work shirt with PW stamped on the back and on each arm. Though slight of stature, he carried himself as if he was in charge. He stood at attention as a hundred more travel-weary clones, dressed alike, descended and moved to form lines twenty across and five deep.

This exercise was repeated for each of the twenty additional train cars, until two thousand men stood, silently, only the dust moving around their feet.

She thought it was journalistic curiosity that drove her desire to be there the moment the Germans stepped off the train. The truth was more likely that she wanted to see and spit at, the Nazis that had killed Sam and so many Americans. These men were described as violent, dangerous, animals. She wasn't expecting them to look quite so broken down.

Bea commented, "I didn't think they'd be so young."

Margaret was at a loss for words.

"Achtung!" Their commander shouted and established control of the crowd and startled the girls.

Though the military uniforms had long been stripped, the regimented behavior of the soldiers had not, and their heels all clicked together, right arms flying into the air at a precise salute.

"Heil Hitler!"

The sound of two thousand voices shouting in unison was breathtaking. The Italians never were organized. They all seemed to be on vacation from the war. But the Germans had a hierarchy and it seemed rules were to be followed even in captivity.

Under the watchful eyes of the armed guards, the Germans turned and began to march the two miles to the camp. Margaret and Bea got back into the car and sped down the road to beat them there. It was going to be a long day.

eℓe

"Heir est dein paket. Nehman sie einin." Bea had taken German in high school and thought she would make sure these boys understood they were to take only one of the packets that included a change of underclothes; a toiletry kit filled with a toothbrush, toothpaste, soap, and a razor; a bedroll; and two postcards.

"Your number," Margaret said sharply. Though very few of the soldiers spoke any English it was easy enough to understand that she was asking for their prisoner ID number. It was part of her job to ensure compliance with the Geneva Convention, each prisoner had received their provisions, and the enlisted men were directed to their 40 square feet of living space while the officers were directed to their separate living quarters.

Bea was smiling at each one and using her limited high school German and kept saying "Willkommen."

"You don't have to coddle them, Bea."

"You don't have to be so cruel, Margaret."

The two friends felt very differently about the prisoners. Bea's extended family owned farmland outside of Gering and were short on labor with all of the local boys overseas. Her family was of German descent, and these boys all looked like her cousins. The Italians, though more playboys than farmers, had been extra sets of hands, and with the sugar beet harvest coming they were missed as laborers. Prisoners of war came cheap, paid 80 cents per day if they worked (10 cents per day if they didn't), and the cost was split by the farmer and the U.S. government.

Margaret simply couldn't stomach the idea of Germans receiving any kindness.

But these men, these boys, really, were her age. Skin and bones, with pallid complexions, they did not resemble the broad-backed Italian men who had recently departed. Some shared the same mottled-red scars her enlisted co-workers brought back from their service. All of them shared the same far-away stares. The slightest twinge of pity began to elbow its way into her mind.

Maybe, just like her, they really didn't have a choice in this whole war thing.

Chapter Twenty-Four

A letter from Bob arrived just after she'd returned home. He must have written the letter in time for it to travel on the same train back home with Margaret and Bea. She realized she might miss him just a bit, though she didn't want to give him any encouragement. It wouldn't take much for Bob to misinterpret friendship for something more, so she would have to walk a fine line. She hoped his letters would keep coming because he did always give her a laugh.

So many of her classmates had married their high school sweethearts. Bea was due to do just that, but Margaret couldn't see herself spending a life hearing the same jokes she'd been hearing since eighth grade. Even if some of those jokes were still funny.

March 24, 1944 - On My Way To Somewhere in the Atlantic
Dear Margaret -
Please pardon the paper, but I'm in my "office", with no other paper available, and writing on Gov't time. Probably should have thought to pack some stationery. Just as long as it is readable (which I doubt), it really doesn't matter what I write on. (I hope.)

I must say it was an unexpected pleasure seeing you in Omaha. I had just received a letter from Aunt Gladys a few days before in which she talked about seeing you in Gering. Hmmm ....get around, don't you?

I was awfully sorry I couldn't stay and talk with you a little longer. Sure wish we could have had a proper date together, but I had to leave at nine o'clock Monday morning. I meant to ask you where you were staying, but in the excitement, it slipped my mind. I thought about calling you Sunday evening but didn't know where to reach you. Life certainly has funny ways of crossing people's paths.

You know Margaret, I'm kind of at a loss for something to say. The last time I saw you before Saturday, we weren't exactly on the best of terms. I realize it was all my fault, and I'd like to say I'm sorry and hope that you will let the past go unmentioned. Is it a deal? (Couldn't have just said this in person, now could I?)

As you undoubtedly know, I'm still free and as crazy as ever. Seems that no girl can stand me very long. Must be my repulsive character or personality. Anyway, looks now like it has all worked out for the best. I'm going overseas and when I come back, I can start from scratch. I'm gonna travel around a bit before I settle down, and no woman likes to be on the move too much. Who knows, I might even drop in on Gering. There is even a possibility that you'll be there. Course you'll probably be married with half a dozen kids, but at least I can say hello.

Well Margaret, time for me to get back to work again. Be sure and write me before too long. Take care of yourself, and remember the picture you promised you'd send me. Bye for now.

Love, Bob.

Now write!

Margaret could hear Bob's goofy vocal cadence in his letter. He even talked in parenthetical asides in person. They'd never had a reason to write letters to each other and she got a kick out of the fact that he was true to his jokester form even on the written page. Responding to him was appealing because she knew she didn't need to be proper, or even all that kind, as he was more friend than flame.

April 4, 1944 - Gering, Nebraska
Bob,
Only you would apologize in a letter after seeing me in person. Guess I'm scarier than those Germans that you're heading off to fight. Hope you find that bravery in between bouts of seasickness on your journey. But let's let bygones be bygones. You've always been good for a laugh and I'm grateful for the distraction of that weekend in Omaha even if you were too scared to come and find me on Sunday. Or maybe you were too busy checking out the other fish before you sailed the seven seas. Let's not kid ourselves—you're definitely getting some mileage out of that "free and crazy" bit. Enjoy your travels and remember, I'm not 'most women' so who knows, travel may be in my future too.
Until then,
Margaret
PS - Remind me again what you've done to earn a photo. I thought those were just sent to war heroes. Ha!

Chapter Twenty-Five

June 1944

Franklin brought the evening paper in with him from work and handed it to Margaret without a word. The headline of the June 6th paper screamed INVASION in bold letters taking up nearly the entire front page. She had no way of knowing if this was where June, Bob, or even Thomas might have landed in Europe, as in the absence of communication they could be almost anywhere.

Once she'd finished reading the paper Margaret got out her scissors and set to cutting out articles about the major battles where she might know someone and inserting them into her journal pages. She combed each Time and Life magazine for articles written by any of the female war correspondents. It was a sort of torture to think of all that they were experiencing in contrast to her relative safety behind bars. Since Sam's departure, and death, she'd had months without a direct connection to the war, and, she thought selfishly, it was more exciting if she was following someone who was truly in it.

"Do you think this is it? Is it the final push?" Margaret was curled up in the corner of the davenport diagonal from her father's leather club chair in the corner of the room next to the window.

He lit up a pipe and took his time responding.

"There is no set timeline in war, Magpie. With each battle, there is a dance of sorts with a few steps forward, a step or two back, and we know better than some that thousands of families are going to wake up for many tomorrows wondering after their loved ones."

"What I wouldn't give to be there. I feel as if there's so much more that I could be doing than just counting bars of soap."

"Now, " He gently cajoled her. "You are doing your own part here. What you're doing is helping our community survive the absence of the young men who usually help with harvest. Without that labor, our town would fall into a depth of economic destruction we haven't seen since the Dust Bowl."

"It's just not the same. These articles are our primary link to what is happening, and I just feel disconnected because I'm not writing about it."

"What exactly is keeping you from writing about it? Did you forget your typewriter back in Lincoln?" Franklin was laughing.

"Oh, sure Dad, I'll just write an article for my own newspaper, *The Margaret Murphy Chronicles*." Margaret knew that she was being a little melodramatic.

"Think creatively kiddo. If you have a story to tell, then tell it. You're working with thousands of German prisoners every day. Not too many people are having that experience. Write it down. I'm sure Jack would publish it. Or at least he'd give you some feedback."

She looked at her father. "You genuinely think Mother would allow that?"

He winked. "Who cares? We're at war. You're home. That's all she can demand of you."

Before she picked up Bea for their carpool in the morning, she headed to the *Gering Courier's* office downtown. She figured if a car was there it was very likely that it was Jack's, the editor of the paper, and she'd give him a copy of her portfolio of articles from the *Daily Nebraskan* and see if he would give her an outlet for her writing.

What she didn't realize is that her father had already talked this over with Jack at the Elk's Club a few weeks back and that Jack had read all of her college columns.

"Well, good morning, Margaret."

Jack was a reedy man, frail, yet somehow still had a bit of a belly. His round wire-rimmed glasses were perched low on his nose as he worked to edit the articles for this week's paper. "How can I help you?"

"Mr. Ellison, it's nice to see you, and my apologies for dropping by unannounced. I was wondering if you would have any interest in having a guest columnist's perspective of what it's like to work at the prisoner of war camp? I have a portfolio of my work at the *Daily Nebraskan* if you'd like to see an example of my writing."

"Miss Murphy, I've read them all and have just been waiting for you to come in and ask. The first rule of journalism: you have to ask for what you want. The second rule of journalism: hire talented writers, and readers will follow. So, yes, I would welcome having you write for the *Courier*. What's your fee?"

"Fee? I was just going to write these for free." Margaret had not expected that she could be paid for this work.

"Third rule of journalism: don't do it for free. I can't pay much, but how about four dollars an article so you can say you're a paid journalist?"

Margaret tried to not look overly excited, "Thank you Mr. Ellison. I have a draft of an article that I can deliver by the end of the week

Behind the Wire — Margaret Murphy, Gering Courier

Just a few miles outside our little town, up a long and dusty road full of cockleburs and tumbleweeds, sits a prison. This is no surprise to anyone as complaints have been loud and frequent about the treatment of these German invaders to our community. As someone who has lost a family member to the German bombs, I'll have to admit I was on the side of the frustrated citizen for several weeks as the men who'd surrendered to us or were captured, have poured into our peaceful valley since May. Indulge this writer as she gives you a brief tour of life behind the wire.

Well fed, healthy, their morale unshattered, the Germans are thinking of the next war. The physical aspects of the various prisoner of war camps are similar throughout the country. The four-square-mile area is surrounded by barbed wire about ten feet high. Knotting up the knapsack securely are guard watchtowers; hemming it all in is a perimeter guard of sentries post-

ed within easy sight of one another. The wire fences are not electrified, but escapes are rare and recapture almost always inevitable.

All phases of prisoner-of-war life are outlined by the regulations of the Geneva Convention, which was signed by the U.S., Germany, Britain, and Italy in 1929 (the Convention was signed but never ratified by Japan). According to representatives of the Protective Power (the Swiss who periodically visit POW camps here and abroad) that the U.S. is probably doing "four times as much for the German prisoners as the Germans do for the U.S. prisoners in Germany, but it's the only way to get decent treatment for U.S. prisoners."

The German enlisted men are housed in long, low barracks similar to those used by U.S. soldiers. There are approximately 40 square feet allotted to each prisoner. Within this area, he must line up his shoes and clothes. He is allowed a chest or trunk, which he can buy or make himself. He sleeps in double-decker beds and is supplied with a G.I. mattress and blankets. On the wall, he may hang pictures of his family and girlfriend. This collection has had many American pin-up "queens" added to it. He may, if he cares to, have a picture of Hitler and a small swastika, but these are limited in size to 6" x 6" maximum. The officers do not live in barracks; instead, they have apartment-like arrangements of two bedrooms and a living room for every two officers.

There are approximately three thousand German prisoners at each POW camp—fair-skinned or swarthy, men of all sizes and shapes. They started pouring in after the African campaign. When they first arrived, they were the dirtiest, mangiest-looking bunch of men that one would care to see. Malaria and venereal diseases were prevalent. They had no personal belongings, such as razors, soap, etc. As the grime and fatigue wash away, some of their inherent arrogance returns. They don't resent their captivity or resent the Americans so much, but merely rationalize their capture as an "accident of war." The prisoners are segregated into compounds, one for enlisted men, one for non-coms, and one for officers. There is no fraternizing among the groups. Each compound is divided into companies headed by German company leaders and American company commanders; over them is the German compound spokesman, or "fuehrer," and the American compound commander. All orders and negotiations are carried out through these men.

The U.S. makes an allowance of ten cents a day for all prisoners, whether or not they do any work. In addition, enlisted men who perform labor for pay receive an additional eighty cents a day. The officers' pay varies according to rank and ranges from $20 to $40 per month. No cash is given to the prisoners; all allowances and pay are issued in the form of credit or coupons redeemable at POW canteens within the stockade. Because the majority of the prisoners are certain that we will lose the war or be so weakened by the war that our currency will become valueless, they go on payday binges, buying medicine, soap, and jewelry, to hoard against inflation. The prisoners at one time even requested that women's ready-to-wear, and baby clothing be sold. No doubt they wanted to stock up for "after the war".

The U.S. Government furnished the men with blue denim fatigues and a slate-blue or khaki-colored uniform, on both of which PW is boldly stenciled in orange or white. Enlisted men

are required to work; they do routine jobs around the camp;
cook, rake, work in the warehouse, do repairing, carpenter
work, gardening, electrical work, drafting, etc. One sees them
everywhere, some working in groups under obvious supervi-
sion, others, more or less on their own. For any work keeping
them from farm labor, these prisoners are paid at the same 80
cents a day rate as those hired out for farm detail.

Prisoners must be fed "rations" equal in quantity and quality
to that of our troops. As a result, the Germans have gained an
average of 8 to 12 pounds a year. If the diet was left entirely
to them, it seems the Germans would eat most of their meat
raw, but naturally, this is prohibited. The prisoners are very
persnickety about the food that is given to them, claiming that
the food is not adequate or good enough for them. However, this
is preposterous inasmuch as the food that is received by them is
at many times better than that served to our own men.

About 20% of the Germans are religious; half of these are
Lutheran, and the other half are devout Catholics. Their ages
range from 17 to 45. Their health, on the whole, is good, although
medical men claim that physically they are "burned-out" from
the vigorous training and battle in Europe. They are slightly
shorter than the Americans but are finely built, and some are
even somewhat good-looking. Emotionally the men are at a
low ebb. There is very little singing in the camp. Their greatest
preoccupation and worry is that their women at home are no
longer faithful. They are uneasy about the general breakdown of
morals in Germany. The German prisoners are a mass of mental
contradictions. The majority of them believe that eventually
German supremacy will be achieved. Many of them are thinking

in terms of the next war. About the only thing all of them are irrevocably agreed upon is their terror of the Russians.

The reality is that we need these workers in our fields. We have sent our men overseas, and the industry in our community is dependent on labor helping with all of the aspects of farming; planting, hoeing, weeding, thinning, and all the down-and-dirty work we don't see American citizens lining up to do. We know this is hard work and we should have some gratitude that our government has found a way for us to comply with the Geneva Convention while also helping maintain our economy. We understand that the powers that be in Germany are not treating our boys with the same care, and it is tempting to descend to the depths of depravity and think in terms of "an eye for an eye" but that would make us no better than the abhorrent enemy.

Chapter Twenty-Six

"You've made them sound like humans." Margaret knew her mother was not happy now that any illusion that Margaret wasn't working at the prison was now impossible to uphold. "Humans that are handsome and have," she paused as if choking on a word, "those diseases."

"Turns out, some of them actually are. Many were given the choice of service or death. I started out feeling the same way. These were the people who killed Sam. It took me seeing them as boys my own age and understanding that no one is really given a choice in war. Many do not want Hitler to win the war; some even want to come back to the United States when this whole mess is done."

"Glad to see you're softening up there a little Megs. I enjoyed the article." Her father tilted the paper down and tried to catch his daughter's eye. "Tell me—how much got taken out by the censors?"

"I was pleasantly surprised. They want the facts out to the community that we're kind without coddling. I wanted to include a bit more about the fact that there are punishments among the ranks. The true Nazis are cruel to the prisoners that refuse to swear allegiance to Hitler. We must keep them separated, for everyone's safety."

Her mother realized neither of them was going to involve her in the conversation and huffed out of the room on that note. Margaret shook her head.

"She's just worried about you."

"No. She's just worried about her precious reputation. I need this war to be done so I can get on with my life! Writing this article was the most alive I've felt in months and just makes me miss school that much more."

"Patience, Megs. We'll keep our chins up and everything will work out in the end."

Margaret sighed as she retreated to the safety of her room. She was worried about Bob and June since they had both shipped off to Europe. She was still waiting for news that Charles had deployed and since she hadn't received a reply from her last note she decided to just wait to hear from him. She hadn't heard from Bea or Bob since the storming of the beaches at Normandy and knew that her imagination would run away from her if she didn't just sit down and write to both of them.

June 30, 1944 - Gering Nebraska
Calling Bob Hale, come in Bob Hale.
Keeping this letter lighthearted in the hopes that you're doing well on the shores of France or deep into German territory and haven't fallen into a hole. One must remind oneself that a boy who was bad at communication does not necessarily grow into a man who's figured it all out. Especially if that man forgets to pack paper on the journey across the sea.

I realize we're supposed to keep these letters to you all full of encouragement and sunshine— "You can do it." "We're keeping the home fires warm for you."— and all that. But I can tell you that's a bunch of bunk and I'd love the opportunity to fight you on it. Besides, if I wrote you a letter that sounded like that, you'd think I'd hit my head. I'm including an article I got published in the Courier. (Back at it, writing away. New York Times, here I come. Ha!) A byline is as good as a photo, don't you think?

One funny story from work: the prisoners decided to go on strike. Turns out they didn't want to weed the sugar beets in the oppressive Nebraska heat for less than a dollar a day. The head of the labor department in the camp had a counterpunch and decided to give them just bread and water during the strike. Three days later they determined they missed bacon and eggs and got right back to work. I guess it's not that funny when you get down to it. Maybe that should be the subject of my next article.

In all seriousness though, we've all been waiting to hear from you. The invasion push followed by your silence seems to give away hints about your location which we all hope is not at the bottom of the sea.

My Best - Margaret

And now for June. She needed to update her friend with the comings and goings back home. She also wanted to fill her in on how Bea was struggling because she hadn't heard from Ted. As a result, she was having a hard time concentrating on her work and was being threatened with a demotion from the personnel office to the typing pool. Margaret knew telling her,

"Hey, they let us know right away that Sam was missing and dead. If something was wrong, you'd know it." She instead just said, "I'm sure he's fine." Repeatedly. She wanted some advice from June on how best to care for their friend or even just get her to relax a bit, but most of all she just wanted to hear from her.

June 30, 1944

Dearest June,

On this, the last day of YOUR month, I have held out hope that you would have had a free moment to write a quick note to Bea, or me, to let us know that you are doing okay. I promised Bea I wouldn't worry until July 1st. So, you have 14 more hours. Get on it.

If your time is limited though, please just write to Bea. She's so scared about Ted and his whereabouts. I don't know how she's going to survive this war without having a full-blown case of the vapors.

News here is limited except that I am, officially, a paid war correspondent. Nothing so exciting as what you're doing but Jack Ellison at the Courier hired me to write articles about my perspective on the war as a guest columnist. Money will be going straight into the "I must move out of my parent's house" fund.

Please stay safe,

~M

Chapter Twenty-Seven

July 1944

Support staff had been given extra time off for the Fourth of July holiday. She and Bea had spent the weekend out at the lake boating, lounging on the sand, and reading books. They didn't listen to the news or talk about the war and it was incredibly relaxing.

Fully recharged, Margaret was ready to go back to work. She had an extra smile for every soldier she passed and felt more lighthearted than she had in months as she crossed through the barracks to her desk. She was as surprised to find a small wooden dog perched on the corner of her desk.

It was a hound dog, approximately two inches tall. He sat hunched forward, his painted pink tongue hanging out nearly as low as his long lop ears. His skin seemed to hang off him, his ribcage exposed, his tail tucked between his legs. He rested perfectly level on her desk as if care was taken to make sure that his hind legs were even and his front paws sturdy. The wood was soft, lightweight, almost like a piece of driftwood from the cottonwood trees down by the North Platte River. His sorrowful eyes watched her as she worked, and she kept reaching out to run her finger down the bridge of his nose.

The dog had been placed right in front of her framed picture of Spike that had taken over her engagement photo's spot. She chuckled. Invitations to dinner had been plenty since that photo was removed. The weekend getaway reminded her that maybe it was time to say yes to one of two of those potential suitors. Bea would be happy to hear that her icy shell was melting a bit. Now she just needed to discover who left this adorable trinket.

Word had come from on high that they were to expect another push of prisoners in the next month, which could only mean that there was another massive endeavor in Europe. Chapman was in meetings all day, so Margaret had the office to herself.

Margaret wished there was a note to go along with the dog so she could know which soldier to thank. She was initially sure it was from Paul "Shorty" Bianchi from Long Island, so she headed to the mess hall to grab a cup of coffee and do some investigating. As she expected, Shorty was holding court with a couple of new transplants from the Pacific.

All 5'5" of him had confidence that belied his vertically challenged stature. Injured in Pearl Harbor, he walked with quite a limp but joked that it gave him a swagger. His sense of humor made him a delight to work with, but his brash East Coast accent hurt her ears. Besides, she was sure his mama wanted him to marry a good Italian girl back home. When she confronted Shorty about the dog he laughed and said, "You've got a PW sweetheart, sweetheart. They're the only ones with time on their hands to carve. I'm too busy counting prisoners when they get back from the farms."

Margaret tucked the carving into the pocket in her sweater and went back to the office, now more confused than ever. She kept her distance from the prisoners. Apart from the janitors and cooks, few prisoners were given access to the common areas of the camp.

In her journalistic mind, there was a story here, and it was worth the risk to get more details. She found a pocket German/English dictionary as well as a small map of Germany and placed them on the corner of her desk where the dog was placed. Inside she tucked a note, "Danke für die Hunde. Thank you for the dog."

Now she'd wait and see if a reply came.

Chapter Twenty-Eight

The camp was in an uproar. Count this morning revealed that, sometime during the night, two prisoners had gone missing. Their bunkmates were being questioned, the night guard crew was under extreme scrutiny, and there were even questions that maybe they had been gone for longer than just one night and somehow the count had been wrong for several days. Oh, the panic that would ensue if the public knew of Germans free and wandering their community!

The civilian workers were called together in the mess hall and given strict instructions to go home for the day and not give any information to anyone about the missing prisoner. They were to say the camp was running military exercises and to return tomorrow after a plan could be developed. Truthfully, the military was concerned that the prisoners might have had help from someone on the inside and were going to wait and see if any civilians didn't return the next day. There were rumors of women in the typing pool falling for the prisoners at other camps across the country.

Margaret worried that the dogs would be a red flag. There had been no response to her note though the dictionary had disap-

peared. Over the last couple of weeks, more dogs had appeared.
A dachshund, a Scottie, a wolfhound, two pups gently chained
together, and her favorite, a long basset hound. The ears, carved
from the same cottonwood as the first, were nearly as soft as
Spike's. A delicate tongue peeked from the mouth and though
it seemed impossible, this two-inch piece of wood seemed to
be almost happy. She would quickly whisk them into her desk
drawer and then tuck them into her waistband on the way out
at the end of the day. At home, these little canine trinkets were
nestled in a small metal box tucked under the bedding next to
her journal.

With Shorty's help, Margaret had narrowed down the sculptor
to one suspect, a prisoner named Rudi. Rudi had arrived with
the third trainload of prisoners. An inch or two under six feet,
but hunched over in the way that chronic pain steals inches
from even the strong. His hair was darker, and he looked more
Slavic than many of the other prisoners. Margaret imagined that
he'd been conscripted into the German army when his town was
overrun and that, like so many, he was not unhappy to be put
back together in a U.S. military hospital and shipped overseas.

Due to the nature of his injuries and compliance with all of
the rules of the camp, he was placed on the office janitorial staff
instead of farm labor and had more freedom to come and go in
offices than most and would have had the opportunity to place
the figurines on Margaret's desk.

There was no doubt that if Rudi was one of the missing prisoners that they would find the dictionary in his possession and
in it a note in her handwriting. She had no desire to go before

the camp leadership for questioning about fraternization with
the enemy.

Chapter Twenty-Nine

August 1944

A letter was waiting for her when she got home. Margaret found herself hoping it was from Bob. She shook her head and laughed at the thought that she could end up with her small-town sweetheart after all, much to her chagrin. She was disappointed it wasn't Bob or June—though it was good to hear from Charles.

July 19, 1944 San Diego

Dear Margaret,

Why do I let so much water flow under the bridge? It makes it so hard to try to connect things up. If I wrote every time I meant to or thought about you, I'd write too often. The spirit is willing, but the flesh is weak. I do miss you and think about you often.

I'll be a full-fledged MD in 2 more months and can get time to do some of the things I want to do. I am learning a great deal though, and I guess that's the most important thing.

The President and Eleanor were both here last week, but I don't suppose Margaret would stand up and cheer about that. He was surrounded by SS men, and I barely got a glimpse of him. She spent a great deal of time amongst the patients.

Where are you going to spend your vacation this year? Isn't it about time for it? Somehow, I connect the 3rd of September with your birthday, is that right? I've been trying to remember. It's late, Margaret, and I must get a note off to the folks before I hit the rack, so I'll say good night. Write soon.
Love, Charles.

So, Charles was thinking about her often. She could do worse than have a cute doctor in San Diego thinking about her. She was glad he understood her great frustration with Roosevelt and his war strategies. Honestly, the First Lady would do a better job of planning a war response and we'd probably be out of this mess.

August 15, 1944 - Gering, Nebraska
So good to hear from you, Charles. Even if you had to celebrate our President. I'm coming around a bit on the old man simply because I like his wife and he lets her talk. If he could just get us out of this darned war, then I'd probably become a full-fledged fan.

I do so enjoy getting your letters but completely understand that medical school is time-intensive and cumbersome. I guess I'm just happy to hear that you're still stateside and secretly hope that you'll be able to remain here for as long as possible. I watch the boys who are sent to us, both German soldiers, and the Americans who are released from active duty to become guards and they all have this far-away stare as if they've seen the depths of hell and the images are perpetually floating before their very eyes.

I suppose that's not a very kind thing to write to a soldier. I will do better to keep my thoughts positive.

I think often about you and the counsel you gave me all those months ago at the train station. Forever is a long time to be grateful, for since that day I've begun building a life I can be proud of here in western Nebraska beyond where I left my life in Lincoln. Life is nothing if not an adventure, and I look forward to our continued correspondence as the adventure continues.

As to holiday vacation, not much to report or look forward to. Bea and I spent a week in Omaha before her fiancé (Ted) shipped off to Europe as a final hurrah and goodbye to June. We're hoping to hear that he's arrived safely in France and is helping capture and send some new German farm labor back stateside. June finished her training in New York and was sent to the front, though we don't yet know where. I guess they don't give the nurses as much time to get up to speed as they do doctors!

I'm writing a column for the Gering Courier *and this week is going to be all about sugar beet harvest. Almost as thrilling as the liberation of Paris, I know. I'd love to be covering the story of a couple of missing prisoners. I guess since it's going to be in the papers, I can tell you. A couple of weeks ago we were two prisoners short when it came time for roll call when they returned from work duty. The family that was hosting them was called in to make sure they weren't conspiring with the enemy since they didn't notice they were two hands short at the end of the day. Turns out they had the truck drop off prisoners two by two at each corner of their land to work more efficiently, and two of them just walked away. The whole town is in a tizzy over where they might be. They may have made it to you in California by now for all we know!*

My birthday is the 18th of September. You have a good memory just to remember the month! Maybe you'll send me another note by then.

All my best,

Margaret

Chapter Thirty

September 1944

With the prison still on high alert about the two missing prisoners, security was tighter than ever. The military had sent in military police from Washington to help bring order to their operation. Bags were searched coming in, and again leaving, with more vigor than before. She was grateful she'd seen Rudi wandering the halls and was hopeful that he'd found somewhere to dispose of, or hide, the dictionary.

"You do know you're not going to find them in my handbag, right?" Margaret had tired of the additional scrutiny. They went through everything in her bag, including the paper she'd brought in with her latest article. Chapman enjoyed reading them and helping her brainstorm future articles. The prisoners had simply walked into a cornfield. They could have very easily found a farmhouse that had been abandoned during the Depression and have been hiding in plain sight. One could live for quite a while on the plentiful fish and wildlife along the North Platte River.

Today's work was to be focused on a new methodology of tracking the coming and going prisoners so that this wouldn't happen again. She was expected to take notes, her least-favorite activity, and she was prepared to put up a fight with Chapman when she entered her office. Instead of his war-weary familiar face, she rounded the corner and found herself face to face with a soldier she'd never seen before sitting at her desk.

"Who are you?" Still amped up in preparation for an argument Margaret couldn't tone down her curt reply.

He reached out his hand, "Captain Harold Burke here. It's a pleasure to meet you, Miss...."

"Murphy. Margaret Murphy."

He grinned down at her from what felt like a very long distance. He really was quite tall. "Well, Miss Murphy, Chapman here has been filling me in on what a helpful contact you've been here in the community. I'm here to help with the financials at the camp as he prepares for his transfer and he said you're going to be the one to help show me the ropes since you've made him look good enough to promote."

Margaret turned to her boss, "Chap?" This was the first Margaret had heard of a promotion. She was proud but knew that she'd have to start all over with a new boss to develop a rapport.

"I've been meaning to tell you. I'm heading back to help open a camp just an hour away from my home. I will get to see my kids and wife on weekends. It's time. You and Captain Burke here will keep this place running."

Margaret felt like a rug had been pulled out from under her. Chapman had been so lenient with her in giving her access to research and write her articles on government time. She knew nothing of this Burke fellow and, while he was much better to look at than old Chap, he was a distraction she didn't want. Her latest article was being published today and she already had ideas of how to incorporate stories of the missing prisoners or her growing canine sculpture collection into her next article. This new fellow changed that plan and she decided she'd stick with more vanilla articles until she figured out his temperament.

For now, she just handed Chapman the paper and said, "I suppose this is the last one of these you'll read then. Maybe you can leave a list of ideas before you go." For all of the losses in the war, this one was going to hurt. She'd worked for him for too long for it not to sting a little.

Sugar Beet Harvest: A Sweet Deal for Farmers and Prisoners Alike — Margaret Murphy, Gering Courier

If you've lived in the valley for more than a year you can feel the pulse of anxiety that runs through our community each summer. Will there be hail? Will it be rainy enough? Will it be hot enough? When is the exact right moment to dig these precious fibrous lumps from the ground? Do we have enough hands to do the digging?

Though we can no more control the weather than we can control the war in Europe and the Pacific, we have an answer to that final question. The answer to our labor shortage with all of the young men off serving our country is to bring the young men captured in Europe back stateside. Instead of writing about the individual farm practices of digging, sorting, and transporting the beets to the various processing factories that pepper the valley, I visited with several local farmers who were benefiting from the POWs and will work to profile these families in future columns.

The Hannigan farm is located just northeast of Scottsbluff and has been in the Hannigan family for several generations. Tom is the grandson of German-Russian immigrants who, legend has it, arrived in the Mitchell Valley and immediately felt like they were back home in their native land but without the oppressive rule, and poverty, that caused them to seek refuge in America. They had spent some time in New York after their arrival and could never feel settled without the view of the horizon. Through hard work, the Hannigan family now farms over 500 acres of primarily sugar beets and corn.

They are, or were, your typical large farm family. Four sons, and three daughters, were all taught to handle the various responsibilities of farm life that this "city" girl has never had to understand. They do not use the word unfortunate when they say that all four of their sons were of enlistment age, as they were proud of the fact their ancestors left the fascist ideology of Hitler and his ilk behind. They knew that their German roots would be difficult to hide, as they were frequently the providers of the delicious streusel and bierocks at our county fair. They encouraged all four of their sons to enlist straight away after Pearl Harbor so there would be no question as to their allegiance.

Tragedy did not take long to strike the Hannigan family, and, as everyone in the Valley knows, two of their sons, Erik and Peter, died tragically when their ship was sunk on the way to the Pacific. Their youngest two are somewhere in Europe fighting against soldiers who may even be their cousins. The absence of these four strong hands left quite the void, but how could a family who has lost so much to war have any tolerance or acceptance for these prisoners of war to work on their land?

According to Mrs. Hannigan, "I just look at these boys and I see Erik, I see Peter. They're too young. They're hungry. I'm used to feeding a large household and I was feeling quite out of sorts until the POWs showed up. Yes, they're helpful in getting the crops harvested, but I never knew they would also help me mourn. Each of these soldiers has a mother who is as scared as I am. I just hope that if any of our boys are captured, they're given the opportunity to be shown just a tiny bit of kindness."

Her clarity of conscience is admirable. It has taken this author months to see the humanity in any of this. Maybe Roosevelt could talk to the mothers on both sides, and we'd get this whole thing buttoned up and everyone could go back to their own lands and harvest their own beets.

Chapter Thirty-One

S tarting the day in chaos was becoming par for the course. It was ridiculous how it seemed like every guard was looking for a crisis to solve just to feel needed. Luckily, her new office mate, nay boss, Captain Burke, was entertained by her annoyance.

"Captain Burke, I presume that you also need to check this handbag for the secret prisoner-shrinking ray gun?"

Burke laughed, "I hear that the brass upstairs has found ways to shrink those ray guns and make them look like lipstick."

"Speaking of." Margaret opened her bag and took out her new tube of Montezuma Red Elizabeth Arden and her small pocket mirror that she'd purchased as a reward for the two columns she'd written and sold.

He'd been there for several weeks and they'd developed a routine of somehow flirting without talking. He would a show of sorting through papers on his desk while surreptitiously enjoying the morning show of lipstick application. She figured that when he got stationed in Nebraska after his time in Northern California, he thought that he would be surrounded by "wind-weathered women in overalls." Every day he seemed more surprised at her wit, her intelligence, her understanding of his quirks. She also knew her wavy hair looked auburn when the sun came through the window in the afternoon as she leaned over the ledger at her desk and she'd catch him staring at her and then try to hide it. All of his covert observation of Margaret was equally matched by her observation of him. Without saying anything, Margaret had noticed at their first meeting that Harold needed it quieter than most. Almost imperceptibly he would jump every time the door opened too far and hit the back of the wall. He did a remarkable job masking it most of the time, but it was there nonetheless.

Harold Burke looked like a man who should walk through life with the confidence of someone who has never seen a struggle. Tall, nearly 6'4", his dark brown hair was sprinkled with the salt and pepper of a man approaching his mid-30s. He walked ramrod straight and though thin, he still filled up a doorway. He was imposing and handsome and, in the safety of his office, was organized and calm. His left arm was just a bit off-kilter, but he fought to keep that fact as under wraps as possible. He'd been stationed in Italy before he was brought home to a camp on the west coast due to a shoulder injury.

She was curious about him and wanted to ask him more questions about where he served, about San Francisco, about everything.

But it would be inappropriate for her to approach him, right? She needed to talk to Bea. Was she curious about him for a story? Or was there something more to the slight uptick in her heartbeat when she opened the door every day?

Margaret shook her head. Enough of these thoughts. Back to work.

"So, Captain Burke, what's the story on the commotion this morning, and how will it change the quartermaster process, again, from yesterday to today?"

"Miss Murphy, you can call me Harold when it's just us in the office."

"Captain Burke, until you call me Margaret, I will not."

"That would be inappropriate, Miss Murphy. How about this? Just call me Burke."

They both laughed. This was as close to flirtatious banter as they'd had in their months of working together.

"They did catch one of the prisoners, so we'll need to update the supply counts and communicate—again—with the commissary. He'll be in solitary for a bit, being grilled about where he was, who he saw, and how he escaped," Burke tried to remain neutral about how ridiculous the process would be of changing every number for the simple re-addition of a prisoner that had only been gone a few months. "We'll need to send a notification to the Regional Quartermaster, the State, and then make a report that can be included in the numbers that go to the federal overlords."

Margaret was hoping to have time to write the story about the capture with the juicy details, but it sounded like her day would be spent behind the typewriter doing anything but using her creativity.

Thankfully, a letter had arrived from Ted for Bea at home and Bea's mother wasted no time in calling the camp and reading it aloud to her. She was full of conversation on the drive home from work that afternoon. It was lovely to have Bea in much better spirits. Margaret bit her tongue as she tried to not remind her that they had not heard from June yet though her mother had not been notified of anything and the rule truly was becoming "no news is good news."

"In just these few months he's accumulated enough points that he'll be home in no time. We've decided that we're going to go ahead and get married the first time he comes home." She clapped her hands together. "I could be a mother before this war is over!"

Margaret loved Bea and her romantic notions, but it just seemed so foreign to her. Who would want to have a child in the middle of a war? Everything felt so disjointed.

"How about, step one, you become a wife. Talk about children after the war."

"We're not getting any younger, Margaret. We need to think about these things. We could be almost thirty by the time this thing is over."

"Do not say such things. I am about to be twenty-three. If they can't get this figured out in the next seven years, then I will enlist and figure it out for them." She pulled up to Bea's house. "I'll see you tomorrow morning when we do more of the same."

"Yes, but you get to do the same with a dreamy Jimmy Stewart lookalike. I have to work for Captain Grumpypants who smells like cheese."

Margaret watched Bea skip up her front walk. It was so good to see her friend's suffering abated. She didn't know what would happen to her friend if Ted died.

She still hadn't heard from Bob and, since his parents had moved to Omaha when Bob left for college, she knew that until news got to his Aunt Gladys in town she would not be told of his whereabouts or wellbeing. She tried not to care so much but figured he deserved another pen-lashing since she couldn't call him out on the phone and didn't know where to send a telegraph. For all she knew, he might have been moved to the Pacific.

September 10, 1944
Robert William Hale,
Yes, I'm using your full name. I know you're not dead because no one has come to tell your family. I'm pretty sure you're not even missing. So, you best be writing to me, or your Aunt Gladys or someone to let us know that you're doing okay. I never thought I'd see the day when I wanted to hear from Bob Hale. So there!

Also, we lost a couple of the Nazis you sent back to us. But then we found one of them again. Ha! You'll get a kick out of my latest article.

If I promise to send a picture, will you return this correspondence?

She who never thought she'd ask Bob to start talking,
Margaret

Then she wrote another letter, this time to June.

September 10, 1944
June,

How are you, future Dr. June? I'm sure you've turned every soldier into a fan, and I hope you're still laughing even though I'm sure the things you are seeing are impossible for us safely stateside to imagine. I endeavor to believe that you are near Paris now and have celebrated the liberation with every last drop of champagne you can stomach. We toasted a glass to you all.

Please take a photo with a French stranger and send it home to us so I can scandalize mother (and Bea!).

Dear friend, I miss the balance that you bring to our triangle. Without you here I threaten to become a romantic. Don't you dare tell Bea or she will make me pick a wedding dress. All I'm saying is that someone has intrigued this cynical friend of yours and, dare I say, I would not turn down a chance to get to know this person better. That's all the details I dare give for now because I'm confident Bea could smell romance from her home blocks away.

Speaking of noses... I'm including a draft of the article that will be in the paper next week. Likely this version won't pass the war reporting rules muster, but hopefully, it brings you a laugh.

I hope you stay safe and know that we miss you with every bit of our beings. We are hopeful that the liberation of Paris is a sign of an end that is sooner rather than later.

The other side of the equilateral triangle,

~M

She had developed quite the evening routine. Write a letter or two to Bob, Charles, or June, write in her journal a few ideas for articles, and join her dad on the porch for discussions of the news of the day from the prison, and bank, and exchange sections of the newspaper.

By a Nose — *Margaret Murphy*, Gering Courier

If you had the opportunity to go anywhere you wanted in this wild western United States of ours, where would you go?

Would you wander north to the badlands of the Dakotas, living off the land like pioneers and native people before us? Sleep under the stars?

Would you trek southwest to the Rockies? Would you work to power through the altitude climb and the ever-changing temperatures to witness the sheer beauty of a never-ending horizon where you're above it all?

Or would you work to go as far west as possible, as fast as you could, to make it to the ocean?

Or maybe, just maybe, you would head east for the relative anonymity that could be found in the bustling cities of the Midwest and the Northeast.

It's quite possible that one of the prisoners that escaped a few weeks ago is on one of those journeys. It's more likely that he, like the prisoner that returned to us (ahem, was recaptured by us) is simply cold and hungry somewhere and about to wander back up from whatever canyon he's been trying to find shelter in these last few weeks and ask for something to eat as if he hasn't caused a bit of trouble in the world.

That is what happened this week at Camp Scottsbluff. Mr. German Prisoner, we'll call him Franz, got hungry for the incredible food that our staff, under the direction of Mrs. Patricia VanNyss, can concoct out of the military rations that are sent to us. She does make the most delightful chicken and dumplings and, as the story is told, the smell of that chicken roasting wafted the mere two miles from the camp where dear Franz was freezing, and he decided to just give himself up.

He swears he does not know where his compatriot is, but rumor has it that cabbage buns are on the menu next week and maybe the military will set up fans to send those scents wafting in every direction to encourage another surrender.

Chapter Thirty-Two

October 1944

The sounds of soccer in the open yard were accompanied by a cacophony of honks, screeches, and drum beats as prisoners auditioned for a place in the prison yard orchestra. Even with the liberation of Paris and the advancing troops in Europe, Hitler still was holding out hopes that he would win this war. As part of the German morale program, he'd ship crates of instruments as well as art supplies to his comrades so they would feel that their Fuhrer had not abandoned them.

"Burke, can't you do something about that racket?" Margaret was in the middle of balancing their supply register and was struggling to focus through the sounds of the oom-pahs of the one tuba and the blaring of the multiple horns and clarinets. Every prisoner wanted a chance to be a part of the band. "Hitler is going to kill us with the screeching of woodwinds, isn't he?"

"Nothing we can do, Miss Murphy." Burke had continued calling her Miss Murphy with a rather silly, almost Irish, accent.

"Could they at least play something with rhythm? Is there German swing music?"

"Oh, you like swing music?"

"What self-respecting youth today doesn't?" Margaret and Burke had fallen into a more familiar rhythm in their conversation.

"I'm a touch older than a youth, and I like swing. There's a band playing at the Officer's Club this weekend, are you going?" She was hoping Burke almost stumbled into the question he really wanted to ask.

"I haven't asked Bea what our plans are. She's my social coordinator. Without her, I'd probably hole up with my dog and just write all weekend. Who's playing?"

"Some band called the *Syncopated Surgeons* or some such nonsense."

"Oh! We saw them in Omaha when we dropped off June!" Margaret was more jubilant than usual. "Yes, Bea and I will be there. I'm sure of it."

"Would you need...would you like...could you use, a ride?" Burke knew Margaret had her own car. He was kicking himself.

Margaret grinned. He might not be saying the exact words, but his meaning was clear. Boys, even thirty-something-year-old men, were so predictable.

"That would be fantastic. Can we pick Bea up as well?" She was hoping he'd say no and it would just be the two of them.

"Absolutely. Should I ask Captain Fowler if he'd like to join us?"

Margaret knew Bea would be none too thrilled by an evening with Fowler, but resigned herself to the fact that it would be a double date since he had not actually used the word "date". Feigning a casual response she didn't feel, he replied,

"Here's my address, pick us up at seven. I'll have Bea come to my house."

On the ride home, Margaret made her case to Bea to go out for the evening.

"Remind me again why I'm agreeing to an evening as a third wheel that is riding along with the spare tire of 'foul-mouthed Fowler' of all people?"

"It keeps Mother from asking too many questions. It's casual, she knows his aunt or something, and it keeps her from asking why I didn't just invite Burke in for dinner. I'm not ready for that level of pressure. Neither is Burke, I'm guessing because he got his tongue tied in a knot just asking me if we were going to the club tonight and didn't use the word date. He just asked if I wanted a ride."

"Have you talked with your folks about the apartment?" Bea was growing anxious to get away from home as well.

"No, that's why you're here for dinner," Margaret grinned. "She won't yell if she has to be polite."

"You manipulative so-and-so!" Bea laughed. "Fine. How are we going to play this?"

"You complain about the cost and then I'll suggest we just split it. Maybe Mother will think I'm being charitable." Margaret knew it wouldn't be an easy fight.

"I make as much money as you do! And my parents are on board and willing to help!"

"Yes, but she doesn't know that."

"Speaking of the apartment, they need an answer soon, so let's hope we can convince them."

"Doesn't it just seem ridiculous that we must do any convincing? We're in our twenties. We have our own money. Women are traveling the world writing, flying planes, and nursing, and just because our parents have tethered us to this small town we are still asking for permission?"

"I agree with you. I do. I also know that if I feed into the energy of your diatribe, we're going to have a mother-daughter knock-down battle, and not only will we not get an apartment, but we will also not be allowed out of the house with Burke and Fowler."

"You understand me too well." They pulled up to the house. "Let's go change."

They'd decided that Bea would just borrow one of Margaret's dresses in order to avoid explaining to Bea's mother that this was not a date. Bea called her and arranged to spend the night at Margaret's. While her parents were more permissive than Margaret's she knew her mother wouldn't love the optics of Bea attending a dance with someone new.

Margaret pulled a couple of dresses out of her closet. One was a royal blue shirtwaist dress with small pearl buttons and a fitted waist, the other was a plum-colored dress with elbow-length sleeves and a rounded collar. "Do these dresses look appropriately 'this is not a date' for tonight?"

"Well, obviously you're going on a date, so the blue one is 'date adjacent', and your eyes will do that magic that makes them change color, which will turn this 'not a date' into a date." Bea's romanticism threatened to come through. "And the plum one is just dowdy enough for me to look like your chaperone instead of giving Fowler any ideas."

"Bea, I'm not sure you could be dowdy on your worst day, but I agree about the dress. It has the right amount of Rebecca energy for this evening. She'll be grateful to see someone wearing it."

"You do know that you're going to owe me one? I'm only here because I think Captain Burke is the first man you've been remotely interested in since Thomas." Bea, while she wanted Margaret to find love, wasn't sure an evening out with Fowler was worth it. God forbid he say anything that got back to Ted before she could write to him and explain the whole thing.

"I owe you more than one, let's not forget you're about to help me with the apartment battle."

The girls joined Franklin and Rebecca for dinner and didn't do much more than casually mention the apartment. Even though Bea had been friends with Margaret since they were four years old, Rebecca still regarded her as a guest and would not get as riled up if there was a guest present, so when she responded, "Oh, that's an interesting idea."

Margaret knew it was code for "No." But Franklin came through with a "When I was your girls' age, I'd been living alone for three years" story, and Margaret knew that she had him hooked.

Her mother started to interject just as Margaret saw a car pull up, and before Burke or Fowler could exit, she and Bea ran down the front porch to prevent introductions from being made. She hoped her parents would fight it out after they left.

Chapter Thirty-Three

The Officers' Club was situated on the opposite side of town at a building overlooking the North Platte River, the de facto border between Scottsbluff and Gering. It was a simple, large, domed Quonset hut, but the military had splurged for wood floors and nicer light fixtures, and it very nearly gave the impression that you were entering a dance hall or a tolerable hotel ballroom. A small stage was situated along the wall furthest from the entrance, and several low tables surrounded the periphery. A few high tops bordered the bar that looked like it had been picked up from a western saloon and plopped in the corner. Drink sales were the source of income that covered the operating expenses of the club, and each drink cost a ticket that you'd purchase at the door. Every officer was given four tickets a week and would have to purchase additional tickets for their dates or for their own imbibing.

Margaret could tell that Burke and Fowler had helped themselves to a couple of beers prior to picking up the girls just to calm. She was hoping that the more festive atmosphere, and another drink, might help him relax enough to talk to her about anything except what was happening at the camp just a few miles away. The band, however, was very loud, and Margaret felt the shift in his energy as he scanned the room. Though the music was fun, and she was hoping to get a dance or two in before the end of the night, she wished he felt more comfortable.

"How about we grab a drink and maybe a cigarette before the night gets too cold out there?" She threaded her arm through his as they went to grab cocktails.

"Two gin and tonics, please?" Sam had once written that these were the go-to drinks of the British soldiers he was stationed with, and though they tasted of chewing on a juniper branch to her, it seemed like it would be a more sophisticated order that Burke might find enjoyable.

As the bartender prepared their drinks Margaret watched the dance floor filled with couples who were all likely pretending to be present and relaxed. Everyone in this room was damaged by the war and was pretending to be okay so that they would not feel like shattering. It's no wonder Burke seemed unsettled.

With drinks in hand, they wandered outside where rough-hewn picnic tables and benches were set up under a net of portable military-issue lights strung from one central post to give the illusion of a tent.

"It was awfully loud in there, don't you think? Hard to get used to after the quiet of the prison." Margaret hoped that her acknowledgment would make him feel more at ease.

"I will sound quite old if I agree, now, won't I?" She could see Burke was trying, with all his might, to relax. He swallowed his gin and tonic in one gulp. Nerves were beginning to soften. He smiled at Margaret. "So, tell me, Miss Murphy, what is keeping you here in this tiny town?"

They had not spent any time talking about their personal lives, and for the next twenty minutes she entertained him with stories of her mother's demands and her father's connections and left out the pesky details of a failed engagement and her feeling that the cosmic timing of war could not have come at a worse time for her. She realized that those complaints would fall on the deaf ears of a man who was obviously injured during battle. "And you, Captain Burke, when you're not bossing around daydreaming journalists and correcting their accounting skills, what do you do for fun?"

"When I was a kid, I liked going hiking with my brother and my dad outside of Tacoma." They were overlooking the river, and she guessed he was feeling a little nostalgic for the true rivers of the Northwest where he was born and raised. Though the Platte was pretty and the area had more hills than anyone expects, it had nothing on the lush green of Washington state.

They settled into a conversation about places to hike in western Nebraska and made plans to go to the hills south of town next weekend. With plans in place and a couple of drinks under his belt, Harold was relaxed enough to suggest that they head back inside for a few dances.

Margaret was intrigued by this man and was looking forward to next week at work and the following weekend out in the hills.

Later that night, Burke dropped off Bea and Margaret. She figured because Fowler was still in the car for a ride back to the barracks, he couldn't muster up the courage to do more than open her door for her when they pulled up to the house.

Chapter Thirty-Four

L etters had arrived from Bob and June that afternoon, but she hadn't even bothered to check the post when she got home from work. She was distracted by preparing for the night out. Even though she was flooded with relief that they were both still alive and finally communicating, she berated herself for being distracted from the people who truly mattered to her.

Her parents had already retired to their bedrooms. Margaret curled up in her reading chair in the corner of her bedroom with the letters, to read them out loud to Bea who was lounging on the bed. They missed June desperately, so that letter was absolutely their priority. Both letters were postmarked in early October.

"It's annoying how the postal service doesn't seem to care if we've spent the month as anxious wrecks waiting to know if our loved ones are okay!"

"I agree, but can we not get into a whole military efficiency conversation and just read them?" Bea was impatient to know where June was. She'd written her almost daily with no reply.

October 8, 1944

Margaret Murphy, my most missed Miss west of the Mississippi,

I'm here, but can't tell you where that is, I'm safe, but can't tell you how close we've come to that not being true, and I'm happier than I've ever been. I'm useful here. I'm learning something new every day. My sense of humor comes in handy to distract injured soldiers and deflect the advances of the desperate. Oh, the stories I could tell you! You know I'd rather put on a "Showtime with June" short play so I will save some of the stories for the next time we're all together. Just remind me: "seasick soldiers by the seaside" and I'll know exactly what story to share.

M, I'm worried about Bea. She has written to me every other day, unlike you. (Not a competition, but c'mon, for a writer you'd think your best friend would get a few pages every now and again.) You are the strong one of the three of us, and I need to know that you're taking care of our girl. She hasn't heard from Ted since that first communication that he landed somewhere near where I landed, and I haven't been able to get word of him either. I'm sure he's still alive because they're pretty swift at notifying family if they're not. (We nurses get to help with that whole process. That, I don't love.) I just don't want her gentle soul to be hardened by all of this. You, on the other hand, I hear might be softening up and saying yes to a couple of possible future Mr. Murphys. (Yes, I will demand he takes your name. It's just too good.)

I trust you will do what your bossiest friend demands and report back.

Your forever friend,

June

Margaret could hear June's voice as she read through the page. The letter reminded her of the loss of those nights of laughter. She wondered how someone was supposed to grieve laughter.

She and Bea decided to draft a joint response so they sat up on the bed together, passing the stationery in between each other.

June, our dearest, our bossiest, our funniest friend,

Your letter arrived on a day that we're together so you're getting two for the price of one in this response.

M-Obviously, the postal system has failed as I have written to you, though not as obsessively as our friend Bea, so I will forgive you the nag. And I will also apologize, as I have not written to you as often as you deserve. I find that I start to worry when I don't hear from all of you that are overseas, and I worry that I'm writing to a memory of a person. I suppose that's just residual grief from Sam's death.

B- HI! You had us worried that something had happened to you. I told you that it was no big deal that you might not hear from Margaret as often. And I'm FINE now and have toughened up quite a bit, thank you very much. (Though I love your concern and now I'm crying. Guess I'm not that tough.)

M – As to Bea, yes, I watched her start to change. She was a little shorter with everyone, including me than I've ever witnessed. Thankfully, Ted turned up in Germany somewhere and managed to get a telegraph off to her, so she's back to planning that wedding. I will work to fill the void that your departed levity has left behind and keep her innocent and pure. She will, undoubtedly, want to give the report on the fact that I forced her on a double date this evening with my boss at the camp and another soldier. The band that played in Omaha the night before you left was playing, and he asked, in a way, if we would go.

B – It was a date. He picked us up and, even though he brought along a complete slug of a human, you could tell that he really didn't want Fowler or me in the car as he booted Fowler to the backseat and Margaret sat up front. Fowler is this horrible man whose every other phrase is some stream of obscenities.

M – I don't think it was a date. Maybe it was a date? Or, as you say, any night out that doesn't end with a kiss is just an appointment.

M&B – Oh! How we miss you! We hope you feel the love we're sending all the way across the Atlantic.

Be safe,

Margaret and Bea

It was gutting to miss a friend so deeply.

Margaret debated waiting to open Bob's letter and reply until Bea left in the morning but Bea was having none of that.

"Now let's see what the boy who has loved you since Kindergarten has to say."

"Love is a strong word for what Bob feels." Margaret was worried about the letter saying that as well but played it off as it didn't bother her and started reading.

October 10, 1944

Dearest Margaret –

Hi, Beautiful! Just a short note to give you my new address and let you know that I'm okay. Not that you might care. (Ha! Ha!)

With censorship restrictions on, there is very little I can tell you. They give us a million things we can't say but fail to mention just what we can say. I am allowed to say that I'm not on the east coast and that it's been a hell of a ride. Now, are you just loaded with hot information? I know, I shouldn't kid. This is the time I've been waiting for, for a long time. I'm really not kidding though. In fact, I'm fairly satisfied.

That's about all for now Maggie. I sure would like to hear from you. Need something to smile about. Also, I believe there was some mention of a snapshot How about it?

Love, Bob

PS - Say hello to Bea for me.

"It's like he knew I'd be here! And, what did I tell you about love?" Bea was so transparent in her desire to see her friends settle down that it didn't take long for her to forget about the date.

She opened her desk drawer and pulled out a V-Mail form. These were introduced to help streamline the international mail service by mailing these folded note cards to a central processing center, which would then be scanned to microfilm, thereby, reducing air cargo weight.

Well, there you are. Good to hear from you. I'll reply via V-mail in the hopes it arrives more quickly. They're encouraging us to use these. I was tempted to hold off on replying to you to punish you for taking so long, but darn it if I'm not just happy to "hear" your voice again after all these months.

Instead, I'll just punish you by not sending that snapshot and making you read a V-mail. Hope your eyesight is good. Ha! So there.

Life here is fine. Not much new to report. I'm enjoying my job because it makes me feel as if I'm engaged in the relative importance of the war effort somehow. I've long resigned myself to the fact that I will never be a war correspondent on the front lines, but instead have shifted my mindset to find some sort of joy here at the moment. I'm restless to get back to school or to get back to some sort of "normal" but for now, this is where we are. Right?

Now, write.

Margaret

P.S. – Bea says hi.

"Megs you're just torturing him."

"Yup, it's a gas isn't it?"

Chapter Thirty-Five

M onday morning, Margaret wasn't quite sure what to expect after the Officers' Club. It didn't really qualify as a date, or at least Bea said it didn't, because he didn't ask her for anything more than if she needed a ride and didn't walk her to the door. He didn't seem too affected by the fact that she took turns dancing with several of the officers who asked, she figured he wasn't that interested in her as anything except a coworker to have fun with before heading back to Washington state at the end of the war. They had plans to hike the Wildcat Hills that weekend, but it seemed like he might invite Fowler along, and Bea had told her in no uncertain terms that she would not be joining any future endeavors. Or hikes. Bea hated hikes. She knew that he was playing it too casually with Burke since she was curious about him but, truly, was somewhat terrified at the prospect of getting to know him better. She'd heard that he had been forced to leave his station in San Francisco due to a breakdown and she wanted to have enough time of calm to know that his issues had subsided. His last assistant, unfortunately, ended up in the line of fire from his meltdown and Margaret didn't want to see that side of him.

It seemed that Camp Scottsbluff was exactly that respite for him. Except for the escaped prisoners, there was very little drama. Situated in the quietest corner of the most sparsely populated state he'd ever visited, she knew the only jarring sounds were the train whistles as they went through town.

"Good morning, Miss Murphy. The weather's looking good for our hike this weekend."

"Might be a little chilly with this never-ending wind, but I'll make sure to let Bea know to bring an extra sweater." Margaret and Bea had decided this would be the easiest way to see if Harold meant for the hike to be a date or just a more casual outing.

"Oh, I didn't realize Bea was joining us?"

"She doesn't have to; I just wasn't sure..." Margaret trailed off. She'd never felt unsure about conversation with anyone, let alone a man. Why she couldn't just say "Let's make it a date" was beyond her.

Harold took a deep breath and said, "I would very much like to spend the afternoon just with you, on a date, if you'd be so obliged, Miss Murphy."

"I'd be honored, Captain Burke." Margaret knew this might complicate her work at the camp and that she'd likely be transferred to the typing pool if anyone found out. Though, with all of the local boys gone to war, more and more of the single women at the camp were coupling up with the soldiers stationed there. Pretty soon they wouldn't have any departments left to transfer people.

ell

Margaret had decided to meet Burke at the trailhead. The Wild-cat Hills was just south of Gering and there was a road you could drive up to the top, or you could park your car at the bottom to hike through the trees up to a stone picnic shelter and overlook. The ground was hard from previous freezes, but it was a mild fall day and there was no snow on the ground. Margaret was wearing trousers and an old barn jacket, which she used when she went out to friends' farms with their horses over the warmest turtleneck she could find. This might possibly be the least date-friendly outfit she'd ever worn on a first date. She'd clipped her hair back so the wind, which was light enough to be called a breeze by people who lived here, wouldn't whip into her face.

Burke pulled up shortly after she did. She was standing in between her car and a truck, and he couldn't see her from his car. She watched as he gripped the steering wheel with both hands, looked into the rearview mirror, and said something to himself. How someone that old, and definitely charming, could still be scared to talk to a girl was quite entertaining.

She decided not to make him suffer any longer and crossed the parking lot towards him, "Happy Saturday, Harold." When he grinned back at her she found herself wanting to do, or say, anything that would make him smile like that again. That smile did not exist in their office or at the dance.

"Good morning, Margaret."

She stopped in her tracks. "I was completely expecting to have to correct you after you used my whole name! You're making progress."

"I can learn new tricks occasionally. Now, tell me, where are we hiking?"

"There's a path over here that leads to an overlook where you can see all the way out to the prison. Did you bring a heavier coat?"

Burke shook his head. "I'll be okay."

Margaret felt bad for questioning his attire but knew that people from out of the area didn't realize just how quickly the wind could come up in this part of the country and just how biting it could be. The constant dust overshadowed the amount of humidity they had and the cold, once it hit, cut straight to the bone.

"I'll be okay. Besides, I brought some hot chocolate for when we get to wherever we get going." He gestured with his thermos.

Hiking wasn't a great activity for conversation, as the trail was narrow through the Ponderosa pines and junipers and steeper than Burke had anticipated. He was born and raised at sea level, and he almost struggled to keep up with Margaret. She kept looking back, and each time he'd smile, so she figured he was okay.

It took about a half hour before they reached the primitive picnic shelter. It was built during the Great Depression by the Civilian Conservation Corps. They also constructed another shelter out at Lake Minatare that was an exact match. Margaret thought if this date went well, maybe they could head out there another time. As they rounded the curve Margaret was happy to see that it was a truly clear day and there was no smog from the Great Western Sugar factory smokestacks.

"There it is. My favorite view in the world. I know that sounds corny because I really haven't been to that many places, but it truly is." Margaret sat on the edge of the table with her feet up on the bench and motioned for Burke to join her. He went to sit on the edge of the table next to her and cracked his head against the log overhang.

"Son of a..." Burke stopped himself before he continued.

"Oh no! Are you okay?" Margaret was biting her lip, trying not to laugh. She reached out to touch his head.

Burke blushed. "I'm fine."

"I guess your legs are just too long. Take a seat on the bench like a normal human."

Burke sat on the lower bench, and they were nearly the same height. They both turned and looked out at the valley.

"What do you think?"

Margaret didn't notice that Burke was looking at her instead of the view when he said, "It's one of the most beautiful things I've ever seen." She turned to look at him, and he got his wits about him "Would you like some hot chocolate?"

"Yes, please." She was impressed that he'd stacked two cups on top of the thermos. The cocoa smelled delicious as he poured them each a mugful.

"Would you like to jazz it up a little?" Burke withdrew a small flask from inside his jacket pocket.

Margaret didn't want to seem like a killjoy, so she held her cup out towards the flask. They'd had drinks together at the Officers' Club so why did this feel different?

Burke poured a small amount into her mug, sensing her hesitation, but was a little heavier-handed with his.

She took a sip. Somehow, he'd made this hot chocolate into something that tasted like the holidays and her reservations went out the window. "This is delicious."

"Peppermint schnapps, the perfect drink for winter."

"I've never had it before. I'll have to make one of these for Bea at our Christmas get-together." She turned to him. "Tell me all about where you like to hike and how it compares; maybe someday I'll head out there."

"It's rarely this cold, but it's green year-round. I have a feeling that I'm going to enjoy Christmas here because it might actually snow. We rarely get snow on Christmas." Burke was shivering.

"Are you cold?" Margaret knew that men didn't like it when you laughed at them, so she stayed as neutral as possible.

"No. Not at all." He took a drink and paused for a moment. "No, Miss Murphy, that is a bald-faced lie. I am freezing."

Margaret let out the laugh that she'd been holding in, "Next date, we can be inside somewhere."

Burke threw back the rest of his hot cocoa. She joined him and they headed back down the hill to the cars.

By the time they got there, the wind had picked up, and Burke looked miserable. She'd had a scarf tucked in her jacket pocket that she'd loaned him because she could just tuck the lower half of her face into her turtleneck and tip up the collar of the barn coat.

She could tell that he wanted to say a more proper goodbye, but he was also shaking and in desperate need of a handkerchief. "You're going to catch your death if you don't get in a warm car immediately. I'll see you on Monday!" She opened her car door and hopped in before he could stop her.

As she drove away, she watched him wave at her with the scarf. She felt like she was playing a game and was having quite a grand time.

Chapter Thirty-Six

M argaret had nothing planned for Sunday except to sleep in, wash her hair, and catch up on writing to her friends. Bob had responded with a V-Mail. Serves her right. Those things were so tiny and hard to read. She'd borrowed her dad's magnifying glass.

November 2, 1944 - V-Mail - Somewhere between France and Germany

Dear M,

The rapidity with which I'm answering this letter of yours will probably astound you, but that is the way I have to do it. I try and answer every letter the minute I get it, because if I have the time then, I might not be around later. It shouldn't make you feel bad, cause I got your letter this evening, and I'm answering this evening. Fast worker that Hale fellow.

It was really swell to hear from you Margaret, and you'll never know how much mail means to me now that I've lost contact with most of my friends or lost a few of them altogether. It won't always be so easy for me to sit down and knock off a letter, so don't be too surprised if there is a gap. Just keep writing away unless you hear a reason to stop, and I'll do the same. I don't think it is possible to set a schedule for writing, cause I never know how often I'll be able to, and when I'll be able to. Can't really plan if I'm going to be writing from a trench or a cot and it's hard to write by lanterns as if those are allowed. It would be swell if you'd just sort of set aside one or two nights a week and drop me a letter. I'll try and do the same from this end.

I'm glad to know that you enjoy your work, and I know what you mean when you say that you get restless after a certain length of time. I love to move about on my own time, do what I want, and go where I want. Being in the army has sort of cramped my style, but I'll get back into the swing of things when this mess is over. The army gives every man $300 at the end of their enlistment, and I'm going to use that money for nothing but having a good time traveling.

That just about finishes up the news I can tell from this end old dear. I'll write more the next time I write, and I'll write more often.

As Ever, Bob

She'd just taken out a fresh sheet of stationary when she heard a familiar yell. "Margaret Elizabeth Murphy, come out here this minute." Her mother's voice shrieked from the front room and carried through Margaret's closed door.

"Mother, I am nearly twenty-two years old. What now?"

"I have just been informed that Nan Pierce and Rose Marsh saw you out in the hills south of town last weekend, on a hike with some man, wearing slacks no less!"

The things that shocked her mother were, if you looked beyond their ridiculousness, sometimes entertaining.

"So, am I in trouble for the pants? The location of the hike? The man?" Margaret knew that she was walking on thin ice with her mother with the attitude and thought she'd covered every base by planning the hike when her mother was out playing bridge. Unfortunately, she had not accounted for two of her mother's bird-watching friends who happened to be out on a hike of their own. News travels so fast in a small town that she should have expected this confrontation and cut it off at the pass.

"It's not enough that you're hurting your father's reputation by working at that prison. Or that you're thinking of moving to some home for unwed women."

Franklin was sitting in the corner chair, smoking a pipe, reading the paper, and he tipped the edge down to see how this confrontation would play out. He rarely intervened in this age-old battle between Margaret and her mother.

"Now wait a minute, Mother. Daddy helped get me that job by setting me up with the airfield construction project. His reputation is just fine. I think it's you who's embarrassed by my work. And mind you, it's just an apartment complex. In Scottsbluff, Nebraska. It's not in Paris." Margaret simply didn't want to rehash this fight, so she thought she'd try the distraction technique again that had worked so well with Thomas all those years ago in college. She took a deep breath.

"Besides, Mother, Harold Burke is a Captain at the camp, and I think you would very much like to meet him. I was thinking of inviting him to dinner since he cannot go home for the holiday. Would you be open to at least meet him before deciding that he is not worthy of seeing me in trousers?"

Franklin finally interjected. "I had the opportunity to meet Captain Burke at the Elks Club. I didn't realize that he was who you were hiking with yesterday."

"You knew she was hiking! I swear. The two of you will be the death of me." Rebecca huffed off into the kitchen.

"Margaret, you just antagonize her sometimes for fun, I think." Franklin shook his head.

She understood that she and her mother were so vastly different in many, many ways, but their constant confrontation was the source of much heartburn for her father. "Oh, Dad. I just wish she understood that I'm doing the best I can with being at home. I'm working, I'm writing, and I am happy to be getting to know Harold. He's very interesting. I'm not saying it will amount to anything, but after all this time, I'm almost having fun."

"If he puts a smile on your face, that's all that matters to me, Magpie. We need more reasons to smile. Feels like the news is bleak leading into the holidays. What do you hear from your 'pen pals' across the pond?"

Margaret never hid the fact that each of the letters was anxiously anticipated and that, while Harold was here and interesting, Bob had arrived in Europe and Charles was headed to the Pacific. Each held a piece of her heart, and, after Sam's death, they were all hopeful that both would come home safely.

"You know how Bob has always had a sense of humor? Never could take a thing seriously?" Bob had come over for several dinners with her parents when they were dating in high school and was always clowning around. Franklin found him a hoot. Her mother not so much.

Franklin nodded.

"He's losing bits of that and it's hard to watch. Each letter sounds a little less like him. More distant. Almost forced. I'm worried about him. I work with so many men that came back from fighting mostly whole physically but not quite all there mentally. I just cannot imagine that happening to Bob." Margaret was shocked at the depth of emotion as she started to choke up thinking of Bob losing that charming, and annoying, wit.

"Charles, on the other hand, I don't hear from as often. He's been in school and training. I'm assuming he's headed for Japan and that scares me. How we can navigate two wars essentially at the same time is beyond me. I wish that Roosevelt and his cronies could just come up with a plan to end this once and for all."

"Oh, me too, Maggie. Me too."

Chapter Thirty-Seven

A Lesson in Gratitude from Behind the Wire — Margaret Murphy, Gering Courier

*W*hen the wind is whipping through the plains of western Nebraska it sometimes takes with it a feeling of gratitude and tries to blow it all the way to Chicago. It seems almost fruitless to chase down things to be thankful for during a war. But it is the season for gratitude and thanksgiving so with that prompt, please indulge this writer on a list of a few things to be grateful for this Thanksgiving of 1944.

I am thankful for our freedom. Unless you've been living under a rock you've seen the images that are coming out of Europe of how Hitler has treated those he conquered.

I am thankful for the Geneva Convention. It is tempting at times to take out our rage at Hitler and his ilk on the prisoners that are here. However, it is in treating them with care, compassion, and humanity that we show that the tenets of what it means to be an American will not be destroyed by war.

I am thankful for the postal service. We were given the task of keeping up the morale of our soldiers as they fought against tyranny by writing them lighthearted letters from home. For me, dear reader, I have found just as much of a morale boost for

*myself hearing back from childhood friends and have developed
a stronger understanding of the world that they're living in and
what they're fighting against. They will return to us different
men and women than when they left, but these letters help us
transition with them.*

*I am grateful for our close-knit community. With a population
as small as ours, the degrees of separation between each family
and our struggles are lessened by our connection. We each have
loved ones in or lost to, the war, and we have rallied to be
supportive of each other.*

*May we find that 1944 is the last year we must celebrate
Thanksgiving during wartime.*

Thanksgiving was small this year—just Margaret and her parents. Her aunt and uncle had gone back east to Chicago to visit her aunt's family. Everything was very reserved.

"We should have just made a chicken. All this work for just the three of us." Rebecca complained as she looked at the leftovers from the turkey dinner that their housekeeper had so kindly prepared.

"We didn't prepare anything, Mother." Boredom in Margaret was as dangerous as boredom in prisoners, and she was looking for a fight.

Rebecca took the deep breath she always took before launching into a speech.

"Would you two just cool it for once?" Even Franklin's temper was at the surface.

Margaret retreated to her room to write to June.

November 27th, 1944

June,

Oh, to be able to transport myself to your side, wherever you may be, and enjoy all the action. I feel like a broken record here. Work is fine, Captain Burke has become a regular date (well, appointment since there is no more physical contact than dancing) to the Officers' Club, but I'm positive the Cupid of our crew, Bea, has filled you in on those details.

Are you safe? I do worry about you. I know you have been passionate about medical work since we were in high school and dissected those frogs. How you have the stomach for it all is beyond me. So, I suppose, for as bored as I am and as tired as I am of living with Mother and Daddy, my life is pretty easy. Chin up Megs, no complaining! (I can hear you now!)

Bea and I are hoping to get an apartment in a few weeks. She started the conversation with the folks and, well, we'll see. Cross your fingers.

I hear through the western Nebraska grapevine that Milt is cranking up the awards. Quite the hero you have there. Is he still your hero?

To safer days in the future. Happy Thanksgiving and a, hopefully, Merry Christmas, to you.

All my love - Your sister - Margaret

Margaret felt like a hypocrite sitting in her very comfortable room, in a very safe part of the country, acting like a bit of a brat to her parents. She'd just written an article about gratitude for the paper, for goodness' sake. Gratitude seems like a minute-by-minute thing during times of war.

She regretted not inviting Burke to join them for Thanksgiving. She debated it but, even though he'd been friendly since the hike, he hadn't asked for another date. They'd had good times at the Officers' Club, but it never amounted to anything except conversation that was a touch more casual than in the office, a few drinks, and a couple of dances. He couldn't handle the noise and crowd inside for more than a couple of songs before a cigarette and drink break was needed. She and Bea always just met him there, so it was more like a work happy hour than a date. She wasn't sure why he was so intriguing to her.

Chapter Thirty-Eight

December 10, 1944
   Dear Margaret,

After many hectic weeks here, I am again able to say hello and chat a while. First a brief resumé of my activities since your last fine letter in September. Most of that month I spent on the sick list with awful sinusitis, 4 weeks in the hospital in all. I had so much penicillin in my ample behind that I'm only just now not tender. On the last day I was in the hospital I got my orders to the Marines. I left for Camp Pendleton 2 days later. When I got there, I was assigned to this unit. A short month followed of rather boring but grueling activity during which time the folks came out for a visit. On the 6th of November, we boarded a Navy transport and headed southwest. 15 days later they pushed us off on this tropical paradise.

Since then, we have been "camping out". I am assigned to a grand outfit, a Medical Company which functions as a field hospital. It's the best duty in the Marine Corps for a Doctor and I feel very fortunate.

We have been spending alternate weeks in the "boondocks" (jungle) on field problems. Off weeks we spend setting up and organizing the division field hospital. It's still a bit of a mess but it will be quite a place. Next week our company is being moved to a new place. Here we only have tents with no decks, a shower where we pump our own water, no beer, nothing but an exquisite setting, white beaches, the blue Pacific, stately palms, mosquitos, land crabs, etc. There we have cottages on stilts on another fine beach, a beautiful (to me) hospital (army built), and 6 bottles of beer a week. Paradise! The only thing missing is a book or two. Any recommendations?

This evening I'm on the eve of a week in those "boondocks." It will be fierce but it's a relief to be away from the confusion of this place and we'll have a swell time.

This letter is to wish you a wonderful Christmas. Right now, you must be planning it all. I'd give anything to be there for the season. I wish I could send you some of this sunshine. We have more than enough and I'm sure you'd enjoy it. I would enjoy sitting with you, quietly reading, and listening to the sound of the surf in the distance. I'll send you some pictures as soon as they are developed of some of our treks then you'll know more about where I am situated. Give my kindest regards and best wishes for a happy Christmas to your Mother and Dad and have a lovely one yourself. Happy New Year will arrive in due time. Until then Adios. Write when you can, I'll be glad to hear from you.

Sincerely, as ever, Charles.

Margaret decided that she would put together a care package for Charles and include a few books. She considered *A Bell for Adano* but thought that a man at war might not want to read something about a different part of that same war. She settled on her copies of *The Lady in the Lake* and *A Tree Grows in Brooklyn* knowing that he'd probably already read both, but it is always soothing to reread things during times of great anxiety.

Dear Charles,

I'm happy to hear that you are sitting by the seaside and enjoying the beach. It's cold and blustery as always here. We're having a bit of a hard go here because not a single one of us is free from concern about loved ones around the world. I was holding out hope that you would maybe just graduate straight into being an instructor of other doctors and you would never need to sail away from safety.

The very least I can do is send you a small package of books that you've likely read, magazines that you may enjoy, and a copy of a few articles that I've written. Please send me all of the requests for reading material that you, and any of your fellow soldiers, might enjoy. I am more than happy to provide.

Merry Christmas and soak up some sunshine for me.

My Best,

Margaret

Before the war, Margaret enjoyed the holiday season. She treasured the memories of waking early, quietly heading to their living room where the eight-foot tree was nestled just to the left of the fireplace. She'd plug in the lights to the tree and lay on the ground watching the colors become more brilliant as the bulbs warmed up. She thought she'd try to recreate that peace.

This year she was tracking Bob's trek across Europe, guessing at his locations, and Charles's trek across the Pacific and was certain that this could be the last Christmas for at least one of them. By this point she, and most of America had started to become numb to the news of death. The garish light of the bulbs on the tree magnified her sense of despair. She struggled with the idea that neither Bob nor Charles, was anything more to her than friends even though their letters were becoming clearer that they could each become more than just pen pals.

She felt a little conflicted as she'd begun spending a bit more time with Harold outside of work.

Chapter Thirty-Nine

"Ground rules for this evening, no war talk, no boy talk, no work talk," Margaret pronounced. Bea and Margaret had finally carved out a time for just the two of them to head to the movies. It had been too long since they'd had a free night without the distraction of a work event, a column to write, or an occasional date with Harold.

"Counterpoint: we will talk about the movie, and our lives, and then we will talk about boys. No war talk, but I need the scoop on you and the captain. I need to know if he's going to whisk you off to the west coast before my wedding." Bea sounded a little anxious about the answer.

Arsenic and Old Lace, starring Cary Grant, was being held over at The Egyptian Theater in Scottsbluff. Movies that came out in other parts of the country seemed to make it to their small art house several weeks later. The newsreels before the movies were always timely, which frustrated Margaret that they couldn't deliver the movies just as quickly.

"I'm not going anywhere anytime soon. I promise. Besides if Ted knew how much you loved Cary Grant, I swear to you Bea, he would call off the engagement and there would be no wedding."

"If Cary Grant knew my name, I would call off my engagement myself," Bea sighed.

The girls grabbed their popcorn and settled in to watch the movie.

The café around the corner from the movie theater was open 24 hours and catered to the sugar factory and railroad workers, but on Friday nights it was typically full of people looking for a pie and a coffee after a movie. The city had chosen to pare down its Christmas light display on Main Street in solidarity with the rationing of supplies; there were still enough lights to make it almost seem festive. Margaret and Bea linked arms and walked to the café.

"Okay, so that movie was hilarious, but I can see why Cary Grant hated his performance." Bea absolutely loved the movies and typically limited her news to the entertainment pages in *Life* magazine. "He was so very over the top."

Margaret enjoyed the escapism of a movie but never really critiqued them beyond whether they entertained her or not or if she felt manipulated by them. "Do you think they're just releasing silly movies like this around the holidays to distract us from war?"

"Come on, ground rule number one. No war." Bea knew that it would be a struggle to keep Margaret from deep diving into the politics of the world they were currently living in. "You promised. In fact, you made the rules!"

"I did. So, in lieu of war and work, which is just about all that I think about, what should we talk about? The new apartment we're getting after Christmas to get away from our mothers?"

The café was not crowded so they took their seats, waved at their high school friend Sheryl who was working behind the counter, and ordered a piece of apple pie a la mode to share and two cups of coffee.

"Do you really think your mother will allow it after the pants meltdown of 1944? I keep thinking she's going to pull the rug out from under us."

"Like she did with my education? At this point, what can she say? I have my own money, my own job, and we're twenty-two years old." Margaret knew her voice was filled with false bravado.

"The question really is, will you be entertaining gentleman callers named Harold Burke at this apartment?" Bea didn't want to get lost in the practicalities of the housing drama but instead wanted to redirect Margaret to the discussion of the first serious prospect of a beau since she called off her engagement.

"Oh, Bea. Harold is an enigma. Just when I think I have him figured out and think we're potentially turning into something more than coworkers that occasionally hike or go to the Officers' Club together he seems to withdraw. I've invited him to dinner at the folks' for Christmas, and I'm hoping he'll let his guard down just a little bit."

"I heard that he got transferred to our camp because he had some sort of issue with nerves at the last place." Bea always got the latest scoop from the typing pool who seemed to have a complete disregard for confidentiality.

"He does seem to startle easily, which has become a bit of a game for us in the office. I wait until he's deeply engrossed in a ledger, and then I slam my drawer shut just to see him jump. He kind of looks like a daddy longlegs spider." Margaret and Bea laughed at the idea of this super tall string bean of a man as an arachnid. "Either way, he's someone here who's interesting to get to know. I miss talking with interesting people. Speaking of interesting, I've been writing with Bob Hale quite a bit."

"You don't need to say his whole name, Meg...I'm well aware of the history of Bob in your life." Bea shook her head. "If, after all this time and all that drama, you end up with Bob, I will just eat my hat."

"Bob is a lark. He's never going to be more than a lark. He's good for a laugh and I like hearing from him to make sure he's still alive. And please don't judge—do you remember that soldier at the train station when you forced me to go with you guys after Sam died?"

"That dreamy doctor from California that you snuck off to talk to in the park?"

"Yes. Charles. He's started writing from San Diego where he was training, and he and I have started exchanging book recommendations. I send him new books once I've finished reading them. I think I might write an article for the paper about setting up a more formal book exchange with our soldiers. He seems to really like it."

"So, what I'm hearing is that you have Bob on the hook in Europe for a laugh, Charles in the Pacific for intelligent conversation, and Harold here for dancing and romancing. You, dear friend, are starring in your own *Philadelphia Story*."

"I don't know about the romancing part of it all. I think I've outgrown all of that."

"Margaret, dear, I don't think you can outgrow something you were never into. Where I was always looking to be swept off my feet, you've always watched dating activities as if you're an anthropologist studying monkeys. Pragmatic to a fault. Unfortunately, you've also got the looks of Katherine Hepburn, and men can't seem to recognize that they are no more than a lab experiment to you. When you and Thomas got together it was obvious, to me at least, that you were using him as leverage against your mom."

"I tried! I tried the whole girlfriend-fiancé, thing. I went to New Orleans, I truly tried to love him. But, God's honest truth, I don't think I've loved anyone before. Maybe it's just not who I'm cut out to be. I'm cold-hearted Margaret, perfect for international writing for the *New York Times*. Unencumbered by any man."

"Let's start by just getting an apartment and see if your mother has a stroke. We can talk about the *New York Times* after that. Sound like a plan?"

Margaret took a sip of her coffee. "Absolutely."

Chapter Forty

The prisoners, with no work to do in the fields in the winter, were at risk of becoming bored, and bored prisoners were harder to control. The higher-ups in Washington had informed the camp commander that they would like the prisoners to decorate and celebrate Christmas. One of Eleanor Roosevelt's initiatives was to "Americanize" the prisoners, and they provided decorations for the barracks and Christmas music to show how free things were here. The one caveat was that all carols had to be sung in English, so the activities lieutenant had been practicing with them all week. They were due to have a talent show of sorts for the staff this afternoon. Margaret shook her head at the cognitive dissonance of celebrating Christmas with carols sung by a choir of mostly German prisoners of war. They had called for a short day of work so that everyone could gather for lunch and entertainment.

"Did they not account for the fact that we might have actual work to do and might not have time for revelry?" Margaret asked as she entered her office.

Burke just grinned. "Do you ever just relax, Miss Murphy?"

"Do you ever work that hard, Captain Burke?"

"As a matter of fact, I do. We're told to expect another shipment of prisoners right after the holiday, and with us going to a short staff for Christmas break, we might as well get a jump on things. Either that or we'll have to work through the weekend, and I'll miss that famous dinner that your mother is preparing for us." Margaret had finally found the bravery that eluded her at Thanksgiving and had asked Burke to join her family for Christmas dinner, which he enthusiastically accepted.

"Ha! As if my mother is cooking. She's having our housekeeper cook for you. She'll take the credit, for sure, but she absolutely would not be the one whose food you would want to eat. If it was up to her, we'd eat a canned pear and a slice of ham and call it good. 'Better for your figure, you know.'"

"What time do you want me there? And what should I bring?"

"Five is fine. Daddy will want to do drinks before dinner. I'm going to head to the commissary to get a cup of coffee. I haven't warmed up from the drive in. Do you need anything?"

"I'd love a refill. Thank you kindly, Miss Murphy." Burke winked at her as she took his cup and walked out.

Margaret wandered down the hall lost in thought about the wink. Did the wink make her feel anything? Was she flirting with Burke because that's just how she'd been conditioned to talk to men? Why must she overthink everything?

As she turned the corner, she ran directly into a prisoner that was twisting greenery around a door surrounding the commissary. Burke's coffee cup went flying and shattered on the ground. Both she and the prisoner started scrambling to pick up the pieces. She recognized him as the inmate she suspected of carving the dogs.

"It's okay, I've got it." Margaret wasn't sure how to communicate with him that he didn't need to clean up her mess.

"Miss, I am Rudi."

"Oh, you're ready?" She looked at the mess of greenery around him.

"I am Rudi." He pointed at his chest. Margaret felt like an idiot. She knew his name was Rudi.

"Oh, I'm Margaret. Thank you for your help."

Finally seeing him up close she realized he was a frail young man, maybe in his mid-twenties. With slightly curly dark brown hair and the sharp features of some of the Russian immigrants, Margaret wondered if he was one of the prisoners that had family on both sides of the war. She grabbed another mug from the counter, filled two cups, and went to reach for the bottle of milk Rudi was holding.

"Margaret." It was like Rudi was practicing her name. He handed her the bottle of milk.

"Yes. Margaret. Thank you." Margaret smiled.

"Thank you." Rudi smiled. Margaret wasn't sure if he just didn't know any more English or was just quiet. Either way, she needed to get back to work, and she turned and hustled down the hallway. Spending too much time talking to the prisoners, even prisoners who had more leeway to move around was not looked upon favorably.

Chapter Forty-One

Christmas 1944

"Mother, Daddy, this is Captain Harold Burke."

Burke had arrived promptly at five o'clock. What Margaret didn't know is that he had pulled up around the corner fifteen minutes earlier and fortified himself with a small swig of liquid courage in the form of a flask of whiskey tucked in his glove box.

"Captain Burke, what a pleasure it is to finally meet you. Franklin here said he had the opportunity to talk with you at the Elks Club?" Her mother simply could not let it go that she was the last to know anything.

"We shook hands but there were too many people there to truly get to know anyone. I'm looking forward to talking with you both tonight. Miss Margaret here has been just an invaluable member of our team in the Quartermaster's office, and I'm so grateful she extended an invitation to join you for the holiday." He handed a bottle of wine to Franklin and a small package of chocolates to her mother. "I wasn't sure what to bring, so I figured sweets and wine would fit with anything."

Margaret observed her mother begin to soften. Burke was well-mannered which mattered more than maybe it should, and the dimple in his cheek when he smiled at her mother didn't hurt either.

"Let's go grab a drink in the front room before dinner. We can pick up where we left off at the Elks."

Dinner went off without a hitch. Her aunt and uncle had joined from across the street, a raucous game of charades was played, many cocktails were consumed, and everyone left more lighthearted than they'd been in a long time. It almost felt like a normal Christmas.

"Mother, Daddy, I'm going to go walk Harold to his car."

"Be careful out there, soldier, it's starting to snow."

"No worries Mr. Murphy, I've got good tires and they plow the roads to the camp. Thank you again, Mrs. Murphy, for the dinner it really meant a lot to my mother to know that I had a place to spend Christmas."

Harold and Margaret walked down the block to where Harold had parked.

"Why did you park so far away?"

"I got here way too early. I guess I was nervous."

"Nervous? About what?"

"I just wanted to make a good impression. Miss Margaret Murphy, I think I'm falling for you, and I just don't want anything to mess this up." He gently took her hand. "Would it be okay if I kissed you?"

This was the first time anyone had ever asked. She could reasonably say this was the first time she'd been kissed by a man. Thomas was a child when they were engaged. Every other casual suitor she'd had over the years had been a fumbling fool. At nearly ten years her senior, Harold was obviously more experienced than most. The kiss, in the still light of the streetlight, as the snow came down gently, felt like a scene from a movie.

As they stepped back from their embrace, he gently stroked the side of her cheek, "Margaret, you are a wonder. Thank you for the merriest Christmas I've had in quite a while."

"Happy to help a soldier out." Margaret stumbled for a romantic retort. It just wasn't in her vocabulary. "I'll see you on Monday." She stood on her tiptoes to kiss him one more time and then turned and ran up the block to the house.

She stood on the front porch as he slid behind the wheel of his car and watched him drive away.

Not exactly sure how to wallow in romance, Margaret wondered if this could be something more than just a camp fling. There was no way she was going to be able to sleep, so she sat down to write a few letters.

December 24, 1944

June, June, come in, June. It's your best friend and I have an urgent question. What does one do when they've developed a case of the feelings? I would describe my symptoms as flushed cheeks, a more rapid heartbeat, and severe cognitive decline. Please let me know exactly what I need to do to make this go away.

My vulnerability is your bonus Christmas gift. You should have received the care package from Bea and me.

Please respond. I will wait patiently by the mailbox.

Merry Christmas, Happy New Year, and Come Home Soon.

Yours forever, your friend ~ M

That kiss had absolutely turned her into a cliché of a woman. She'd bumbled through her good nights with her parents, and her aunt and uncle chuckled at her flushed cheeks which she blamed on the weather when she came back inside. Sleep wasn't going to come easily, so she figured she might as well send a note to Bob as well.

Probably 1945 by the time you get this - Gering, Nebraska
Hi-di-ho and Happy New Year Hale,
Trying to send all the happiness I can muster across the miles to you. Was hoping to hear news from you for Christmas. Gladys brought by some of her world-famous fudge and news that you were doing well (as well as can be considered) and we toasted you and your family with each bite. She was going to try and ship some over to you, but something tells me it won't be the same. One of the boys that I work with said he received a cake from his mom for his birthday, and he had to lie and say that it was delicious even though it was more pancake than cake and was a bit fuzzier than cake should be.
Oh, discussing moldy cake is not really how we should kick off the new year now, is it? But looking back at the four years since we headed to school I guess if you had to pick a dessert that summed up the fact that we were still at war in 1945, it would be something putrid.
Are you still not sleeping? I worry about you. What's that? Margaret has a heart for an old friend. Shhhh...don't tell anyone. There's a softy under this cantankerous exterior.
Send me some descriptions of the world you're witnessing. I'm living vicariously through you. The Monument is still in

the same place. Chimney Rock hasn't moved. Nothing much has changed on our end.

Keep that chin up, keep your head down, and stay safe.

Looking forward to an update.

All my best—Murphy

Margaret worried that by leaving out the story of her developing relationship with Burke she was leading Bob on about her intentions. Her rationale was that men did this all of the time. For all she knew, Bob was writing to a half dozen women.

Chapter Forty-Two

January 1945

The weeks had passed since Christmas, and Margaret and Burke were finding more and more reasons to shut the door to their office for private conferences that involved more kissing than she'd ever experienced or enjoyed, in her life. She was going to run out of lipstick from the constant reapplication. After meeting her parents Harold was welcome at the house and became a more regular fixture for weeknight meals before they headed to the Officers' Club for dancing.

The idea of getting an apartment just so she and Harold could be alone was starting to sound more and more appealing. Happily, her parents had acquiesced. She and Bea were picking up the keys to their place on Friday after work.

This level of distraction in the workplace simply wasn't healthy. She pulled away and sat down at her desk.

"Harold, we need to cool it at work. Someone is going to catch us, and I'll have to go to the typing pool."

"Why would you need to go anywhere?"

"Because you know as well as I that I would take the brunt of the blame for any violation of workplace fraternization rules.

I am, after all, a woman and men are incapable of controlling themselves around women."

"I cannot disagree with you there, Miss Murphy." He leaned over the back of her chair and kissed the side of her neck softly. "I am incapable of controlling myself around you."

She felt the imprint of his lips between her collarbone and her ear for the rest of the day as if it was tattooed on her permanently.

Luckily, there were things to keep her busy, or at least things that made her look busy if a superior officer walked down the hall. Burke was even more lenient with her time to write articles.

Being busy and having secret kissing sessions also helped to keep anxiety at bay. Margaret hadn't heard back from June and had to really work to control her emotions when there were long lapses in communication. Just because there were six weeks between Sam's last letter and his death didn't mean that every time there was silence coming from the other side of the world that her friends were dead. She figured she'd do what was asked and just keep writing even if there was no response. She planned to mail her latest article to June since it was inspired by her bravery.

The Women of the War — Margaret Murphy, Gering Courier
Our community has sent hundreds of our young men off to the dueling fronts in the Pacific and Europe. We hear stories of their heroism on the radio and watch newsreels before our movies showing the chaos in which they're living. What we're not seeing

is the women behind the scenes who are making as big of an impact as the men with the guns.

From our small community, we have several nurses, a few Red Cross supply drivers, and even a pilot who ferries planes back and forth for the Navy—all women. Many are, thanks to the pressure from our First Lady, military officers, and are paid as such. They will come home with the same rank and some incredible hands-on experience that will, undoubtedly, benefit small communities across our great nation.

What would be better than a nurse who has the nerves of steel, honed during battle, as your surgeon's right hand? Who knows, maybe we'd even open up the surgical suite for female doctors? After all, our community was home to Dr. Georgia Arbuckle Fix who is buried in our West Lawn Cemetery, one of the first female doctors in the country.

We see posters of Rosie the Riveter and the smiling faces of actresses on USO posters. What we aren't seeing is that, for instance, the prisoner of war camp is staffed primarily by civilian workers, many women, who handle many behind-the-scenes operations. Women across the nation are doing jobs that we've never even considered. We're playing baseball, we're driving tractors, we're building airplanes.

So, if you know a woman who is working to make the best of this war, and I dare say we all do, give thanks and pray that this New Year might come with an end to this conflict.

Chapter Forty-Three

Prisoner intake had slowed during the holidays but had ramped up after the first of the year. The days flew by so quickly that even Burke's obsession with canoodling in the corner of the office had gone by the wayside. Margaret had to admit that she missed some of that passion and sneaking around.

She was planning her next attack on a defenseless Burke and suggest that he come to see the new apartment now that it was all set up. He'd spent the weekend helping Bea and her haul boxes. When she entered the office, he was standing, red-faced, holding a small wooden figurine of a poodle.

"I caught a prisoner trying to sneak in here to put this on your desk. He said your name. Explain."

"Oh, they're harmless. One appears on my desk every once in a while. I like dogs."

"How does a prisoner, a German Nazi dog himself, know anything about you? Have you been talking to him? Have you given him gifts too? How could you do this?"

Harold's speech had become stilted, rushed even. His reaction, in Margaret's opinion, did not fit the situation.

"Harold, dear, they mean nothing. I know nothing more than his name is Rudi. He's been here since the first trainload of prisoners."

"His name is Rudolph Hahn, and he was an officer in the German army and is worth nothing more than the manure that this godforsaken town reeks of constantly. I am disgusted with you, Miss Murphy. I have half a mind to report your fraternization to my superior and have you terminated immediately."

This was completely out of left field. Burke had never shown any sort of temper.

"How about this, Captain Burke," her voice dripped with her Scotch Irish rage, "I'm going to leave now. Tell people I've headed home ill if anyone notices. I will expect an apology when you get your damned wits about you."

With that, Margaret grabbed the figurine from Burke's hand, turned on her heel, and stormed out of the office. She stopped by the switchboard on her way out and waved at Bea.

"Margaret, what's wrong?" Bea had enjoyed the reprieve from Margaret's temper due to her new relationship but could see that something had peeved her. "Why do you have your purse? Has something happened?" She didn't look forward to another frantic drive like the one when Sam died.

"Captain Harold Burke is what is wrong. I'm going home. Do you think you can get a ride with another one of the girls? Tell anyone who asks that I'm sick."

"Absolutely. No problem at all." Bea knew better than to push. She figured they would talk about it later. "I'll see you tonight."

Margaret threw a warning glare at the soldier doing the exit security, daring him to ask to search her bag. He just tipped his head. He'd heard rumors that she was coupled up with Burke and wasn't about to potentially anger his superior officer.

She revved the engine of her car and backed up with a little too much confidence, narrowly missing two soldiers walking across the parking lot. She laughed. Would running them over count as a civilian or soldier accident on the placard hanging outside the entrance?

One of the many upsides of having her own apartment was that she could go in, slam all the cabinet doors she wanted, and no one would bother her or question her anger. She had every right to be angry. Burke was out of his mind with his accusations. Sure, she could have told him about the figurines, but why would she willingly get a prisoner, who was harming no one, in trouble?

Margaret put the kettle on for coffee and spooled a fresh piece of paper into the typewriter.

The Fragility of Man — Margaret Murphy, Gering Courier
At what point in a relationship does possessiveness come into play? And, if the goal of a relationship is possession, what is an independent woman to do? We are but mammals designed to couple up with other mammals to ensure the survival of the species but must that survival come with the headache of the fragile emotions of men?

She knew that this ranting would be crumpled and tossed into the trash, but it felt good to write it all down.

I thought I'd found a good one, a tolerable one at least, some-one who was a little more mature and wiser to the ways of the world.

Even with his jumping at the slightest noise, Harold had never let on that he was one to lose his temper with her. Sure, he scared the other soldiers when things weren't done correctly in their department, but that was strength, right? He could give the soldiers orders all day long and still soften into the gangly man who kissed like that was the only thing he studied in college. Damn. She was going to miss those kisses.

These dog figurines were just tiny pieces of art. Made for me. Just for me. By someone who didn't expect anything in return. Why must men suspect that all other men are their direct com-petition? Are men nothing more than angry gorillas in uniform looking for someone with which to mate?

The apartment was filled with hand-me-down furniture from her parent's basement, old cups, and saucers that her mother didn't want any longer. To Margaret, it was the coziest, most peaceful place she'd ever lived. The sorority house at NU was loud, and her house at 14th and O was spacious but there was never privacy. Margaret made herself a cup of coffee, pulled the paper loose from the typewriter, and crumpled it up in a ball to throw away when there was a knock at the door.

Margaret opened the door to a forlorn Harold Burke staring at his shoes. She started to pick up the fight where they'd left off when she noticed that he was crying, tears silently running down his face. This was new. She could count on one hand the times she'd seen a man cry.

Her father was never one for emotion, jovial to a fault. When Sam died the whole family was, of course, devastated, but as Franklin watched his brother fall apart, he went the other direction into a solve-everything mode, and there were no tears. The only men she'd ever seen cry were the very young prisoners as they were being processed, but they were quickly shushed by their superiors.

"Harold." Margaret decided to keep her head as level as possible and stay curious about why he left work to chase her and how the rage-filled man could go so quickly to this broken individual outside her door.

"Margaret, can I come in?" She knew that the rumor mill would work overtime if he was seen coming into her apartment, but rumors be damned. She let him pass.

"Can I get you a cup of coffee?" Margaret shut the door behind him, and Harold walked over to the sofa. Watching his limbs fold in upon themselves Margaret decided to just sit quietly until he started talking. If journalism classes taught her nothing else, it's that the story is told in the moments of silence and that Harold needed to lead the direction of the conversation.

He sipped his coffee, hand shaking slightly as he placed the cup back on the saucer and dropped his face in his hands.

"I owe you an apology."

"Yes." Margaret bit her tongue from lashing out at him with the vitriol of his words in their office.

"It's just that I like you far too much to lose you. These last few weeks have been some of the best since this damned war started, and I've gone and messed it all up by screaming at you about some dumb dogs."

"Harold, is this really about the dogs, though? The reaction felt a little more like you were trying to go to war with all of Germany. Don't get me wrong, I'm still angry as all get out that you spoke to me in that manner. But, I have also had more fun these last few weeks than I have since the war started, and I care enough about you to hear you out. So start talking, Soldier." She worked to keep her voice a bit light—leaving the door open to encourage him to share.

"Do you have anything stiffer than coffee? I might need to Irish this up to make it through this story."

Margaret pulled down a small bottle of whiskey that she and Bea had used to stock their "bar cart", which was really just a small collection of half-drunk liquor bottles from their parent's collections.

Harold poured a healthy ounce of whiskey into his hot coffee and took a bracing drink directly from the bottle. He stared at his hands. Margaret sat down gently on the opposite end of the sofa.

"Go ahead. I'm here to listen."

"So, you know I served in Italy, which is why I was allowed to work with German prisoners. What you don't fully know is why I'm not still in Europe doing the work I should be doing. I should be killing the Nazi bastards. I saw and looked away from, things that no human should have to see. I didn't do anything, really. Everyone that I killed was supposed to die, I guess. Until you've killed a man you don't really know. And there was too much, so much, and there was a boy and his dog, and it's too awful." He wasn't making much sense, his rambles being mumbled into his hands where he had rested his head.

"Asking a human to kill another human, even if the cause is righteous, is horrific. I don't know if I could do it." Margaret didn't know the right words to say.

"You do what you're told to do. What you're trained to do. The world was going to be overrun by fascists if America didn't step in." His voice took on a relatively monotonous tone as the deep military indoctrination took hold.

"You mentioned a boy? And a dog?"

Harold shook his head as if to remove a nest of cobwebs from the memory.

"We were just supposed to take an airfield. It was summer. We were hot. Many of the boys were green. Everything was okay until the sniper started picking us off one by one. I got nicked and couldn't keep going. Ben got killed, Scotty got killed and our commander lost his mind. Screaming at us to find the sniper. I needed a medic to bandage me up so I stayed back as the boys set off. It didn't take long. Their sniper was just a soldier with a rifle and a hell of an aim." The whiskey was starting to take effect, and his speaking had slowed to a more recognizable pace.

"This soldier wasn't all that they found. He was camped out in a bombed outbuilding with some thirty other men, boys really, only two of them in uniform. He had the only gun. The youngest couldn't have been more than fourteen."

Margaret could see where this was going and felt ill, but let him continue.

"In the time it took for me to get bandaged—because I guess it was more than a nick—I watched as my fellow soldiers lined up these men and executed every last one of them. Even the boy. And his dog. I didn't do anything. I didn't stop them. I couldn't have stopped them. Instead, all of us were given easy postings back stateside in exchange for our silence. The only problem is that I can't sleep, I don't eat, I drink too much, and I was kicked out of my last posting for throwing my assistant under a desk when I thought we were being bombed during a fire drill. Camp Scottsbluff is my final stop in the war, and it was supposed to be quiet, no conflict, and it was until I saw that dog."

Margaret reached her hand over and set it gently on his knee.

"I'm sorry. Not for the dog, but for the fact that you had to see those things and that you have had to carry that for such a long time on your own."

"Do you forgive me?"

"Do you promise to never do it again?"

"Watch as people get executed? I sure hope so." Harold was still unsteady in his response.

Margaret reached over, touched his chin, and turned it towards her.

"Speak to me like that. You cannot speak to me like that ever again."

Harold sheepishly made eye contact. "You don't think I'm horrible?"

"I do not think that you are horrible. I think that you were made to see, and do, horrible things in the pursuit of whatever freedom this war is designed to protect. You were simply doing your job."

Harold's eyes glistened with the remnants of his tears. "Miss Margaret Murphy, you are, quite possibly, too good for this world and definitely too good for a man as damaged as I am."

Margaret moved in closer. Bea was going to be at work for several more hours. Harold stood up abruptly. "I should be going."

"Should you? I think we still have more things to discuss that maybe aren't appropriate for an office environment."

She reached her hand out for assistance to get up from the sofa and pulled him closer to her as she stood up. "Maybe you could stay for a while longer? Bea won't be home until five thirty, and since I'm sick, I'm down for the count and have taken to my bed."

"Margaret? I don't want to misread this situation. I didn't come here for any reason other than to make sure that you understood why I was so awful and beg your forgiveness."

"Harold, I need you to understand that I am in complete possession of my faculties, and now that I am no longer angry with you I have lost my urge to write, but I seemingly have not lost my urge for this." With that, Margaret stood on her tiptoes and pulled his face down to hers.

All the stolen kisses at work, the long goodbyes in the car after their dates, and the close dancing at the Officers' Club had set the groundwork for what she knew she wanted. She did not hold any old-fashioned beliefs that marriage needed to come first. Harold lifted her up by her waist and carried her into her bedroom.

She knew that their age difference meant that he likely had vastly more experience than she did in these endeavors. The song *"It's Been a Long, Long Time"* kept running through her head as he gently unbuttoned her dress and kissed her once, kissed her twice, and kissed her once again after each button. He placed her dress on the bedside chair, stepped back, and looked at her. She was standing in a new slip she'd splurged on after moving out now that her laundry was her own.

"Oh, Miss Murphy, you are a vision. And I ask you once again, are you sure this is what you want?"

"Shut up and get over here, Burke."

Chapter Forty-Four

Who knows what time even is when you're in the throes of lovemaking? Had it been thirty minutes? Hours? Was it tomorrow already? Everything was new, and different, and felt like it should have been this easy all along. Somehow their vast height difference didn't matter on a horizontal plane. He was stretched out on his back with his left arm behind his head, his right arm around her naked back holding her pressed up against him. Her head rested on his bare chest. She ran her hands across his chest, just above his left shoulder blade to the puckered silvery skin of a scar.

"I imagine that it's hard to escape the memories of hell when you were given a badge you see in the mirror reminding you of that horrible day."

"Doctors told me I should be grateful that it didn't hit me up a few inches in my jugular or over a few inches straight through the heart. It took me a long time to not wish that I'd just been taken out before seeing the worst of humanity."

Margaret lifted herself up to straddle him. She gently kissed him and said, "So it would have killed you if it hit you here," and kissed his throat, "or here," and kissed his chest where his heart would have been. He sat up, wrapping his arms around behind her so they were sitting up face to face on the bed. He looked directly into her eyes. "I'm so glad I lived to see this. Every bit of it was worth it for this moment."

Mid-afternoon, Margaret and Harold determined it would be best if he returned to the camp as if nothing had happened. He held a high enough rank that he could simply say he had a meeting in town.

Grinning at her as he finished buttoning his shirt, "I'm assuming you'll be well enough to be at work tomorrow, Miss Murphy?"

She tied her robe around her waist—there was no sense in getting dressed again—since she was home sick, after all.

"Just the quick flu, after all. Mild fever. I will be fully recovered by tomorrow morning. All I needed was some bed rest."

"And are we still on for Friday? Dinner at your folks' to keep them off your back?" Harold had gotten to know her mother well enough to know that it didn't take much to set her off or keep her happy, and if future afternoons with Margaret could be anything like this, he was happy to play the game.

"Yes, suppose we'll skip dessert and head to the Officers' Club after."

"If we're renaming your apartment the Officers' Club, absolutely."

Margaret was glad that they had moved beyond his meltdown back into their more flirtatious banter.

Harold bent down to kiss her deeply. "I will be counting the minutes until I watch you put lipstick on this beautiful mouth tomorrow morning. Thank you for all of this. Thank you for understanding that I'm not a terrible person. I do believe I love you, Miss Margaret Elizabeth Murphy."

"Oh, Harold." Margaret kissed him back. She enjoyed the afternoon, loved getting to know him, and hoped he would not be bothered by the fact she wasn't effusive in her return of the word love. She felt like there was still a lot to understand about the whole subject before she could commit to that.

Later that evening, Bea entered fully expecting Margaret to be planted behind her typewriter banging away on an article. She truly did some of her best writing when she was fired up about something or other. Instead, she was surprised to see Margaret curled up in the corner of the sofa, in her dressing gown, reading a book. She looked up as Bea removed her coat and smiled more broadly than Bea had ever seen.

"Margaret Murphy, you didn't! Oh, please tell me you did!" Bea and Ted had been engaged for the entirety of college and the war. They had spent many evenings together when he was home on leave and had, in fact, used Margaret as a cover when they were in Omaha. "Tell me everything. Was the temper tantrum all an act just to get out of the office?"

"Actually, no. He genuinely was a complete ass. It's complicated, but I think he's a little more broken inside than he lets on. For what it's worth though, I think I fixed him this afternoon. A couple of times."

The girls both laughed. If their mothers had any idea.

Bea kicked off her shoes and snuggled up on the other end of the sofa. "Okay, start at the beginning."

Chapter Forty-Five

The events of last week made working together in a small office even more challenging. They'd set ground rules as to how they could address each other in the hallways and were convinced no one was the wiser about their relationship. They were wrong. Burke, who was usually quiet and reserved, was whistling in the hallways. Margaret, who usually saved smiles for special occasions that required manipulation of the weaker sex, was smiling at everyone, guards, prisoners, even the cranky women in the typing pool. Everyone could read between the lines and knew that if these two were both this ga-ga, there was something going on.

She and Bea drove into the office together every day and had developed a system where, a few days a week, Margaret and Bea would leave at the same time as Burke and then pull over just outside of the camp where Margaret would switch cars and ride home with Burke, and then Bea would take the car and find something to occupy her time for a bit after work to give the lovebirds some solitude. Bea knew Margaret would do, and had done, the same when Ted visited on leave. Friends provide fantastic cover stories for overbearing mothers.

"How long before you guys are official and fill out the required fraternization forms?" Bea didn't want her best friend to get into trouble but also understood that the moment anything was revealed she'd be transferred to the typing pool or, God forbid, the kitchen.

"I am not going to fill out any such form, and I've informed Burke as much. I enjoy my job, we're careful, I can do the work in my sleep, and working in that office gives me time to write when things are slow."

Bea looked out the window.

"Anyhow, I am assuming this is just a camp romance. You hear of them all the time. He's at the mercy of the government as to where he's stationed, and I am at the mercy of my parents. I mean, c'mon Bea—Mother just agreed to an apartment without too much of a fuss, and it took me barely a week to end up in bed with a man! Her head would explode if I told her that I was going to follow him anywhere without a ring on this finger, and I don't want a ring on this finger. I want the war to end. I want to go back to school. I want my own life."

"Okay, so what is the plan for this evening?"

"We'll do the old car switch-a-roo outside the camp, I'll run home and change," she turned and winked at Bea, "and then Harold and I will go to the folks for dinner, and I'll be home by curfew, okay Mom?"

Bea laughed. "Oh, when you talk about the 'running home and changing' bit I just really miss Ted, if you know what I mean. I'm grateful he's going to be back on leave soon."

"If only our mothers knew that we knew what that meant!"

Chapter Forty-Six

Harold was helping Margaret put on her coat. "Dinner was lovely Mrs. Murphy. Mr. Murphy."

"Please, call me Franklin, you've been to dinner in our home enough to let down your guard a bit."

Letters had arrived at their home for Margaret from Charles, Bob, and, much to Rebecca's delight, Thomas. Charles and Bob had obviously not yet received Margaret's letters with her address update. There had been no communication from Thomas for years. Rebecca had held them back until just before Margaret and Harold were leaving.

"I have letters here for you from your old beaus, have you not shared that you're living on your own now?"

Margaret grabbed the letters from Rebecca's hand. "Thank you, Mother. They are just friends. You know that."

Margaret knew that her mother was concerned about how close she and Burke were becoming. Though they worked to disguise any affection they had for each other, she figured that their body language showed her mother that there was more to their relationship than that of work colleagues. Because her mother was never one to let things go, Margaret was not that shocked by her mother's meddling.

"Oh, you're so silly, Margaret. You know those boys are crazy for you. I swear, Captain Burke, I know she's book smart, but she can't tell the true intentions of men for anything."

Margaret stormed off to the car. "Mrs. Murphy, you don't know the half of it." It was as entertaining to Burke as it was infuriating to Margaret when her mother got under her skin. They had a rule that she could only huff and puff about her mother until they reached the train tracks and then they would switch topics.

Burke slid into the driver's seat. Margaret was holding the three envelopes in her hand, unopened, and tapping them nervously against her leg.

"So, do you want to tell me about my competition? I know that we're rather new and have rushed into a few things without talking about what either of our histories or futures might be." He was far more levelheaded than Margaret expected. She was a little surprised.

Margaret took a deep breath. "They're not competition. Not really. I'm sure they're getting letters from and writing to, many women all around the world. We were asked to write to keep morale up, and I started at the beginning of the war as an outlet to fill the void left by not writing for the paper." She turned the question back on him, "I'm assuming you have left a trail of lovelorn women pining for letters across the northwest and in Italy."

"Margaret, I genuinely agree with your mother. Maybe for the first time. Could be the only time, because she is a handful. But you know nothing of men. We don't write letters to women we don't care about. We get bored on the front lines, but not bored enough to write thick letters to beautiful women that we have loved unless we think those women might be waiting for us when we return."

"That's not the case here." Margaret stubbornly refused to believe that she could not receive letters from friends simply because they are men or men she dated.

"Do you want to tell me about the guys? Please believe me when I tell you, I'm not threatened. They're wherever they are. I get to see you, really see you and hold you. I'm here now and I hope to be here for a while."

"Is it okay if we don't talk about it? Can I just assure you that I'm not leading anyone on, and can you just not ask me questions about them? Ever since my cousin Sam died, I have steeled myself, knowing that I would lose people close to me in this war. So far, he's the only one that I know personally that has died. I wrote to him right up until the day that his plane went down. I plan to do that with at least two of these."

"But not the third?"

Margaret had not yet told him about her previous engagement. Like she'd told Bea earlier that day, she thought that Harold was going to be called to a different camp and didn't figure he needed details about that chapter of her life. His openness and lack of judgment, especially after the whole Rudi sculpture fiasco, caused her to internally debate whether she needed to keep those details under wraps.

They drove in silence for a few moments. He took the long way back to Scottsbluff so that the train track cutoff could come a little slower and Margaret could keep talking. "Mother was threatening to make me drop out of college before the war started because I was writing columns about how women deserved to be treated on campus. Well, and how I kicked a wide receiver in the nose."

"Of course you did. I can see it now." Burke looked over and grinned. "Though, I'd probably like to do more than that if I knew the details of why he deserved a kick."

"Those details don't really matter. What matters is that I knew my chances of staying in school were greater if Mother thought that the chances were high that I'd land a husband."

"Ah, so you were engaged to letter writer number three. Did you love him?" Burke was tentative in his questioning.

"I was fond of Thomas. He was a good dancer and was going to be a pharmacist, and my parents liked him well enough because he came from a prominent family. We got engaged the week after Pearl Harbor which was, quite possibly, the most cliché thing I have ever done in my life."

"When did it end?"

"I called it off a couple of months before you arrived at camp. I had traveled to visit him in New Orleans—his mother as our chaperone because 'appearances are everything'—and his immaturities were boundless. He might be the only grown man I've met to throw a temper tantrum in a restaurant. I have no idea what this letter says as I haven't heard from him since the engagement ended, but I guarantee it won't be well-written, intriguing, or spelled correctly in many cases. Can you imagine me, a want-to-be writer, married to someone who cannot spell?"

"That I cannot imagine. Can you see yourself getting married someday?"

"Maybe. Surely. Isn't that what all women are supposed to want? Right now, the world is falling apart, and I struggle to see why doing anything more than distracting ourselves is healthy."

Burke pulled over into a parking spot near her apartment and turned in the car seat towards her. "Miss Murphy...are you saying that I'm just a distraction?"

She turned towards him. "Yes. A delightful one at that. Now, walk me to my door like a proper gentleman so some busybody in this town can see you returning me to my building at a suitable hour and a message can be returned to Mother that everything is on the up and up."

Burke ran around to the passenger side to open her door. As she stepped out, he leaned down to kiss her. "Don't worry, the coast is clear. I just needed to remind you of the distractions I am more than happy to provide."

After a few more stolen moments in the lobby of her apartment building, Margaret said her good nights and sent him on his way.

Chapter Forty-Seven

B ea was at their kitchen table writing a letter to Ted.

"How was dinner? Any mama drama?" Bea had known the Murphy family her entire life and the Rebecca-isms were legendary.

"I genuinely thought we had escaped scot-free, but then she handed me these right as we were walking out the door." She held up letters from Thomas, Bob, and Charles. "I think she fully expected to start a fight with Harold and me. He is, however, too much of a gentleman and was fine since they're all just friends. Well, except Thomas. I have no idea what he wants. I haven't heard from him since I called things off."

"Which one are you going to read first?"

Margaret held them up like three playing cards. "Pick a card, any card, I'll start with that one. Luck of the draw."

Bea reached over and grabbed the envelope from Bob, then Thomas, which left Charles for last. Margaret grabbed her stationery set, turned on the lamp in their small living room, and curled up in her favorite spot on the sofa to read.

January 17, 1945 - Somewhere in the middle of it all
Dearest Margaret!

Received your most welcome letter this evening. Also received your Xmas card. Guess maybe my correspondence just "ain't what it used to be." Back in the states I could keep up by missing a little sleep, but up here I lose all my sleep, and still don't have time to write. I'll do my best though, and you'd better do the same. (Ha! Ha!)

I'll forgive you about the snapshot this time, but I expect you to get one in the mail before you receive this letter. After all, you wouldn't want me to forget how pretty you are would you? By cracky, according to the reports I've been receiving you're now one of the prettiest gals in western Nebraska. Sure wish I could jump in my old "Red Beauty" for a quick trip to Gering and check for myself. (Ha! Ha!) You always were darn good-looking. I've always been known for being a good pick (Wow!) I may sound like I'm trying to be witty, but really I'm serious. I'd give a whole flock of Francs right now to be able to take you out to dinner, a show, and a dance tonight. It's been so long since I've seen a good-looking girl that I've almost forgotten what one looks like. These French and German girls are sure not what they are cracked up to be. I'll take any GI Jane or any American gal, period, in place of a dozen of these gals.

Wish I could tell you more about where I am, but for security reasons it is not permissible. You should be reading of us in the paper before too long however. Let's just say that the song "Somewhere Over the Rainbow" is going to take on a different meaning. Hint hint. I can say that I've been seeing plenty of action, and that I dislike it more every day. After every battle, I can't seem to sleep for a few days. Guess maybe I'll get used to it before long.

I'm sure sorry we didn't have a chance to see more of each other the time we were both in Omaha. I'd give anything to go back, and I would have made sure we could have talked over old times over a drink or two.

Speaking of drinks, I'll take that date for "Tom and Jerry's" the first Xmas I get back. Boy, sure would have been nice to have those "heart-warmers" this Xmas. As it was, it wasn't such a good situation. We did have a turkey dinner, but it is hard to enjoy food when you're ducking. If you know what I mean.

I'm going to take the $5,000 I'll have saved when this mess is over and do nothing but travel. If I can't get someone to marry me, I'll travel alone. I'm going to take in California, New York, Florida, and Washington, and just cover the states again. Could I interest you in a quick trip about the U.S. in a convertible? Good!

Well, it is getting late, and I'm getting tired. Keep those "sugar" reports coming beautiful, and <u>don't forget the snapshot</u>. Get me! Okay, so it is bye for now.

Cuddles, Hale.

Bob was getting more flirtatious in his letters but, even for Bob Hale, seemed to be running a little manic, and she could sense the stress even in just how his penmanship had changed from previous letters. What was once the jaunty, carefree script of a boy who didn't much care if you could read his writing had now become very severe with too much pressure from the pen on the fragile paper, often resulting in slight rips.

Margaret decided to write back a more lighthearted letter. There was no harm in giving him something to smile about. She had extra prints of the portrait her mother demanded she take yearly. Every newsreel and article showed the horrors of Europe worsening by the day. A photo in the pocket of a dear friend was harmless.

Cuddles, eh? Getting a little forward in your old age?

I would take a trip anywhere, with just about anyone, just to get out of town. We're under gas rations again for this final push, and sometimes I try my luck and take the long way home from the camp just to feel like I've been somewhere new.

What paper is covering the escapades of Robert Hale? I have scoured the Omaha World-Herald *for news of you and haven't read anything...is Judy Garland fighting alongside you? Has Hitler laid down a Yellow Brick Road?*

Here's a picture. You've worn me down. Don't laugh too hard.

Your road trip buddy,

Margaret.

P.S. - Bea and I got our own place. You can write to me at Lincoln House, Scottsbluff % of your friend who is finally free from under her mother's thumb!

The next letter from Thomas was much thicker. She could not even imagine what he had to say to her that couldn't have been said in a postcard.

Dear Margaret:

Hi Ho, Cheerio and Tweet Tweet. Whataya know, Toots. This is a great day here in Merry Old England. The weather is grand

and has been for the past week. The only trouble is that you and I can't jump into that Chevy of mine and dash off to a picnic.

It was just a year ago yesterday that we were restricted in New Orleans, we left there a year ago the 15th at arrived at Cp Kilmer, N.J. the morning of the seventeenth. We sailed on the "Athlone Castle" if I have never told you the name on the 22nd and arrived in Liverpool, England of the 4 April. We took over the Hospital on the 15 May after spending some six weeks in Llandudno, North Wales. The year has gone by quite uneventful as far as moving around is concerned. We have however had a lot happen to us in the past year, and I hope it doesn't go over that too much before we are going home again. I am afraid it will be quite a spell though before we will get back home.

We received the latest dope on what happened the other day and it's supposed to be The Real McCoy. It seems that as soon as the fighting is over on the continent General Eisenhower will tell how many many needs for the army of occupation and General MacArthur will tell how many additional troops he needs in the Pacific and the CBI theater for the final blow with Japan. They will then select the troops for the occupation Army and start sending the troops to the South Pacific. The transfer of troops and supplies is supposed to take at least six months. After that they will start sending troops back to the States for final diposition which will take from 6 to 18 months. The point system will be used for the troops going back until I figure if we are one of the lucky outfits to go back it will also be about a year until they get around to us.

How are things with you Margaret? I was just hashing over you're last letter and I'm sorry to say that I haven't heard from *you since then and also sorry to say that I have not written you since then either.*

I'm now special service officer. The old man and I had a little row and things are a bit rough all the way around so I lost my job as mess officer which I was not in the least sorry to lose. I have been happy ever sense. I have charge of all the entertainment and shows, reading material, magazines, music, trips, anything else that can be thought of for the unit.

Well honey there isn't much more I can tell you. I like to see you and I'm really looking forward to getting home in the next year-and-a-half. Hope so. Right when you have a spare moment. I think of you often.

Love, as ever, Thomas.

There was no reason for this letter. She had not left the door open for future communication. Over the last year, she received a letter or two from his mother, so she knew he was still alive. In reading through this exchange, she was amazed that they could have walked down the aisle before he ever wrote her a letter, and she'd be stuck for all of eternity with a man that simply couldn't figure out the difference between right and write. His responsibility in the war seemed so mild compared to Bob's or Charles's, or even hers.

Infantry and surgery felt real and necessary. To oversee magazines for the enlisted men seemed like a way to hide, but somehow Thomas could both be a coward and a jerk based on the fighting he referenced. Margaret once again felt she'd dodged a bullet and decided that no good could come from continuing the correspondence with her former fiancé.

Now Charles. She was glad he was the final letter. His writing was always so much more fun to read.

January 21, 1945 - South Pacific
Dearest Margaret,

There has been another lag but it's shorter, do you notice? I enjoyed your letter as much as I always do enjoy them. Thank you for sending me the articles you've written. You have talent. Always have.

I am still as busy as ever. I guess I've never written to you without saying that, but it's still true. Now that they think I know something I'll have to work harder than ever to keep the truth from them. I know I'll enjoy the books you sent because reading material is scarce. The folks have sent several magazine subscriptions, but they have not started to come in yet. I wish I could send you some cigarettes because we have plenty but it's against the law. I can send Cuban cigars—does your dad need some? I'll not wait for an answer to write because it's too slow.

Things here have changed only for the better, so far as concerns me at least. I have been made the executive officer of our "D" medical company. That means second in command and assistant to the CO, but you know that's what's wrong with me. We have a 100-head hospital unit and 101 enlisted men. It's more responsibility than I like but it seems like a great opportunity.

I wish you could see this beautiful place. We are right on the sea in a great coconut grove. The days are steaming hot, but the nights are lovely and the sunsets rival, if not surpass, western Nebraska's. Shrieking red parakeets and white cockatoos fill the trees and almost any time you can see a canoe full of natives go-

ing by loaded with pineapples and papayas to trade for crackers and corned beef. The stars make the sky a blue silver and the palms etched against it make a breathtaking sight. The waves are whispering back and forth across the beach in a lulling, monotonous way. It's still 7,000 miles from home, and from you, and that's a sobering thought.

Our quarters are quite nice now, with screens and wooden decks. We are about ready to leave, apparently, because that's the way it usually happens. I wish you could see it. You'd love it. For all the beauty, it is very hot here by my Coleman, and I'm awfully moist.

I am now in the midst of training my 8-man team for evacuations of casualties—I wish our real work need never start but maybe we can help. I hope by now you have got your smile back without an effort. Nothing so bad. It can't get worse—you know that too. Margaret, I don't want you to think you need only answer my letters. I know you have little news too, but I'd like to hear from you often. I do cherish your letters. I would not mind a photo to remind me that, even amongst the horrors they are training us for, there are things of beauty that are worth fighting for.

This afternoon the chaplain wrangled steaks and we had a steak fry at the beach. We had a swim in the warm teal ocean and the best meal I've had in months. The steaks were perfect, and there were cokes, ice cold, olives, cheese, nuts, and oranges. After we had eaten, we sat on the only real south sea island beach I have ever seen, pure white coral sand, and sang while a full moon rose over the palms. It was almost too beautiful. I missed you.

Before too long there'll be quite a lapse while I take a little vacation cruise so please don't think I've forgotten how to write. Now M, cheer up and don't work too hard. Write when you can, both to me and for the papers.

Lovingly as ever, Charles.

This was the first letter from Charles that was more direct about any affection he might have for her. Maybe her mother, and Harold, were correct. That did not mean that she wasn't going to continue to communicate. She had yet to meet someone that wanted to talk about books with her. Burke was not dedicated to the more intellectual pursuits or even movies for that matter.

Charles,

I'm so glad you got the books. I'll send you more and I hope you don't mind if I read them before I send them to you. Would love to hear your thoughts on those that I send. I miss real conversations. The soldiers at the camp are all rattled and lonely. Most of them would rather drink a beer and go dancing than sit and discuss a book.

I can hear the sounds of the parakeets from here and almost feel like I'm there with you enjoying the waves and the warmth of the island. It makes me long for the choppy surf of Long Beach and our lazy summer days.

While I'm grateful for your intelligence and talent and have no doubt you're the best doctor to head to the Pacific, I would be lying if I didn't tell you that my heart is heavy with worry. I suppose if I would just stop reading the news then I might not be burdened by the knowledge of the challenges you're about to face.

Stay safe my dear friend.

Margaret

Bea watched as Margaret finished writing another letter. "So, when are you going to tell them that you're off the market?"

"I was never on the market. I am not a piece of fish that can be bought." She sealed the envelope.

"Oh, you know what I mean, you scamp. One look at you and Harold, and anyone who wasn't blind could see that there are definite fireworks."

"The reality is, Bea, that it's likely that one, or both, of these friends of mine—and they are just friends—will not be returning home. Each day the casualty list mounts. It seems like they make three steps ahead in Europe just to be handed their asses. The Pacific fleet seems to be pelted by kamikaze pilots and warfare unlike any other. I'm not going to stop writing to either of them. I'll talk books with Charles, and I'll reminisce about childhood with Bob. It's completely harmless."

"And you're sure Harold is absolutely fine with whatever you wrote to these harmless friends? And I noticed that each of them got that stunning new photo your mother forced you to have taken. The one that reminds us all that we will never look half as good and now will be handed around bases in Germany and the Pacific as 'the girl I'm fighting for back home.' You've got too many irons in the fire if you ask me."

"I didn't ask." Margaret got up and went into her room and shut the door a little too firmly for Bea's liking.

Chapter Forty-Eight

V alentine's Day, 1945
      Margaret entered the office to find a card on the center of her desk with her name scrawled in beautiful penmanship. She hurriedly opened it in case it was from Rudi or someone who might upset the calm that she and Burke had going for them right now. He told her yesterday he had made some Valentine's Day plans for them, and she was assuming that they were going to dinner at The Gaslight after work. There weren't many options in town right now.

My dearest Miss Murphy,

I am sorry to say that I will not be at work today. This is to say that I've already made plans with Bea, and she is standing outside this door waiting for the keys to your car.

We have been charged with going on assignment to Fort Robinson as their Quartermaster department is in shambles. Or, at least that's the story I have told your parents as to why we are going out of town on strictly government business. I might have fudged and said that several assistants and soldiers are going.

I could not do this job, or this life, without you.

I'll be waiting for you at the gate, my love.

Harold

She opened her door, and Bea was standing there with a smile like a cat who caught a mouse. "I packed a bag for you. It's in Burke's car. Have a good couple of days."

"A couple of days?" Margaret was still recovering from the frosty exchange of a few nights ago with Bea. They'd driven to and from work together without the normal banter. Margaret was annoyed that they were fighting over a boy. Bea just wanted Margaret to be happy, truly, but also really wanted her friend to settle down officially with Burke so they could all stop sneaking around.

"I have no idea beyond the specific instructions I was given. Your keys, please?"

Margaret exited into the parking lot and saw Harold leaning against the car.

"So, tell me, Captain Burke, how did you manage to finagle this whole thing? And are we actually going to Fort Robinson?"

"We are indeed, Miss Murphy, though we do have a brief side trip to the branch camp in Chadron planned. We'll be home by Friday afternoon just in time to button up the week here. Completely on the up and up. I just couldn't do the work without my secretary, war wounds and all."

"Harold, your injury is to your left arm. You are a rascal." He walked around and opened her car door. On the seat was a single red rose.

"You didn't think I would forget it was Valentine's Day? I couldn't very well bring you a whole bouquet at work, but I thought this might do. You're always talking about how you want adventure. This is the best I can do right now but I think we'll find our way to combine some pleasure with our work."

If he was looking to speak to her heart this was certainly the way to do it. She hadn't been out of town since the trip to Omaha so long, long ago, and while Chadron, Nebraska, was hardly Europe, it was the effort in planning that made all of the difference.

"Oh, Burke, I do love an adventure."

"And, Miss Murphy, I do love you."

Chapter Forty-Nine

F ort Robinson POW camp was about 80 miles north of
Scottsbluff. The scenery was mostly desolate prairie, just
as dry and empty as one would imagine after a relatively dry
winter. The remnants of snow drifted on the side of the fields.

They had settled into a very comfortable conversational
rhythm. Margaret was worried that they both would be too
distracted by the simple pleasures of their young relationship
and conversation would go by the wayside. She was happily surprised that wasn't the case. She still doubted that this relationship would survive the end of the war, as Harold kept speaking
of moving back home to the Pacific Northwest, and, though she
wanted to travel, she couldn't see moving with someone before
she took time for herself after the war.

"A penny for your thoughts?"

"Just curious as to the details of this getaway. As your assistant,
your travel plans should have crossed my desk."

"Oh, they did. I just got to them before you. We will be staying
at the motel near camp this evening. Tomorrow we will head
north to do a quick tour of the branch camp outside of Chadron,
but it will be too late for us to head home, so we will be forced
to spend another night on the road on the government dime.

And just so you don't get any ideas," he reached over and put his hand on her knee, "we have separate rooms. No impropriety here. Strictly professional."

"Absolutely. I hope Bea packed my stationery so that I can sit in my room this evening and catch up on my correspondence."

"I'm sorry to say that you'll be booked well into the evening with work endeavors. Your boss truly is a taskmaster. Might be an all-nighter."

Margaret was excited that a night away was the surprise. She could tell he was nervous and worried that he was planning something bigger, like a proposal. She stared out the window and was contemplating how to answer a question like that. As they neared the camp, the topography changed. They went from open prairie to hills with pine trees as if the earth had folded in half and the Wildcat Hills near Scottsbluff were just torn apart from each other.

Margaret interrupted the silence. "Did you know that our Army massacred dozens upon dozens of Indians at Fort Robinson and imprisoned many, many more? We were required to take Nebraska history as a course to graduate. Of course, that wasn't the story that we were told. We were told about a valiant battle to protect the Wild West from savages. Absolutely ridiculous. They were here first."

"Tell me how you really feel."

"The idea that for nearly a hundred years we've been imprisoning our enemies out of the sight of the media and the civilization in cities. There doesn't seem to be much scrutiny of the atrocities that can happen at camp. I mean, what's preventing one of our soldiers from going rogue and just killing Germans as our army did to the Indians? I mean, look what our soldiers did with you in Italy."

Burke's jaw tightened at the memory. "That wouldn't happen now. And besides, we're not up here to take a history course, though I'm sure your facts are true, and it was horrible. Can we put that dark nugget of history on the back burner for a discussion on tomorrow's car ride? I have a surprise for you."

They pulled up to the security gate, complete with the Safety-First sign that was so familiar, though they'd gone zero days without a military incident.

"Wow, they're even worse up here than you guys are down home!"

"You guys? Aren't you one of us?"

"Absolutely not, soldier, I'm a civilian. We've made it almost 50 days this time!"

As Burke rolled down the window to talk to the gate agent, she was surprised to hear dogs barking. Not just a few dogs, but a true cacophony of barking that sounded like hundreds of dogs. They continued through the gate and around to the main entrance.

"There are dogs here? Why are there so many dogs?"

Burke seemed thrilled she was lighting up at the sight of the dogs.

"Now, they're not all for you to play with, or take home, but this is the top canine training camp for the Army, and we are here on a reconnaissance mission to determine if Camp Scottsbluff could run a training program that is similar, though on a smaller scale. Or at least that's the idea I came up with to provide some cover."

"You mean to tell me that I get to go play with dogs and call this work? Harold, this is absolutely the best gift you could have given me for this silly holiday. Who needs romance when there are puppies?"

Burke obviously knew just how happy these dogs would make her. He wouldn't want to propose to her behind the walls of a prison so her concern about that scenario disappeared.

They exited the car and were met at the gate by a military officer of the same rank as Burke. They both saluted each other. Margaret never quite knew what to do with her hands when people were saluting.

"Captain Burke, it is a pleasure."

"Captain Antony, this is Miss Margaret Murphy, my absolute right hand in the Quartermaster's office down at Scottsbluff. I need you to know that she's the one who was responsible for getting Captain Chapman in line and promoted, and I have simply had to follow her lead. Her father, Franklin Murphy, has also been an invaluable asset in the community as the president of the bank. I thought Miss Murphy should join me on this trip in order to help calculate the cost and develop a plan for the supplies we may need on hand to build out a K-9 training unit down south."

Margaret reached out her hand. "It's a pleasure to meet you, Captain. I've been looking forward to touring your facility for quite some time. To be honest, I am hoping we can bring a K-9 unit to Scottsbluff to help distract the prisoners from the band they are trying to form," she quickly improvised.

"I'm assuming you would like a tour. Most of the dogs are friendly, so if you're up for it, you're welcome to meet a few if you're a dog person."

"Absolutely." Margaret worked to tamp down her enthusiasm. "This is the first time in my life I've lived without a dog in my home. I have a Brittany Spaniel at my parent's home but can't keep one in my current apartment."

Surrounding the edge of the parking lot was a ten-foot chain link fence and behind the fence were individual dog houses laid out with the same precision as a military cemetery. Chained to each house was a dog. At the edge was a large, fenced-in area where several dogs were playing. In a field just beyond was an obstacle course where several prisoners were training dogs.

"Did you know that we have one of the lowest instances of violence in the camps? We attribute that to the time the prisoners get working with the dogs. Turns out that whether you speak German, English, or Italian, dogs all bark in the same language."

Margaret wrapped her coat around her a bit more tightly. The January wind was not any different up north. The guard opened the gate, and they were walking along the edge of the dog camp. Most of the dogs were German Shepherds, but there were several hunting retrievers and water dogs.

"People from all over the country donated their dogs, we've wrangled up shelter dogs, and we've bred quite a few as well. Some of these are trained for search and rescue. Others are guard dogs. A few are trained as sled dogs to be used in snow emergencies. I can't take you into the guard dog area, obviously, but we've put together a couple of our youngest, friendliest, dogs that might not be good for much more than troop morale for you to meet. We do find that every visitor needs a bit of time with the dogs before we can get down to the business at hand."

He led them into the next outbuilding and waiting for them were two soldiers, each with a leash in hand, tethered to two beautiful Golden Retrievers. Both looked like they were smiling as their back ends shook as if they had minds of their own.

"May I?" Margaret reached out her hand for the leashes and led the two dogs over to a bench near the wall. Both dogs fought for her attention and to be scratched behind their ears. She attempted to maintain some professional decorum as this was supposed to be a work trip, and it took all her restraint not to drop to the dusty floor and have a true cuddle puddle with these two bundles of joy.

The four men were not rushing her, but she knew if she stayed any longer she'd just ask to be transferred to this camp just to be around dogs all day. She finally sighed, grabbed the leashes, and led them back to their handlers.

"I must tell you, Captain Burke, we would need to bring these two down specifically. I'm sure there's room for them in our offices. We'll call them our Officers of Emotional Wellness."

The men chuckled.

"Shall we go see the rest of the camp and talk through some of the logistics?"

"Lead the way." Margaret wanted to grab Burke's hand so he could soak up her happiness.

Chapter Fifty

The meeting at the camp went well, and they had dinner with their counterparts at the Officers' Club. They discussed the possibility of accepting a shipment of twenty dogs and working with them as search and rescue dogs. The guard dogs caused too many biting incidents to be the inaugural K-9s. It was after eight when they got checked into their hotel rooms. They agreed to both go and freshen up after a long travel day, and then Burke would find an excuse to have to come to her room for a nightcap.

Their pillow talk ended after eleven. Burke had no trouble falling asleep and was gently snoring. Actually sleeping together for the first time was something that Margaret had not fully prepared for. She was used to her double bed with two pillows and very soft sheets in her very quiet bedroom. She tossed and turned for quite a while before falling into a fitful sleep.

Sometime between two and three a.m.—the clock was on the other side of the bed, and she couldn't see it clearly—she was jolted awake by the sound of a scream. Every limb on Burke's body was tense and he was sitting straight up. His eyes were wide open but staring at nothing. She reached out to touch his arm.

"Burke, honey, I'm right here. You're just having a dream."

His arm whipped out and pushed her away. His lanky frame was already taking up much of the bed and she landed on the floor with a hard thud hitting the nightstand with her ribs on the way. He kept flailing, though nothing was there to hit, as if he was in a fight to the death. His legs were tangled in the sheets.

"Harold. Harold. It's Margaret. Harold, you're dreaming." Margaret stayed on the relative safety of the floor on the opposite side of the bed as her voice got close to shouting.

He turned his head towards her. "Margaret? Why are you on the floor?" Though he was now awake he was very disoriented. "Are you crying?" He went to stand up, but his legs were so wrapped up in the sheet that it was not a simple endeavor, and he ended up tripping a few times before he made it to her side of the bed. He dropped to the floor next to her.

"You scared me. You were having a nightmare." So much for a quiet night away.

"But why are you on the floor?" Harold was still getting his wits about him.

"You pushed me." Margaret grabbed the sheet that had finally untangled itself from Burke's feet and wrapped it around her naked body. She stood up and walked to the bathroom and shut the door behind her. The adrenaline was fading, and she realized that she was going to have quite the bruise on her side where she landed.

Burke scrambled to pull on his boxers and ran to the bathroom door. He leaned his forehead against the wood.

"Margaret, can I talk to you? I'm so sorry. I had no idea what I was doing."

She opened the door.

"It was as if you weren't even there. Like you were staring at something and fighting with someone only you could see. Do you know what you were dreaming?"

"Not really. Just that I needed to stop someone. I'm so sorry." He sat on the edge of the bed and reached his arms out to her. At this height, they were eye to eye. "Can you come back to bed?"

"I think maybe you should go to your room so we can get some sleep. We still have quite the drive ahead of us tomorrow."

She wasn't sure she'd actually get any sleep at all either way, but she didn't want to wake up like that again.

"I understand." He turned on the lamp in the bedroom and quickly dressed and quietly left while Margaret stayed in the bathroom.

Chapter Fifty-One

They had planned to meet at the hotel diner for breakfast in the morning, but Burke never emerged from his room. Margaret sat staring at her cup of coffee, sipping it occasionally just to give her something to do. She'd ordered an egg and toast, and when it arrived, she discovered she had completely lost her appetite.

Because she wasn't involved in the planning of this trip, she had no idea what time they were due to arrive at the next camp but thought she'd give Harold a few more minutes to meet her before she checked his room. All of this was new to her. It was so much simpler in town when every one of their interactions had to be planned and choreographed ahead of time to ensure privacy. Without the oversight of polite society, there was nothing preventing her from just going to his hotel room and distracting him from the day's agenda with activities that are far more fun than sitting and staring at a congealing egg and drinking cold coffee.

Margaret threw down a couple of dollars for her tab and a tip and went to drop her bag off in the car. It wasn't parked where they'd left it, and it took her a few minutes to locate it in the parking lot. She tossed her bag in the back and headed to Harold's room. She knocked softly, remembering that sudden noises made him jump. "Harold, it's Margaret. I'm here to provide a wake-up call."

There was no answer. Maybe he was in the shower? She knocked harder and could finally hear someone moving around in the room.

The door opened to Harold standing, mostly upright, still dressed in the clothes he'd hurriedly thrown on when he left her room last night. He reeked of whisky, and an empty fifth was on its side on the bedside table.

"I overslept. Let me brush my teeth." He turned and tripped on the chair that was sitting in front of the desk just barely catching himself before he fell into the bed. "Still waking up. Give me a second."

Margaret pulled the chair out from the desk and took a seat, watching him as he fiddled with his Dopp-kit, working to find his toothbrush.

"Did you sleep okay?" Margaret wasn't sure how to handle this situation. They definitely wouldn't be spending time in this hotel room, as it smelled like a bar. She noticed that there were several empty beer cans on the floor on the opposite side of the room.

"Mmmhmm," Harold mumbled around his toothbrush, grabbed a fresh pair of boxers and a t-shirt from his overnight bag, nodded his head at the shower, and shut the door to the bathroom behind him.

Margaret didn't know if she should stay or go or go back to the diner or throw caution to the wind and just join him in the shower in a few minutes. She was maddened by the fact that all of these things made sense at the same moment. She relished the days when she did not care about relationships. If this is what love might be, she wasn't sure she wanted it.

Several minutes later Harold emerged looking, for the most part, put back together and fully dressed. He threw his things in his bag and headed, wordlessly, for the door. Margaret followed. When they got to the car, he struggled with the keys to unlock the door.

"It's already unlocked. I already put my bags in the back."

"Look at you, little Miss Problem Solver." Harold was still struggling with the keys.

"Harold, are you drunk?" Margaret had limited experience with booze outside of a few drunk fraternity brothers. Her parents drank occasionally at social events and, briefly, her uncle had a time after Sam died when his days seemed to be filled with drinking and staring at nothing until her father went over and shook some sense into him.

"Nope. I'm fine. You just think that's another thing that's wrong with me." The pacing of his speech was off just a bit, parsed like he was talking without fully opening his mouth.

He climbed into the driver's seat and waited for Margaret to get in the car. This was very unlike him. He always opened the door for her. Margaret shook her head and got in the passenger side.

Fitting the keys into the ignition was no easier than trying to navigate the door lock Harold dropped the keys, and they fell on the floorboard in between their feet. Margaret reached down and grabbed them.

"It seems like you're still waking up. How about I drive?" She opened the door and got out. There was no way she was riding in a car with him in this condition.

Harold climbed out of his side. "Give me the keys, Margaret."

"Absolutely not. I would rather sit here on the side of the road in nowhere Nebraska than let you drive."

"Fine! Have it your way." Harold moved to the passenger side, using the car to balance the entire way.

Margaret moved to the driver's side and started the car to maneuver out of the parking lot. It was bigger than her Buick, which hardly seemed possible, and the steering was more rigid. It was not comfortable to drive. She maneuvered onto the highway heading north towards Chadron and the next stop, hoping that his head would clear enough to provide direction and he could get his wits about him before their next meeting.

They drove for twenty minutes in silence. The road was becoming curvier as they entered the forest, and each bend in the road caused her ribs to scream out in pain. At a particularly sharp turn, a tight gasp escaped her mouth. She hoped he didn't notice. She gritted her teeth. Burke looked over at her.

"Did I hurt you?" His voice caught in his throat.

"I'll be fine." Margaret had used the remainder of the ice from their nightcap ice bucket, wrapped in a washcloth, on the rapidly forming bruise on her ribs.

"Margaret, stop the car."

"Here? Why?"

"Just stop. Now."

She worried that he was going to be sick and pulled over onto the shoulder. This stretch of highway was not very frequently traveled this time of year.

Burke turned to her. "I hurt you. I cannot believe I hurt you. I would never hurt you on purpose, Margaret I hope you believe me. I am terrible. I should just get out of this car and walk away."

Margaret paused before responding. He was being melodramatic, but she also never wanted to experience this again.

"Of course, I know you would never do anything on purpose. I just wasn't expecting that the first time I ever spent the whole night with someone I would end up being thrown out of bed. I guess I just wonder what was going on in your head. Your face looked so much like when you lost your temper over the carved dog on my desk. It has me worried for you."

"Don't worry about me. You don't deserve to have to worry about me. I will figure this all out on my own, and you can just forget me."

Though it hurt to turn in the seat she turned to face Harold. "Oh? Is it that easy you think? Just get to know you, start falling in love with you, and then discover that you can't sleep through the night without raiding a liquor store?"

"I can't stop, Margaret. I keep trying. I go for days, or weeks sometimes, and then something trips me up. You weren't supposed to see it."

"But I did. Now what? How do we pull it all together for our next meeting?"

Burke stared straight ahead. "We weren't going to go to another camp. We just were going to go to dinner and spend the night at a hotel there. But I think it might be best if we head back. We'll say we were worried about the weather."

Margaret turned the car around on the highway and headed back south. They spent the rest of the trip silently staring out the window.

Chapter Fifty-Two

W hen Bea got back from work on Thursday, Margaret was sitting at the desk in her room typing.

"How was..." Bea didn't get the sentence out before Margaret snapped.

"I don't want to talk about it."

They drove to work on Friday without much conversation. June was on leave and was expected on the train that afternoon, and she was hopeful that June could break through Margaret's shell. June's mother had moved out to a ranch between Kimball and Gering, and the three girls were going to spend the night in their new apartment, and then they would drive her to her mother's in the morning.

"It's been a while since we've had a good old-fashioned sleep-over." Bea was trying her damnedest to get through to Margaret. "I cannot wait to hear all about June's adventures in France. I suppose if I'd taken French in high school instead of German, I could have been a nurse."

"Bea, my dear, dear darling, you passed out at the sight of a bloody nose on the court of a basketball game. They had to get a stretcher." Bea started to laugh, which got Margaret laughing, and once they started, they could hardly stop as they pulled up to the security line at the prison.

"I've missed laughing with you."

Margaret looked at her friend. "I know I've been in my head lately. I promise I'll snap out of it soon. Let's just get through the day and then go get our girl."

They left work at noon, having taken a half day so they could be there with homemade signs for June. Burke had called in sick so Margaret really didn't have anything to do.

"Alright ladies, what do you think?" June had hardly been off the train for two minutes before she removed her hat and showed off a very short, very stylish haircut that made her look so much more mature than either of them with their long waves.

"I think you look like you could be in charge of a whole hospital is what I think!" Bea was bouncing up and down on the balls of her toes. "Oh June, I've missed you, we've missed you, I just, well, I just can't..." And with that dear, sensitive Bea, burst into tears. They all gathered in a group hug. It was many minutes before they regained their composure well enough to make it to the car.

It felt a bit like playing grownups as Bea fussed in the kitchen and Margaret made drinks for the three of them while June washed up from the trip. "Make mine as strong as a British Para- trooper!" June shouted from the bathroom. Margaret poured the gin with a little heavier hand and splashed a little less tonic than normal.

"Alright ladies, where do we start? We have all night, and something tells me that there are stories that I need to hear. I have cleaned out the train dust from my ears and I am ready. Give me the gossip."

Margaret knew that Bea had been writing June more frequently than she, and she was sure that much of her "dirt" had already been spilled.

"Excuse me? Gossip? No, we need to hear the gory details of being a front-line nurse in Europe."

"Not too gory, please! I don't want to hit my head again."

"I promise you Bea I will only speak of entrails in a limited capacity." They all laughed, their triad was complete, and the rhythm hadn't changed. "In all seriousness though it is even more fulfilling than I ever imagined. Every single day is something new. We never want to say we're having a slow day because then, without a doubt, we're peppered by an air attack or casualties come screaming in. I thought I would be overwhelmed by the chaos of it all, but I truly feel like I'm thriving. It is the hardest, saddest, most rewarding work I have ever done in my life."

They each grabbed a plate and their drinks and went over to the trays that they'd set up in their living room. Bea on one end of the sofa, June on the other, Margaret in the reading chair she had pulled out from her room.

"What's the worst thing you've experienced?"

"Well, hello to rising star journalist Margaret Murphy, you're cutting right to the chase." A look flashed across June's face that was so similar to the look she saw on every soldier in the prison. June, almost imperceptibly, shook her head, "How about we start with the funniest? Yes?" Bea and Margaret each nodded and prepared for June to take the stage.

"There was a day we saved twenty-four soldiers who were horribly injured. They were coming in almost faster than we could handle them, bleeding everywhere, guts and bones spilling out from the gurneys."

Bea was starting to get a little green around the gills. "How is this funny?"

"Just wait. We were bandaging and suturing and medicating soldier after soldier when suddenly the door to our ward flew open, and there was the commander of our camp, holding his hand as if it had been blown completely off and hollering to beat the band. He nearly drowned out the sound of the men who had been torn apart by a bomb dropped from a German warplane." June, always the actress of the bunch, stood up to act out the scene, holding her arm in front of her as if it was a baby.

"The doctor who I work most closely with, Captain Dr. Hansen of Atlanta, Georgia, sent me over to examine the commander myself." June took on an affected southern accent. "Nurse Roth, go triage that poor man and let me know what resources we need to divert." She continued, "I went over, asked my commander—whose name I shall not use because he is quite frequently in the news—to remove the bandage from his hand, fully expecting to see a severed tendon or two."

"I ask you again June, how is this funny?" Bea had set her dinner off to the side and had her eyes covered as if not seeing would prevent the hearing.

"Oh, we're getting there. He removed the bandage and," she paused for effect, "in his hand lay a lifeless parrot."

"A what?" both Margaret and June exclaimed.

"An African grey parrot. Turns out that our commander had fought against Rommel and his men and had been gifted this bird by one of the locals. He did not have family, and the Army would not allow him to take the parrot on a ship back to the states, so he just stayed in Europe and traveled everywhere with this dumb bird. He named it Hemingway and had it trained to shout 'ATTENTION' and 'Aye-aye Captain' and 'Sir, yes sir.'" The girls were giggling. June was in her element.

"I could not laugh at our commanding officer. He wanted our 'best doctor immediately' to come and deal with his fowl problem. I had to tell him that, unfortunately, our doctors were all busy with the carnage that he could see behind me, but that, lucky for him, I had received specialized training in ornithology at the University of Nebraska and I could examine his bird."

"You did not." Margaret's bruised side was going to hurt tomorrow from laughing.

"I gently took the bird from his hands and pushed on its tiny chest as if attempting to resuscitate him, gently blowing on his beak, fully expecting that I would have to deliver a time of death notice momentarily and deal with the grief-induced wrath of a rather unstable individual. It was grim."

"Dead birds are not funny, June!" Bea was such a softy when it came to all creatures. Margaret could see by the sparkle in June's eyes that there was a punchline coming.

"Suddenly, Hemingway's eyes pop open and he cackles, 'Fucking hell you bloody cock!' and then flies away straight over the, mostly sterile, surgical field where our surgeon was repairing a very, very damaged leg, and proceeds to shit all down the back of my least favorite doctor. And that, my friends, is the story that I will tell for the rest of my life at cocktail parties about how I spent my time in France."

June took a bow. Bea leaned back in relief, June's stories always pulled them in deeply. They were going to need a minute before they could start eating again. Margaret grabbed her journalist notebook. "Now, this commander. His name please?"

The girls spent the rest of the night hearing more stories about Europe, the soldiers June worked with, and all of the doctors, British and American, that she had trained under. June had decided that she was going back for one more tour, and then whenever the war ended, hopefully soon, she was going to take advantage of the fact that military nurses could use the G.I. Bill to continue her education. The girls were not surprised when she said, "Working be damned, I'm going straight to medical school."

Chapter Fifty-Three

Last evening passed without Bea bringing up Harold and Margaret thought maybe they'd make it the whole forty-mile trip to June's mom's home without any pestering. If only she were so lucky. They made it three miles before June, in true June fashion, gently broke the ice. "So, tell me more about this "canoodling code". Is it like Morse code, but sexier? I hear those lines might be down after a Valentine's trip that was called short by the weather?" She looked out the window. "Must have been a quick-moving storm since the roads are dry."

Margaret looked up in the rear-view mirror and glared at Bea in the back seat.

"No murdering the messenger with your eyes. She was worried but also—sorry to say, Bea—scared of your temper. Spill it."

Margaret took a chance that she could deflect the conversation with a joke. "Yes. It is a sexier form of Morse code. They teach night classes."

"I'm sure they do. I don't know the details, and you don't have to kiss and tell, but I know that those classes were going quite well until you went on a two-day trip that turned into a one-day and now school might no longer be in session?"

"Enough of the innuendo. Hell, if you can't tell your girlfriends, who can you tell? Bea, grab my purse. There's a picture of Harold and me in there from Christmas at the folks'. It's easier to paint a picture if June knows what all the characters in the story look like."

Bea took out the photo that showed Margaret sitting side by side with Burke as Franklin popped his head into the frame. "I've never seen this photo, either." She handed the photo to June in the front seat. "See, I told you he was quite the Jimmy Stewart." June admired the photo.

"I suppose Jimmy Stewart comes to mind. Either way, he's quite tall—a full foot taller than I am—and about as big around as my thigh. The basics: he's thirty, from the Pacific Northwest, he served in Italy early in the war and was shot by a sniper."

"Where was he shot?"

"Italy."

"No, dummy, where did the bullet enter his body?"

"Oh, must we, June?"

Margaret laughed, "His shoulder. Though, Dr. June, I suppose you want to know that it was directly above his collarbone. Through and through. Missed the bone by millimeters and those other important pieces and parts by inches. He was, I suppose you could say, lucky. He escaped with just a scar and a shoulder that seizes up when it's going to rain."

"Obviously it doesn't affect his performance at work or on any extracurricular duties. Why didn't he go back to the front after something so relatively minor in the scheme of things?" June knew the answer but wanted Margaret to say it out loud. The men who she'd help repair physically, the ones who ended up staffing the camps, had issues that weren't healed with bandages. She had worried since June wrote to her saying she was dating a camp officer, but how do you ask your friend if her suitor has a bad case of nerves?

"I think he's losing his mind. At first, I thought he was just easily startled. Loud noises cause his limbs to twitch."

"We called him Daddy Longlegs because Margaret would slam a drawer and he'd jump," Bea interjected.

June shook her head.

"It took him weeks to get up the courage to even ask me to go to the Officers' Club with him and he didn't even ask to kiss me until after Christmas. I just thought he was a somewhat timid gentleman. He studied accounting in college, so he's not exactly a real 'rounder,' but once that first kiss happened, I finally understood everything you two were talking about when it came to kissing. My goodness." Margaret was grinning just thinking about it.

"Finally! We told you there were better men on this planet, and you weren't destined for fish-lips Thomas. So, the kissing was so good that you got an apartment just so you could have some time with him outside of Rebecca's prying eyes? That's some accomplished kissing." June looked at the picture of Harold and Margaret. "Let me take a closer look at this set of lips. Yes, in my medical opinion he would make a good kisser."

Margaret knew June had never liked Thomas and was likely thrilled that she didn't have to see him again. "That's not the reason. Oh, well, that's not the only reason."

"Tell her about sneaking out of work in the middle of the day to christen the apartment!" Bea's love of romantic movies threatened to spill over.

"Actually, Bea, I haven't even told you all of the details but it kind of leads into why we cut the trip short this week and why, I think, things might need to end."

Margaret proceeded to tell the story of Rudi's dog sculptures and the meltdown, how he'd followed her home where, after many conversations and many apologies, she'd made the first move. She ended with the story of being shoved out of bed by a terrorized Harold in the middle of the night, leaving out the very sore ribs she was still nursing. "And that is why I think I'm going to have to call it off with Harold. For as fun as every other bedtime activity is, and oh boy...it is...I was really scared. It can't be normal, and I don't think I ever want to experience that again."

Bea and June were silent for a few minutes. Margaret looked in the rearview again and Bea was crying. "Do you think Ted is going to have the same issues?" she choked back a sob. They were due to get married on his next leave, and the idea of his lighthearted personality disappearing scared her.

"Bea, honey, it's okay. June, tell us something to lighten the mood."

"I'm sorry. I can't. What you saw might have been terrifying for you, but whatever he saw that caused the nightmare was worse. This isn't to minimize your fear. That's real. And, in the same breath, I need you to understand that I have not yet met a person who has served on the front lines who is going to escape without flashbacks."

"Do they go away?" Margaret held out hope that maybe there would be something she could do, or say, to help Harold whether they stayed together or not. "I'll do whatever I can."

"If you find something that works better than whiskey, please let me know." June's hands had been balled up into fists. "Or, if you can figure out what might give a person a little bit of warning before a flashback hits, that would be great too."

Margaret reached over across the front seat and put her hand on June's fist, which slowly relaxed, and she threaded their fingers together. June didn't offer up any details. She didn't need to. It was very apparent that she knew intimately what Burke was experiencing.

"As to seeing him again, that's up to you. I find it's easier to take your leave before Rip Van Winkle descends. Besides, if you do that, you can say 'Oh, of course, I didn't sleep with him before we were married, Mother!'"

With that, they jumped back into gossiping about what all of their former classmates were doing. June never let Margaret's hand go through the rest of the drive. Each of them thought the other might be able to put on quite a show, but they drew strength in knowing they had each other.

Chapter Fifty-Four

M onday morning came too quickly, and Margaret was so rattled that she forgot her coat, and then her purse, and they had to turn around twice to go back to retrieve them so instead of her perpetually early arrival, Margaret entered her office promptly as the clock hit 8 a.m.

Burke was sitting behind his desk. His eyes, when they finally contacted hers, were bloodshot, and his face looked like maybe he'd skipped a shave for the first time since she'd met him.

She shut the door behind her and went around his desk, put her hands on either side of his face, and gently lowered her mouth to kiss him.

"Good morning, Captain. I've missed you."

He had the acrid smell of someone who was working through a heavy night of carousing. She knew that he was struggling, but her words were genuine. She did miss him. If what June had shared was true, and she was sure that it was, it meant that some grace needed to be given to people who had survived a trip to hell.

Burke pushed his chair back. "I'm not sure that you should do anything more than miss me. I cannot believe that I could hurt you. I would rather die than ever lay a hand on you again."

"Don't say that. Don't ever say that. I talked to June, and she said this is very, very, normal amongst soldiers. Actually, not just soldiers, but everyone who's serving. Even nurses." She hoped that by implying that June herself was struggling, he would feel better.

"I have not met a single soldier who has thrown his girlfriend across the room in the middle of the night." Burke stared down at his shoes.

"Have you done a survey? Because I'm afraid the number is higher than just you, Harold Burke. You're worth spending time with, so please know that I'm okay and I just want you to be okay too." Burke's eyes met hers. "I understand work is not the best place to have this conversation, so let's pick this up later this week when we have a free evening to be together. By not talking about it here I'm not avoiding it, I just know that for both of us, work is important, and we still have a dog training brief to write about our trip last week. Does that sound good?"

Burke nodded. She planted a kiss on his cheek, grabbed his coffee cup, and headed to the canteen. So much for a drama-free camp romance.

Margaret dropped by her parents that night. She figured she owed them a visit after the trip to Fort Robinson.

"Magpie! I didn't know you were coming by!" Franklin was always happy to see his only child. "Your mother is out playing bridge but should be home a bit later. There's cold chicken in the fridge if you'd care to join me."

They each made a plate with chicken, a couple of slices of cheese, and some apple slices and went to the living room. "Mother's not here, so let's just eat like 'savages' and not even use forks while you tell me why, exactly, you came by."

Spike sat between them, his head bouncing back and forth, hoping for a bite of dinner.

Margaret picked at her piece of chicken. "Daddy, why does life have to be so ugly?" She knew that she wasn't going to share many of the details.

"Did something happen with Burke? Your mother and I like him well enough, but we were a little suspect of the trip north since you're spending so much time together at, and after, work."

"No, maybe, yes." Margaret wondered how to have this conversation. "It's mostly June. She was here this weekend."

"She's such a character. I do like her. Always a riot." Franklin had favorites among Margaret's friends, and June was at the top of that list. He had been friends with her father before he died. "What's going on with June?"

"She's having some nerves, serious nightmares, after seeing the things she's seen, and she said nearly every soldier she's helped who was wounded has this thing they're calling 'battle rattle.' So, I suppose it's not just Harold I'm worried about, but also her, Charles, Bob, Ted, just all of them."

"And Thomas?" Franklin knew the letters that arrived included one from the ex-fiancé and she was grateful he didn't often interject his opinion on relationships.

"No, he's handling troop entertainment and educational materials for the front from the safety of Wales. If he's traumatized by that, then he's an even weaker man than I thought he was."

"Have you ever thought, Megs, entertainment, and education may be exactly what they all need? You're working for the military. I'm sure they've written some handbooks on what to do in this situation, wouldn't you think?"

"I suppose. The only soldiers I've met lately who seemed happy—and I'm counting all soldiers, servicemen, and prisoners—are the ones working at the dog training facility at the Fort Rob camp."

"So that was a real work trip?" Franklin seemed genuinely surprised. He wasn't born yesterday and she figured he thought Burke had simply come up with a clever way to get Margaret out of town and the spying eyes of her mother's network. Had he shared that out loud he would have been correct.

"Of course it was real!" Margaret was biting the inside of her cheek, which would hopefully slow down any blushing. They were tiptoeing dangerously close to a conversation she didn't want to have with her father. "In fact, my next column in the *Courier* is going to be wholly focused on that K-9 training program." They finished dinner, and as Franklin enjoyed a cigar, she told him all about the program. Spike was snuggled up on her lap the entire time.

"And dare I ask about Captain Burke?"

Margaret looked at the ground. She knew her dad would see right through her. "Oh, Dad. He's pretty broken. I think that the Army thought just sending him home to work in a prison was going to cure everything. The things he's seen are too horrible to even think about."

"But, knowing you, Magpie, that's all you're doing. Thinking. Imagining every possible outcome of any interaction. What is that brain of yours saying?"

"That if I could just find the right thing to do, to say, to read, to share with him that I could fix it all and that if I could fix him, I could fix every single one of the soldiers at the prison, whether prisoner or guard and cure them of that look. You know the look?"

"So, you really think you could fix all of that by just learning something?" Margaret knew he'd be sad that she was hurting, but that he knew there was very little he could do to solve this problem. No amount of money could be thrown at the right person to make it go away.

"It sounds ridiculous when I say it out loud. I don't even fully understand the pain that they're feeling. You know, Daddy, you and Mother really have protected me from anything too real. The closest I can come is when we lost Sam, but even that doesn't quite feel real. He was here, then he wasn't, and then we found that he never would be. Some of these men are teetering in limbo between life and death even after their wounds heal. It's awful."

"And your heart, Magpie? How's that doing?"

"It's complicated. I love so many things about Burke. I don't understand him enough to say that I love him, though. Does that make sense?"

Silence descended on the pair as they contemplated the conflict Margaret was facing. At about ten minutes to eight, Franklin said, "You know, if you'd like to escape before you have to answer any more questions or repeat these stories, you have just a few minutes before someone walks through that door."

"Daddy!" Margaret knew that the tension was palpable between her and her mother, but the escape had never been quite so directly provided. "I guess it's time to go anyway."

"Mmm hmmm. And grab that letter from Charles on the way out."

Chapter Fifty-Five

I t was nice to have a night with just her father. He brought up an interesting point about the military plans for the nerves. She considered revising her dog column to include just a little more depth of discussion surrounding the mental health aspects but decided, instead, that she'd start researching for a larger piece on this "battle rattle."

A Dog's Life — Margaret Murphy, Gering Courier

If I interviewed each and every one of you, I would be hard-pressed to find a single person who could not tell me a story of a dog. We are a strange group of mammals who feel we must have the companionship of other mammals. Most dogs have no purpose other than to provide joy and companionship to their masters. My dog, Spike, would disagree. He believes that he is the hardest working dog in the valley when his only responsibility is to bark so my parents know when the mail has been delivered. And, though I love Spike more than anything, he would be wrong.

The hardest-working dogs are just 80 miles north of Scottsbluff in a K-9 training center on the grounds of the Fort Robinson

POW Camp, which I had the distinct pleasure of touring last week.

Thousands of dogs have come to our Panhandle from across our nation. Many were donated by families because they were hunting dogs with hunters who left for war. Even more have been bred on-site specifically for the task at hand.;

They are training to be guard dogs for our prisons here and abroad; they are search and rescue dogs; they are trained to sniff out bombs and warn our troops; and they do this all for the scraps of food that we can spare and for the scratches that we can give them behind the ears. They are being trained, by the prisoners, primarily to help our men overseas.

We hope to be bringing a few dogs to Camp Scottsbluff to evaluate a search and rescue training program. What I noticed though on my brief trip to Fort Rob is that each soldier who handled the dogs, each prisoner who was working to train the dogs, had a peace about them that I have not seen at Camp Scottsbluff.

Every single man who spends his day behind the wire fence of our prison, whether friend or foe, has seen atrocities that the human mind should not be expected to process. There is a look in the eye—we all know it—of the irreparably harmed. That look is not weakness, or fear, but rather one of understanding the darkest side of man and struggling with the fact that somehow fate chose to save him and damn him to his memories forever.

That look dissipates the moment that a dog lays their soft head upon a knee. So, while I hope that our training program raises a talented group of search and rescue dogs, I hope even more that these dogs will provide a moment of solace to the men who have served.

Once that column was done, she opened the letter from Charles.

She was happy to hear from him. His letters were always more soothing, and she looked forward to a quiet evening of responding to him.

January 30, 1945 (South Pacific)

Dearest Margaret,

It's been quite a spell since you have heard from this end and after this is finished, you'll be none the wiser I fear. I believe I wrote to thank you for the books. I did enjoy them a lot. I ordered a lot of magazines before I left but they have not been getting here. I should think 4 months would be long enough, but I guess not.

As soon as I get enough strength to load myself with my combat gear I'll send you a picture. I don't believe anyone could carry it all—especially over the side of a ship on a cargo net—so we plan to discard all but absolute necessities.

Our existence seems sort of unreal as if we were living in another world. Completely divorced from familiar scenes except for the brief moments reading our letters. I saw some lovely orchids in the jungle the other day, one was yellow with dusty pink blotches, and the others were tiny and pale green. I wish I could have sent them on to you. No, I wish I could deliver them to you in person. They would be as priceless there as you would be here. Watch the post for a package from me with something almost as beautiful as the orchid.

I wish you could see this place. Maybe one day you can. I don't believe you can beat Colorado and I know I'd give a lot to see one of those Boulder snows. This place makes you feel after a while as if you had eaten too much candy.

I am sending you an invitation to a party already passed but I wish you could have been here. The only women were the ones who come with the Generals and all were kind and motherly and not a day under 48. We did have a fine time and excellent food. We cut down 6 palm trees to get the hearts for salad. We even had olives, chicken (canned), roast beef, cheese, ham, and ice cream. The drinks were good and plentiful and everyone thought that it was a success. Our battalion exec made the "invites" and made an extra one for me to send.

I believe I have told you how comfortably we live now. Of course, our plumbing is primitive and our tents have only lanterns but it's not unpleasant at all.

I'm afraid I've just been meandering but there is so little I have to write about. I'm getting pretty hot with a 45 Colt. Write whenever you have time and give me the news. I'll write as soon as I possibly can. Give my regards to your Mom and Dad and have fun.

How are all the POWs and how is your job? You have been there for a long time. Are you a big shot now?

Margaret, would you try to buy the book "Fantastic Interim" for me? They might have it at your bookstore. It's anti-republican but supposed to be good. I'll not make you read more of this drivel but close with all of my love.

Charles.

This letter didn't flow with quite the same ease as others. There were strange grammatical errors where usually he was so precise. Charles was a gentle man, a healer, and to have to train to take the lives of others all while honing his craft of saving others had to create incredible conflict in his mind. She wanted to ask him about this idea of night terrors and if they studied that in medical school.

Charles,

How can war be so picturesque? Each letter you send makes me think you're on a beautiful holiday cruise and then comes the reminder that in addition to being sure with a scalpel you must be sure with a gun. Grateful you're good with both.

The news here is a bit of a mixed bag.

We're seeing more and more soldiers, on both sides of this war, start to come back with quite a set of nerves. I hope that it's just temporary.

On the good news, I've been writing more articles for the paper. Without seeming too indulgent, I've included one I'm working on now for your reading pleasure. You're also going to be featured in a future article, sort of, as an example of what we could be doing stateside to help with morale. An international book club of sorts. Wish we'd started this earlier. I will put Fantastic Interim *in the post as quickly as I can procure it (and read it.)*

It sure feels like things are starting to come to a head, and maybe an end, in Europe. Maybe all of those boys can head down to help you guys out in the Pacific.

Lovingly to you too,

Margaret

Chapter Fifty-Six

Two days passed without much more than a perfunctory conversation between Burke and Margaret. He'd at least shaved the stubble, and his eyes didn't seem quite as bloodshot. The weather was beginning to transition from winter to spring, western Nebraska traded the oppressive wind for spring rains, and everything was really greening up.

Margaret looked up from her ledger. "Would you be interested in going on a walk in the hills with me after work today? There might be bluebirds migrating through." She was hopeful if she could get him moving, she could also get him talking. "I can ask Bea to take my car home."

"Are you sure?"

"Harold, I don't know what else I can say to you. Besides, you can't have a nightmare while walking."

They parked the car at the top of the dirt road in the Wildcat Hills just outside of town. This was the time of year that Margaret liked best. The fields were being turned, the days were getting longer, and life felt full of possibility. It was this brief window where the hills were as green as they ever would be before turning back into dust and yucca.

They walked in silence. Holding hands wasn't practical with their height difference unless she wanted to hold her arm up the entire time or he wanted to slouch down like Quasimodo. She led the way to the lookout spot. Someone had built a primitive bench, which was the perfect place to look out and watch the sunset over the valley. Margaret sat down hoping Burke would join her.

From this vantage point, you could do a short walk to the edge of the canyon and see all the way back down into the valley. On a clear day, you could see all the way from Dome Rock and the Monument out to the airfield and the camp. Burke sat down on the opposite end of the bench.

"Should we find a way to call it a day and go back to being work colleagues with good banter?" Margaret was not going to force, or plead, for something more.

"Is that what you want?" Burke seemed resigned to agreeing to whatever she wanted.

"No. What I want is to know how I can help and for us to go back to having the fun we were having before all of this. I don't like the tension. But I meant what I said. I miss you." She stood up and went to stand over towards the edge of the canyon drop-off. She was concerned she might start crying, and that was not something she would allow to happen over any man, even if they were closer than she'd ever been with anyone else.

Harold stood and walked over until he was directly behind her and put his hands on her shoulders and turned her around. "I cannot promise you that it will never happen again because I don't know how it happened in the first place. I'm losing my mind trying to figure out what I could do differently the next time. But Margaret, I miss you more than I've ever missed anything in my life, and I would give anything to kiss you again right now but don't think I'm safe for you to have around."

"I feel plenty safe with you. Really, Harold, I do. I, too miss this." She stood on her very tiptoes, he leaned down, and they were in very real danger of him getting a kink in his neck or her having a cramp in her calf. They pulled apart, and Margaret ran back to the bench and hopped up on it so that they were eye to eye. "Come back over here, please."

They resumed their embrace as the sunset moved from flaming orange to dusty pink before they finally adjourned to the car.

"Bea said she'd make herself scarce this evening if you'd like to come over." Margaret missed more than just kissing and wanted things to feel normal again.

"I want nothing more. I'm sure you know that. But I don't think I should."

"June gave me a great suggestion. Just tuck me in and take your leave before you go to sleep. That's what she does." She turned and winked at him.

Burke was shocked, "What you women share with each other baffles me but I'll agree with June's idea."

They scrambled back to the car and made it down the hill in record time.

They entered the apartment, and Bea was sitting in the living room with a bridal magazine open in front of her. She was happy to see that her friend and Burke were both sporting smiles and a more relaxed countenance.

"Welcome back. Captain Burke, it's good to see you again."

"You don't have to call me Captain Burke when we're not at the prison, I've told you that, Bea. Oh, and thank you for helping arrange for the suitcases and the car last week. I really appreciated that."

"I do what I can for love. Which reminds me, we're out of coffee and I think the market in Gering has the kind we like and is open until ten. I completely forgot to grab it on my way home." She stood, grinning at the couple, and grabbed her sweater and the keys to Margaret's car. "I'm assuming I can take your car, Megs?"

"You assume correctly."

"I'm parked directly behind you, so if I'm not here when you get back, thank you again."

"Well, goodnight then. Megs, I'll see you in the morning."

The moment that Bea shut the door behind her, Margaret had the buttons on Burke's shirt undone. He was working to pull her sweater up over her head, and by the time they got to the bedroom door they had left a trail of most of their clothing and fell onto the bed. Margaret was still in the bra and panty set that she picked out in the hopes that this was how today would end up.

Burke propped himself above her, kissing her mouth, then her throat, then the space in between her breasts that her bra didn't cover. He slid a hand behind her back and deftly unclamped the soft ivory barrier, pulled each strap down over her arms, and looked down at her. "Margaret, you are ravishing." He lowered his mouth to her, coming close, but not quite, to touch her. She arched her back to try and bring herself into contact with his lips.

"I've missed you, and I'm going to take my time. This was what I wanted to do on our second night away." He moved his mouth instead to her ribs, directly under her breasts, kissing lightly with each movement. He propped himself up again to kiss her and then drew a line with his mouth straight from her lips, over her stomach, and then looped his thumbs through either side of her panties and kept descending.

Margaret could not believe that anything could feel as good as this and was sorry that they had to cut their trip short if this was what it would have included. She was grateful that the light was dim in her room and he was so distracted he didn't see the bruise on her side.

She laid back and enjoyed absolutely everything he was doing. What a way to be tucked into bed.

In the comfortable afterglow, she lay with her head on his chest, listening to his heartbeat. "Can't you just stay? I'm sure things will be fine. Bea won't care."

"I would hold you forever if I could. This is a perfect moment. A perfect memory." He propped up on one elbow and reached around to pull her on top of him, grabbing her by her side.

Margaret gasped. He'd inadvertently grabbed the area on her ribs that were still tender. She attempted to mask the noise by pretending she was yawning.

Burke didn't buy it. "Are you still hurting?" The light was dim so he couldn't see anything. He sat up and turned on the bedside lamp. The bruise had faded, but on her pale skin it had gone from a dark purple to a mottled green and yellow with a blue undertone.

"Margaret! You didn't tell me it was this bad."

"I'm fine. Really, Harold. I just bruise easily."

"This is not fine. It's not okay." He stood up and began pulling on his clothes. "I can't stay. I have to go."

She reached to him, and he pulled away. She grabbed her robe and tied it around her waist as he got dressed.

"Harold, it's okay. I'm sorry I pressured you to stay."

He turned and looked at her, leaned down, and kissed her softly.

"It's okay, Margaret. I just have to go. Know that I love you. So very, very, much." His voice caught as he said the words.

Sleep did not come easily to Margaret that night.

Chapter Fifty-Seven

S he was distracted through breakfast, on the commute, through the security line, and down the hall to her office. Margaret prepped for a day simply focused on the mundane aspects of work and hopefully some writing on supporting the mental health of soldiers. She hoped Burke would share some thoughts on the matter.

He wasn't in the office yet, which wasn't unusual. What was unusual is that there was another card on her desk. There were also two dog figurines that she'd never seen propping it up on each side. She prepped for another surprise getaway under the guise of K-9 research. Another do-over.

She opened the letter.

My Dearest Miss Murphy,

I hope in time you will forgive me. You are the love, for certain, of my life, and it is because of that love that I have left.

It is the middle of the night as I'm sitting in the office wishing that I could find the eloquence that you deserve. The explanation that you deserve. The explanation of why I have to leave.

All I ask is that you trust me in knowing that I am doing this for you but not because of you. You do not deserve to be burdened by me. You deserve the freedom to write, and travel, and go back to school, and to someday marry a man who, if he loves you even a fraction of how much I love you, will love you beyond measure. I was hopeful that man could be me. I purchased this ring the day after our first fight. Hoped to give it to you on our trip. It's yours even though I'm gone.

You deserve every bit of the passion of our last night together without any of the fear. I want nothing more than that for you.

My love forever -

H.

P.S. One more request for forgiveness. I hid these two carvings from you. They arrived the day after we got back from our K-9 trip. I'm sorry.

Margaret felt as if she'd been punched in the gut. What did this mean? Where did he go? She went down the hall to the personnel office to discuss this with Bea but was nearly knocked into the wall by several soldiers from the medical wing running towards the officer's quarters.

"Watch it!" Margaret thought it was no wonder that the enlisted go just a day or two without an accident. Soldiers have no regard for where they are going.

She entered the personnel office and mimed drinking a cup of coffee to Bea who grabbed her mug and came to the door.

"What's going on?" Bea looked out the window as they headed to the coffee pot. There was more and more commotion outside.

"That? Who knows. Probably someone cut himself shaving and they're bored." She handed Bea the envelope from Burke. "I need your advice on this. I guess Burke is leaving."

"But you had a great night last night, didn't you?" Bea handed the letter back to Margaret.

"I thought it was okay. We had a good talk out in the hills and then had a good time not talking back home. Then he got spooked when I asked him to stay."

Both of them were distracted as a crowd was gathering outside of the officer's quarters.

"Want to go see what's going on? My boss obviously isn't coming into work today." Margaret and Bea headed to the gate in between the prison and the officer's quarters. Shorty saw them and came running over.

"You girls shouldn't be here. Especially you, Margaret." His words were shaky.

"Especially me?" Margaret had a horrible realization. "Open this gate, Shorty. Right. Now." Margaret felt like she was floating above herself. The gate opened, and she walked towards the crowd and into the officers' quarters. She'd never been inside, civilians weren't allowed, but she knew instinctively that the crowd was gathered outside of Harold's room. She started to run and push her way through the wall of men when Shorty finally caught up to her and reached to grab her arm.

She shook him off and turned the corner just in time to see two soldiers holding on to each side of Harold's lifeless body while a third used a knife to cut the rope that was tied around the rod in his closet and looped around his neck. He was fully dressed in his military uniform. He was an odd shade of blue that wasn't quite grey but somehow was the color of the lake after a rainstorm. At his feet were two empty bottles of whisky.

She wanted to look away, to run, to hide, but also to be fully present for everything that was happening. There was so much noise going on around her, yet she heard no distinct sounds, just her heartbeat whooshing through her ears. A scream broke through, and she turned around just in time to watch Bea crumble to the ground.

Harold had left. For good. Forever. What now? She dropped to her knees next to Bea. "Can someone help me get her outside? She needs some air."

Margaret felt something snap in her body as if what was before, everything that was real and true in her life, was at the end of a rope, and she was now stranded on the other side, completely untethered. She went into problem-solving mode. Harold was dead, but Bea was not. Bea needed air. Maybe she herself needed air? If she could get Bea some air maybe Bea could start breathing for her. Breathing suddenly didn't make any sense. Nothing did.

Shorty and another soldier gently lifted Bea. Someone tried to put their arm through hers, but she pushed their hand away and walked, her back rigidly straight, to the yard. The two soldiers lowered Bea to a bench as she started to come to. Margaret shooed them off and sat down next to her friend.

"Deep breath Bea. You're going to be okay."

Bea was now sobbing loudly. Margaret rubbed circles on her back. "We should go inside, and get you a tissue."

Bea acquiesced, and they headed down the hall just as the coroner arrived with a stretcher. Margaret grabbed a handkerchief for Bea and stood in the doorway of her office while Bea sat at her chair and her sobs quieted down. "Do you think you can go back to work?"

"I'm sorry, what?" Bea looked up at her friend. "Go back to work? I can't go back to work! You shouldn't go back to work! Harold is dead, Margaret, and you're standing there as if everything is just fine."

"Oh, everything is not fine, Bea. I just don't know what exactly I'm supposed to do now. I think I need a minute. Can you go get your things from your desk and give me a moment to think? I will come to get you when I'm ready to leave."

No one ever fully understood Margaret's need to isolate during times of deep stress, but thankfully Bea knew her well enough to do what she asked.

Margaret looked around the office. There was not a corner of it that didn't hold some memory of Harold. She could still smell his aftershave. His desk looked like he was expected back any moment. She walked over to his desk, sat in his chair, and placed her hands flat on the desktop. If she held still enough, maybe some of his final moments could be absorbed. He obviously sat here while he wrote his final message with the pen that was casually placed in the middle of the desk.

How could someone be clear of mind enough to write a letter, place a pen where the pen was always placed, and then moments later choose to end his life? She pushed back from the desk.

She simply could not handle being in the office for one more moment and opened her handbag and put the dogs, the picture of Spike, and her name placard inside. She straightened up the ledgers and made sure the process manuals that she'd written about how to do her job were placed squarely in the middle of the desk. She inserted a piece of paper into the typewriter.

April 27, 1945
To Whom it May Concern:
I am taking my leave of employment, effectively immediately, from the Scottsbluff Prisoner of War Camp. I have left the process manuals for my replacement on my desk.
Thank you for the opportunity.
Margaret Elizabeth Murphy

Right before she left the office, she turned and grabbed Harold's pen, the dogs, and the ring. She walked down the hall to the personnel office and handed Bea's boss the resignation letter and turned around and left the building for the last time. She knew people would talk. Let them.

Chapter Fifty-Eight

*D*ear June,
    Apologies for the V-Mail. Needed to get to you quickly and too much for a telegraph. Harold is dead. He took his own life. At the prison. You have probably heard as much from Bea, but this is the first time I've written those words down, and if you see ink running on this page it's simply because I am alone in the apartment, crying.

There was a lot to love about him but, to be honest, after our conversation when you were home, I planned to end it when the camp closed. This sounds terrible, and I might need you to burn this letter when you're done reading it and never show Bea. I don't believe that I am the right kind of person to have the gentle patience that is required to support someone who has spent time in hell.

But you've all been there. You're there now. Please understand, I will always be there for you. I know Bob is seeing things that are turning him into a morose insomniac and that Charles isn't even interested in reading or writing as consistently. I cannot continue caring for people who might leave.

What now?

I wish you were home.

~M

Harold's body had been sent back to Tacoma to his family. She included a copy of the photo of them together at Christmas and one at the Officer's Club with a note of condolences. It felt so strange that one day he was here, in her bed, and the next day he was gone. It was a void very different from any she'd felt before.

Dear Mr. and Mrs. Burke,

I am so sorry for your loss. Captain Burke spoke so highly of you both and we had talked of me coming to visit as the Pacific Northwest was one of my family's favorite places to holiday. We had become quite close, he was a wonderful boss and friend to me at the camp. My heartbreak at his death could only be a fraction of yours. I'm sending along a couple of photos of his wonderful smile that might, with time, be a reminder of his times of joy.

Margaret Murphy, Assistant to the Quartermasters Office, Camp Scottsbluff

Chapter Fifty-Nine

S he spent the next week vacillating between wanting to be alone and wanting Bea to quit her job and not leave her side. She was sitting and staring at her typewriter wishing she could will it to provide her with the motivation to do anything when she was shaken from her thoughts by a knock at the door. A young messenger handed her a telegraph.

M-
SO SORRY. YOU WILL SURVIVE THIS. I WILL BE HOME TO LISTEN SOON. WRITE IT ALL DOWN.
-J

There really was nothing more to say, no platitudes of "he's not in pain" or shame of "why didn't you do something"— just a simple acknowledgment that right now life was hard, and that she was strong enough to handle the hard.

June's letter reminded her that writing was her safe space for processing emotions. For some reason, she didn't want to put all of these thoughts into her journal. Margaret decided to write herself a letter. It seemed a little silly, but she didn't want Burke's suicide to cloud the rest of the experiences at the camp. Maybe it was that, once she'd felt everything she needed to feel, and processed through every complicated emotion, a letter could be easily burned.

M,

When Harold left that last night, should I have followed him? Could I have changed any of this? Would I have just been kicking the can down the road to stop him from killing himself? What was he thinking in those final hours? Were things even worse than I knew? Should I have said more to his parents? Should I have sent back the ring I will never wear since the proposal was from a dead man? Do I tell someone that he was tormented by keeping the horrors he saw secret? Should that secret be exposed in his honor?

The questioning mind is an exhausting place to live. The moment when I think all of the questions have been answered my imagination comes up with new things to consider.

How long did it take him to stop feeling pain? I pray the whiskey took him first and the noose finished him off. Will there be a funeral? Should I attend? I have nothing else to do. I don't want to explain that I was having a secret relationship with my boss, who left me a note that I shared only with Bea, that he might not have killed himself if he never saw that bruise. I can't go. My attendance will not improve anything.

Bea has been a comfort and a bother. She has no problems crying and letting things out, but I always end up comforting her. I suppose I've never really found a space where I wasn't the problem solver. June would provide the logic and understanding of the pain of a soldier, and surely some humor, but she is gone for a few more months. She could be gone forever.

My greatest fear is that, before this war is over, I will lose all of them, Charles, Bob...June. I'm terrified that she's seen things that will affect her as deeply, that she will have nowhere to turn for help because no one seems to know how to help, and that she will make choice to quiet her memories permanently as well.

She would never. She could never. Good Lord, how did June know, from thousands of miles away, that she'd force me to cry again? When I type my articles I'm so safe, I'm logical, and I hold reality at a comfortable distance. Picking up this pen, Harold's pen, and writing is more intimate. It's like emotional bloodletting. I'm not saying every thought that is running through my mind, though it feels like it. It makes me wonder how many thoughts are hidden in every letter I receive. Words, which are my comfort, feel like limitations to everything I'm feeling.

I'm sad, of course, but I'm angrier than anything else. Even though I was going to end this, eventually, I now will never have the opportunity. Harold will not have the opportunity to get the help he needs. Needed.

I really should go see my parents. I'm not ready to see anyone. I can't write anymore and I can't leave this letter behind.

What do I do now?

M

There was a release, of sorts, in the act of writing these thoughts down but there was no way she was keeping this letter to be found. Margaret took the lit end of her cigarette, held it up to the corner of the paper, and let it burn while ashes fell in the sink.

The stream of conscious writing lit something up inside of Margaret and she decided to put a fresh piece of paper in the typewriter and begin writing a new column for the *Courier.*

Chapter Sixty

March 1945

She was holed up in her apartment when the phone rang. She hated herself for forgetting it couldn't be Harold. Instead, it was her dad calling from the bank.

"Maggie, it's dad. Can I come to take you to lunch at the café in about twenty minutes?"

"Just you?" Margaret didn't have the energy to deal with prying questions from her mother.

"Just me. That's why I'm calling from the bank."

The café was within walking distance of her apartment, and it was a beautiful day. The clouds were the perfectly white puff balls that you'd see in a painting by a child. They almost didn't look real against the piercing blue of the sky. She wondered how long it had been since she simply took the time to look at the clouds during the day. Life outside of the prison was ridiculous if she never left the walls of her apartment, and she vowed that after lunch she would go for a walk to the park nearby and write in her journal, and then would walk by the library for a new book or two. She was going to be fine. Now to convince her dad of that lie.

She beat Franklin to the café and asked for a booth near the back. She was assuming he would have questions she'd rather not have everyone easily eavesdrop upon. There were at least three people she knew in the café already, and it was impossible to expect any anonymity in this town.

It was just a short wait until she saw Franklin get out of his car across the street from the café and wait for a break in traffic to cross the street.

"Daddy? You never leave for lunch."

Franklin pulled her up from her seat and held her close.

"Margaret. I'm so sorry." Franklin was a master at deflection.

"I'm guessing you're here because you've heard the news about Harold?"

"Of course, I've heard the news about Harold. I kept hoping you'd call, or come home, but then I realized you're as stubborn as they come, and I was going to have to come to you. How are you?"

"That's a hard question to answer. Harold wasn't in my life long enough for it to matter, really, but..." She started to get choked up. "He hung himself."

The news in the paper had just been that an officer had died at the camp. The soldiers and the staff all protected their own and had not shared that detail with anyone in the community. He was not the first officer to end his own life, he would not be the last. There seemed to be an understanding that some of these people had simply seen too much to carry.

"You, Magpie, can do whatever you'd like but if you'd like to tell me more, I'm listening."

Margaret struggled to keep eye contact with her father as she spoke. "Harold and I were dating, and I was starting to really care for him. But I learned that he had a breakdown at his previous camp, and he was on the verge of another here these last few weeks. I thought he was doing better until I showed up at work and there was a letter on my desk saying that he had to leave. I stupidly thought he had gone back to his parents. I simply could not be in the office for one more minute and not cry at work. So, I wrote a letter of my own and resigned that very morning. I'm sorry I didn't tell you. I just needed some time on my own to figure out what is next."

"The other night when you were over, why didn't you tell me more about how he was struggling? You mentioned June's struggles but nothing about Harold."

"I think I was still trying to figure it all out. I was sure it was a problem I could solve or, honestly, I was going to chalk it up to a camp romance and send him on his way. I never considered that it was as bad as this. I figured that someone I cared about was still due to die in this damned war, I just didn't think it would be from an injury worse than just being shot. None of it really makes sense. It makes no sense that we can start a war and then expect humans to be okay with the damage it causes. Bullet wounds and bomb shrapnel aren't the only things that are killing people."

"Sadly, death is required to stop more killing in this case. Hitler would not listen to anything else and, sadly, Japan also seems to only comprehend messages delivered while they are looking down the barrel of a gun."

"Then the military needs to do something for the people that are forced to deliver that message." Tears that were equal part anger and grief threatened to spill out of Margaret's eyes. "Let's change the subject."

"Do you need money for rent?" Franklin was generous to a fault financially but these emotions scared him.

"No, someone taught me to have money in savings. Besides, it took me almost three years to move out and you didn't charge me rent while I lived with you so I've built up quite the savings account."

"Anytime you need anything, you just need to ask. Do you want to come work for me at the bank? You could start this afternoon. Though you'd have to go back and change into a work outfit instead of the more casual trousers I see you're enjoying."

"Daddy, now you're sounding like Mother. What is it with you two and pants!"

The waitress stopped by to take their order. She didn't want her dad to be even more concerned so she said, "I'll have whatever he's having."

"Can I ask what's next for you?"

"I really want to head back to school. I feel like I need some space from all of this."

"I understand. Let me see if can get your mother on board. It wasn't easy the first time. Hopefully, this time is different."

With that, they dove into eating and enjoyed their conversation about how the Allies were making some incredible progress in Europe and Margaret felt like she'd found an ally of her own in the battle to get her degree. She knew he had her back as she worked through this grief.

Chapter Sixty-One

April 30, 1945

Time away from the prison was remarkably healing. Her routine consisted of: a daily walk to the café, journaling about everything going on in her mind, drafting a book based on everything that happened over the last few years, and reading novels and news until Bea came home and filled her in on the daily gossip from the prison. She admired the people that could go straight back to work after a tragedy and was very aware of her privilege of having time to process.

She had just paid her bill and was pushing the door open to head home to tuck into *Cannery Row* before she sent it off to Charles. She was almost knocked to the ground by a man with wild eyes as he pushed past her into the nearly full café.

"It just came across on the wire. Hitler is dead! Adolph Hitler is dead!"

The cheering could still be heard as Margaret ran the rest of the way home, grabbed her car keys, and headed back out to the prison. She'd left just a few days too early to celebrate but was hoping that her friends running security would give her some grace. Bea had been carpooling with another friend from the personnel office so she figured, at the very least, she could say she was just there to pick up a friend.

She raced to the prison, ignoring the speed limit. Everyone in town, including the police, would be glued to the radio waiting for announcements. The mood at the prison was jovial and they just waved her through security. Even some of the prisoners seemed happy to hear the news. Maybe this war was going to finally end. Bea saw her down the hallway and rushed to embrace her.

"Can you believe it?" Tears were streaming down her face.

Margaret was surprised by the fact that even some of the prisoners seemed happy to hear the news.

Someone brought out some contraband champagne and small paper cups were passed around. No one even questioned why she'd left. Everyone seemed to understand that she didn't want to talk about Harold. She could miss him and still be livid that he disappeared the way he did.

She saw Rudi down the hall and wondered what he thought about returning to a country destroyed by bombs. He turned, saw her, and tipped his head in a slight bow with a smile on his face. It would be inappropriate to go talk to him, but knew exactly what he felt from that simple gesture.

"Are you staying until work's done? I'd rather ride home with you."

"I can't," Margaret still wasn't quite ready to be back behind these walls. "I have an article to finish."

She left the prison and though she might head to her parents. She was hopeful the joy of today's news would affect her mother's decision for her to go back to school.

As with everyone else across the U.S., it didn't really feel real to her yet. Her father was thrilled but also concerned about how this might affect the markets. Her mother seemed to have calmed a bit. There had not been a surrender by Germany yet, and Japan was another story, but this felt like the most positive development since before Sam died years ago.

Her mother was surprisingly cordial, simply telling Margaret that she was "sorry about her friend." Suicide was something so very shameful that even saying the word was too much for people like her mother. When asked, she would likely just say that Margaret's boss died suddenly and that they had gotten to know him briefly over a couple of dinners, but not well.

She decided to push the parental interaction to the weekend and instead went back to the apartment to write. The news of the day meant that, hopefully, the war was nearly over.

Chapter Sixty-Two

M ay 4, 1945

"I suppose you'd like a letter from Bob though I really wish you'd inform them that we are not your mail collectors." It was as if her mother had planned to have a confrontation the minute Margaret walked up the back door.

It had been quite a while since she'd heard from Bob. She had to admit that she had let their correspondence lapse a bit, and instead of writing proactively, she waited to respond whenever the next letter arrived.

She knew he was in Germany and was hopeful that he had something to do with the death of the tyrant who'd started this whole war. "That Bob Hale, can't remember an address to save his life. He wrote this the day after Hitler died. We'll never be able to live with him if he becomes a war hero because of this."

Dachau

Can't sleep Margaret so thought I'd try and put a pen to paper to see if it could calm the noise in my head. Kind of hard to believe that it's too noisy for your Hale. But it's silent. Quietest it's ever been.

I don't know when I can tell you things officially but what I can tell you is that I don't want to tell you anything and can I tell you everything? I think I've finally found something that will shut up your friend that always has something to say. Maybe you can listen while I just say nothing.

I hurt my bum ankle but not bad enough to keep me from walking into something that has seared my brain. Remember that day we went to my uncle's ranch for branding? You refused to help make potato salad with the ladies and stayed on the back of the horse while we separated those calves from their moms and heated up that iron and seared that hot metal into the flesh. The smell of that hair burning catches at the back of your throat. I think maybe you even smell fear above all the shit.

That smell is honey and roses to me now.

Oh, honey I wish you were here just to go walk until I was tired enough to just lay down and close my eyes that haven't closed for two days. There's not enough soap in the barracks. We've run out from trying to scrub it all away. Maybe writing this to you made a difference. Maybe it's just ol' Hale being self-centered. I can tell you what though that convertible ride can't come soon enough. Maybe I could go grab one of those jeeps parked out there and come get you? Can you wait up?

Write me just to make sure I'm still real.

Bob

PS - can't remember your new address. Can't even remember my own hardly. Don't know the date. I'm sure your folks will get this to you.

Everything about his letter was disquieting. Firstly, there was not a parenthetical in sight. Second, he had hardly flirted. His penmanship was terrible, but these scribbles were almost illegible.

It was another letter that sounded like a man losing his mind and she dropped it on the table. It was hard to breathe thinking of one of her longest friends struggling like this.

"So, what does Robert Hale have to say? He was a buffoon, but a good-hearted one at that." Her dad liked to scare Bob when they were dating in high school but had a soft spot because he really liked the Hale family. She wished she had a funny anecdote from Bob for Margaret to share, but that was not the case based on her daughter's expression.

Margaret handed over the letter to him. Rebecca came to read over Franklin's shoulder.

"How can you even read this? His penmanship is atrocious." Rebecca was critical of anything less than perfection.

"Oh, I don't know Mother," Margaret rolled her eyes. "Maybe he was in the middle of a war when he wrote it."

Franklin chewed on the end of his cigar. "Dachau. Rebecca, wasn't there an article about Dachau in the paper?"

Rebecca went and grabbed some clippings. "I cut out an article for you from the paper. That woman writer that you're always going on about, Marguerite Higgins, wrote a horribly graphic article. I couldn't make it past the third paragraph, but I knew you'd want to see it. I figured you'd be by sooner or later with everything that was going on."

She handed over the clippings from several different parts of the paper. Margaret felt it might have been easier to just save the paper, but it's the thought that counts.

The Liberation of Camp Dachau — Marguerite Higgins, New York Herald Tribune

Troops of the United States 7th Army liberated 33,000 prisoners this afternoon at this first and largest of the Nazi concentration camps. Some of the prisoners had endured for eleven years the horrors of notorious Dachau.

The liberation was a frenzied scene: Inmates of the camp hugged and embraced the American troops, kissed the ground before them and carried them shoulder high around the place.

The Dachau camp, in which at least a thousand prisoners were killed last night before the SS (Elite Guard) men in charge fled, is a grimmer and larger edition of the similarly notorious Buchenwald camp near Weimar.

This correspondent and Peter Furst, of the Army newspaper Stars and Stripes, were the first two Americans to enter the enclosure at Dachau, where persons possessing some of the best brains in Europe were held during what might have been the most fruitful years of their lives.

While a United States 45th Infantry Division patrol was still fighting a way down through S.S. barracks to the north, our jeep and two others from the 42nd Infantry drove into the camp enclosure through the southern entrance. As men of the patrol with us busied themselves accepting an S.S. man's surrender, we impressed a soldier into service and drove with him to the prisoners' barracks. There he opened the gate after pushing the body of a prisoner shot last night while attempting to get out to meet the Americans.

There was not a soul in the yard when the gate was opened. As we learned later, the prisoners themselves had taken over control of their enclosure the night before, refusing to obey any further orders from the German guards, who had retreated to the outside. The prisoners maintained strict discipline among themselves, remaining close to their barracks so as not to give the S.S. men an excuse for mass murder.

But the minute the two of us entered, a jangled barrage of "Are you Americans?" in about 16 languages came from the barracks 200 yards from the gate. An affirmative nod caused pandemonium.

Tattered, emaciated men weeping, yelling and shouting "Long live America!" swept toward the gate in a mob. Those who could not walk limped or crawled. In the confusion, they were so hysterically happy that they took the S.S. man for an American. During a wild five minutes, he was patted on the back, paraded on shoulders and embraced enthusiastically by the prisoners. The arrival of the American soldier soon straightened out the situation.

I happened to be the first through the gate, and the first person to rush up to me turned out to be a Polish Catholic who was not a little startled to discover that the helmeted, uniformed, begoggled individual he had so heartily embraced was not a man.

In the excitement, which was not the least dampened by the German artillery and the sounds of battle in the northern part of the camp, some of the prisoners died trying to pass through elec-

trically charged barbed wire. Some who got out after the wires were decharged joined in the battle, when some ill-advised S.S. men holding out in a tower fired upon them.

The prisoners charged the tower and threw all six S.S. men out the window.

The barracks at Dachau, like those at Buchenwald, had the stench of death and sickness. But at Dachau there were six barracks like the infamous No. 61 at Buchenwald, where the starving and dying lay virtually on top of each other in quarters where 1,200 men occupied a space intended for 200. The dead—300 died of sickness yesterday—lay on concrete walks outside the quarters and others were carried out as the reporters went through.

The mark of starvation was on all the emaciated corpses. Many of the living were so frail it seemed impossible they could still be holding on to life.

The crematorium and torture chambers lay outside the prisoner enclosures. Situated in a wood close by, a new building had been built by prisoners under Nazi guards. Inside, in the two rooms used as torture chambers, an estimated 1,200 bodies were piled.

In the crematorium were hooks on which the S.S. men hung their victims when they wished to flog them or to use any of the other torture instruments.

The prisoners also showed reporters the grounds where men knelt and were shot in the back of the neck.

Just beyond the crematorium was a ditch containing some 2,000 bodies, which had been hastily tossed there in the last few days by the S.S. men, who were so busy preparing their escape they did not have time to burn the bodies.

Below the camp were cattle cars in which prisoners from Buchenwald had been transported to Dachau. Hundreds of dead were still in the cars due to the fact that prisoners in the camp had rejected S.S. orders to remove them. It was mainly the men from these cattle cars that the S.S. leaders had shot before making their escape. Among those who had been left for dead in the cattle cars was one man still alive who managed to lift himself from the heap of corpses on which he lay.[3]

Margaret openly wept for the first time since Harold's death. No one should have to see these horrors, especially not her happy-go-lucky friend. It was impossible to reconcile the atrocities committed at the German POW camp with the fact that Hitler had been sending instruments to the prisons in America. The U.S. citizens were appalled that the German prisoners were getting cared for with hot meals and warm bedding. When they saw what Hitler did to American prisoners, the Jewish people, and anyone who disagreed with him? It was beyond cognition.

"Thank you for saving this. Bob's part of this liberation group — the 42nd. I can only imagine what he saw."

She went to the desk in her room, which was still set up as if she lived there, and took out a fresh piece of paper.

Bob,

I need you to know how grateful I am that you are still alive and how fervently I hope that you are done. Done with this war. Done with your tour. Done with heading into hell. I read

Margarite Higgins' article about the liberation. I guess since it's in the papers we can talk about it and maybe things won't get censored.

I've been reading about the things war does to the human brain. It sounds like it can change it forever if you don't take the time to work through it all. I don't know how you work through some of the things you've seen.

I have some close experience that I'll tell you about someday that makes it very, very clear to me that you need to do what you can to care for not just your bum ankle but also your mind. I need you, the goofy, fun-loving Bob Hale, to come back to us.

All I can say is that I wish you'd have broken that damned ankle of yours that's given you fits since high school football so you could have stayed on the shores of France. You are too good and kind and terrible and funny to come home without the thing that makes you Bob still fully intact.

I don't know if any of this is making sense.

All my best,

Margaret

P.S. I might also want to, well, hold your breath, and apologize to you for all the mean things I've said over the years to you. You are too good of a friend, and I couldn't bear you thinking I still meant those things from years ago.

Chapter Sixty-Three

B ea and Margaret walked to the movies that night to see the newsreels. Earlier, Ted telegraphed that he had enough points to be discharged but was thinking of going from France to the Pacific to wrap things up over there and wanted Bea to wait for him. She found no consolation in the movie theater, especially with the newsreel at the beginning showing the celebrations in Europe. It looked like the war was nearly over.

"Can you believe him?" Bea asked for the tenth time. "He could come home, but he won't. We can't do any wedding planning until we have a date that he'll be here."

"No planning whatsoever? What, then, is that big white dress that's hanging in our coat closet? Do we have a formal coming up that I don't know about?"

Margaret put her arm around Bea's waist as they walked.

"When he gets here, you and your mother will have it done within days. Besides, we need to make sure June is home, too. There's no way that the two of us have listened to your wedding plans and looked at cutouts of dresses for three years for this wedding to take place without both of us there."

"Are you going to come back and help discharge the prisoners? They need help in the processing department and since it's in a different office..." Bea missed riding in with Margaret and felt that her friend was spending too much time cooped up inside, writing.

"Maybe. Let me think about it." Margaret really wanted to walk into the *Star-Herald* and ask for a job as a full-time reporter. Instead, she was working on a column for the *Courier* on what people could expect of the mindset of men who might be returning shortly. She'd planned on getting Harold's input and permission to share parts of his story. He killed himself before she could ask which she equated to "permission granted." She would be respectful with the details to protect herself, but people needed to know what was coming home to them.

Of Mind and Men — Margaret Murphy, Gering Courier
You are probably sitting in your most comfortable chair with your favorite mug full of hot coffee as you read this column. You might be savoring it in a café while you enjoy a slice of pie. You might be sitting in your quiet office taking a break from the challenges of the day.

You (or I) are likely not someone that has served on the front line of a war overseas. We had four million soldiers that served in the first Great War against Germany and lost over 100,000 precious souls. We are at nearly four times that number in this conflict, both in soldiers and deaths. Thank goodness that conflict looks to be ending now that the tyrannical madman who was running Germany has ended his life. May Japan fall soon.

What this means is that we stateside are about to see a huge influx of men, and many women, returning from Europe with intimate exposure to depths of violence and trauma, unlike anything we have ever considered. This war was fought not just on the land, sea, and air, but also employed some of the basest torture that humanity could imagine in the way of concentration camps throughout Europe where hundreds of thousands of people were killed.

Our military was on the right side of this war, of that, I have no doubt. What I doubt is that we know what war does when it's over. In talking with soldiers who have already returned, I've learned that they are struggling with nightmares more intense than anything they've ever experienced. Their spouses are sharing that nights are filled with their husbands both somehow awake and asleep at the same time, screaming at and fighting with an unseen enemy. Stories are told of wives being thrown from the bed without their husbands having any awareness of what has happened until they snap out of it. Nurses are sharing that they can still hear the howling of the gravely injured even though they haven't been in an infirmary for months. Something as simple as a door slamming can send someone diving for cover. One can only imagine what the sound of a gunshot or firecracker will do.

Very little, if any, research exists to explain why some of the soldiers will come home with these long-lasting scars on their minds. Some will escape with just a memory. What we do know is that it's going to take patience from all of us as we welcome these heroes back into our lives.

Thank you and congratulations to our servicemen and women in Europe. You've done us proud. Wrap it up and make it home safely.

She finished the column, but it wasn't due for a few days. Maybe she should seriously consider going back, hat in hand, to the prison to help as they prepare to release the prisoners. After all, if she wanted to go back to school in the fall, she was going to need money of her own if her mother still refused support. She had reached out to the Dean last week and was assured there was a spot waiting for her when she was ready. August couldn't come soon enough.

She picked up the phone and called the prison's personnel office. With an end in sight, she was ready to go back and help things along. If the men in Germany were going to be sent to the Pacific, then she could do her duty and head back to the prison.

Chapter Sixty-Four

I t was strange to walk through the gates of the prison and head down the same hall towards her old office but stop short and turn, with Bea, into the personnel and processing department. The head of the personnel department had taken pity on her after Burke's death and wanted her to have the support of her friend beside her.

Their job was to make sure they knew where each prisoner was from originally, if he had communication with family back home, and if they were still in that location. Then they would assign the prisoners to trains to go to Fort Morgan, Colorado, to be processed again and put on more trains to get to the coast where they'd be put on carrier ships and shipped back where they came from. Someday.

Though Germany had surrendered, there was still a threat in the Pacific. Japan didn't seem to be backing down an inch. She'd finally received a letter from Charles. His last letter came in mid-February but was written in January. This one arrived around the first of June. Margaret shook her head. After almost four years you think they'd have the mail figured out.

May 13, 1945 - Okinawa Japan

Dearest Margaret:

The last time I wrote I was sitting in a rice paddy near Suku on the northeast coast. Now I am a few miles above Naka and a lot has happened in the meantime. We were not busy at Suku as the casualties were very light but when we moved across the island to Nago I really put in some time. In 3 days and 2 nites without sleep I took care of over 200 patients. I think I might have saved some lives and it made lots of things which have gone before worthwhile. Soon afterward we were moved down to the southern end of the island to help the army above Naha. I am now sitting on the side of a hill overlooking tiny terraced fields and the dark blue sea beyond. They are out there throwing 14 inchers over our heads into strong engaging positions. There is almost a constant artillery barge and the air is full of rocket throwing planes. It's a comfort to be on our side. We are waiting to move up to enter the battered city of Naka. I sure hope all the nice things haven't been ruined because I want to bring home some of them. I shouldn't tell you this yet because we will have a long wait but at Nago I found a silk scroll hand painted of the Emperor Meiji and his shrine. I am sending it to have it repaired at an art shop in L.A. and then on to you. It really is so nice and I hope it won't take too long.

Air raid siren blowing—must watch harder—no excitement I guess they didn't get thru this far.

I got your letter with the picture only yesterday. I was sure glad to see you. You look swell and your smile as nice as ever. I don't know why it took so long to get here but it was plenty welcome. I have been getting the clippings and always enjoy them. So far, outside of a few discomforts this whole thing has not been bad

*but 4 days without fresh food is a long time and I'm sure hungry
for steak, fruit, and vegetables. Sometime I'll send you one of our
K rations. They are good but it's pretty tough to live a week on
them. I am sending some of our ersatz orange juice and another
little gadget which we could not live without. It's a trick one
copied, I hear, from the Japs.*

*Over under a little tree two of the corpsmen are drawing and
comparing diagrams of their home towns to see which is the
smaller. Others are writing letters or reading or "shooting the
bull". Anything to keep busy. The waiting is the hardest part of
it all.*

*Well Margaret, I guess this about winds it up for now so for a
few days adios. I'll write as soon as I can a note tomorrow if we
don't move. Have a good time and write when you can. Give my
regards to your parents.*

Lovingly as ever, Charles.

How one stops in the middle of a letter, casually mentions an
air raid and then resumes writing was beyond comprehension to
Margaret. Reading between the lines you could almost see the
mental gymnastics Charles needed to go through just to make it
through a day. His writing had become choppy and disjointed.

Dear Charles,

*My heart is happy to hear from you. The silence coupled with
my imagination creates quite the anxiety, which I tend to try to
hide at work. With Germany out of the picture, we're prepping
to send everyone back east, and then I'll be out of a job, heading
back to school, and starting life again. Some day? Right?*

Can you even think of what might happen at the end of all of this? Where will you go? I need you to think of the good you will do back home and not of the air raid sirens. Find something to focus on that is not in that rice paddy.

I've been hesitant to send another book because I'm being a bit superstitious. Maybe, if there's nothing left for you to read, the war will simply end. My mother mentioned a trip out to Long Beach. While it's no Pacific Island, I would love to walk the beach with you and hear about everything you've done that didn't fit onto the small pages of a letter, or even worse, a v-mail. The ripples of a wave will be a welcome distraction from the ripples of tragedy and trauma that reached inland as far as western Nebraska.

Please stay safe.

Love - Margaret

Chapter Sixty-Five

O ne good indication that the war in Europe was ending was that mail was coming with less regularity as if the postal service overseas was ceasing to exist. She hadn't heard from Bob since his letter written the day after Dachau. She had worried that he had lost his will to live after the things that he'd seen. There were reports of families hearing that their sons and husbands had taken their own lives after some of the more harrowing liberations. The letter that arrived that day at her parents was the thickest one she'd ever received, and she hoped beyond hope that it would not be the manic ramblings of his last letter.

May 20, 1945 - Kitzbuhel Austria

Dearest Margaret -

Hi beautiful, how's everything in "dar ol' Gering" these days? Still the same peaceful little village that I once knew? Or have you turned it into a wild town? (Ha! Ha!)

Well kiddo, it has finally happened. "Fini la Guerre!" What a great day this is for all the boys over here! In a way we're happy, but it is restrained happiness, cause most of us are sweating out the China/Burma mess and the Pacific. Your apologies are accepted for your cruel statement and with a little luck, I may give you a chance to apologize in person before too long! How about it? Guess I just needed to see some pretty terrible stuff to get Margaret to soften up a bit.

No one knows just yet what will take place now but sure all feel that a few months back in the states will be given to us before we ship out again. I sure hope so. If we do get home on furlough how's about you dropping down to Omaha way for a few days, or to Lincoln? We could have a lot of fun and is sure what I can use right now. What do you say? There are a few more places to go where not everyone knows everything about everything and everyone.

I hear Milt and June finally called the whole thing off and went their respective ways. I hear from Milt occasionally and we've decided to go back to the States and start all over again. We are both free, and way over 21, so we've decided maybe some nice gal will close her eyes and say yes! (Ha! Ha!) (Hint! Hint!)

You know Megs, I sure wish you could see this country we are in right now. It is the most beautiful place you've ever seen. This little town of Kitzbuhel that I'm in now is a resort town, nestled right in the Alps, just 20 miles from the German border, and 22 miles from the Italian border. I guess they sent us here for some R&R. Our only orders were to wipe away the memories of the last few months with sleep, swimming, and some food that almost feels like we've made it home to our moms.

From my front porch, I can see snowcapped mountains, and waterfalls and just about a mile from here is a beautiful lake. A very nice place for a vacation. Wouldn't you like to join me?

I've spent the last three days doing nothing more than sleeping, eating, and sleeping some more.

I'm sitting here listening to my old favorite Bing Crosby sing an Oldie — "Cause I'm Too Romantic" — you know "I'm so afraid of love - cause I'm too romantic..." Ah yes, that's me! (Ha! Ha!) Hell, I've never given love a chance to hit me, so I wouldn't know! I guess I'll just have to wait until I hit the U.S. again. Right off hand, I don't know of anyone who is interested in marrying a "battle-worn" 1st Lt. though! Do you? Guess I'll just have to become a hero and maybe hook someone. Do you go for heroes or just an average guy who does his job and once in a while gets a commendation? Frankly, I'm of the opinion that I'd just as soon do my job and get home. If along the line I get a medal okay, if not, so what! But enough of this talk. Don't know how I even got on the subject.

Right now I'm sweating out the CBI. If I can get home first, okay, I won't mind too much. I hate to think of going straight over. Don't forget my invitation to you in case I do get home first.

Nothing more to carry on about right now. Think over my invitation, providing I get home, and let me hear from you. Keep the swell letters coming and I think I'll be able to do better from here on out. Nothing could be worse than that last letter I wrote—I must have sounded like a loon. I still feel a little loony but will keep the chin up and dance through it all like I do.

With love, Bob

It was better than she'd expected. He was still Bob. Margaret wondered what it was about each individual's personality that made one man see horrors for days and months on end and be able to return to relative normalcy in a matter of weeks or months while another has one truly horrible day and will have nightmares for the rest of his days until he ends his own life.

Maybe the difference was that Harold was sent straight from the front line to a prison stateside with the belief that being back in the U.S. was enough of a break to unsee everything he'd seen, and Bob was sent to a spa. She was happy to see that things had changed in the years since Harold left and that Bob and his fellow soldiers were being given time to recuperate.

There was a lot to unpack in his letter. With each line, she could see more of the old Bob Hale personality re-emerge. He had his false confidence and bravado back. The letters were the most direct he'd ever been with implying that he was interested in her as more than a friend. It wouldn't be fair to keep him on a string. It seemed that every soldier and all the single women she knew were looking to couple up the moment people got off the train.

Bea was right, she should cut it off at the pass so that they could remain friends in the future. Now that she knew the difference between passion and affection, she knew that she would never have the passion she deserved with Bob.

Dearest Bob,

Happy Victory Day. I'm sure you spent V-E Day kissing whatever willing women were in your vicinity. From the newsreels, it looks like a remarkable amount of smooching happened over there. (Ha!)

I spent the day organizing prisoner rolls to align with the newest requirements from the boys back east. I'd walked away from the job for a few weeks. (I'll tell you over drinks. It's a rough one.)

Turns out when the "German" prisoners are not all from Germany we've got to figure out whether we're sending them back to Poland, or Russia, or what part of Germany even, because Russia is being a little stubborn about how Germany is going to be split up. Some of the prisoners are lobbying to stay here. Sounds like things are going to be a lot harder there than the years they spent behind the wire here.

What a beautiful adventure it sounds like you've been on after mucking through Hades (which is what I'm taking to calling the French/German countryside when you're getting shot at). I have gone to the library to look up pictures of where you were in Switzerland and have decided you have landed in the most beautiful place on earth. Those Colorado Rockies have nothing on where you are. Once again, I vacillate between envy and relief. I want nothing more than to travel the world, but I think of what you, and your peers, have sacrificed. Definitely more than I ever could.

You and your battalion did some heroic things. How can things that are heroic and horrific be so connected? I don't know how it's decided that you've done enough heroic or seen enough horrific to be given a ticket home. The math of the military makes no sense to me.

And thank you for those (all of those) invitations. I think I know what you're asking and now that the war is ending, I think it's only fair to share that I think I'm going to stay "free and over 21" for a while longer. I'm heading back to Lincoln in the fall to pick up where I left off. (Haven't told Mother yet, so please don't tell Aunt Gladys.)

I was engaged right after the war kicked off. I think I nearly went down that path again in the middle, but it ended rather abruptly. And now I don't know when, or even if, that needs to be in my future. I guess what I'm saying is, yes to the drink, no to the longer-term things? I might be convinced to go on one of the old-fashioned picnics of our youth. That way I can always be yours in friendship, but our tempers need never fire each other up again.

Now, who sounds like the loon?

With love and affection ~ M

Chapter Sixty-Six

B ob wasted no time in responding via V-mail, so it arrived within a matter of days, instead of weeks.

June 6, 1945 - Thérèse, Austria

Dear Megs!

Hiya sweets! How's the "light of my life?" Fresh, aren't I? Ah well, you have to be bold to get what you want, and so, I'm bold with you. Now, <u>you</u> can figure that one out. A salesmanship class I took once said you have to ask for the sale and be prepared to get told "no" five times before you can close the deal. Guess you've only officially said "no" directly in one letter so I'll keep trying. Maybe if I ask using one of these damned V-mails? You can use your magnifying glass to decipher my scribbles.

Yes, honey, the Rainbow Division did do pretty well over here and someday will do the same in the CBI. I only hope we can bring the boys home for a short time before we go though. Have you made up your mind about my invitation yet? I know you must think I'm taking a lot for granted, and maybe I am, but at least I admit some. (Ha! Ha!) Now, how about it, will you come to see me? (That Bob Hale, he's nothing if not persistent.)

As far as the rotation plan is concerned, I still have several months to go. The point system may not apply to officers, but in case it does, here is my scorebook: 25 months active service (25 points); six months overseas (6 points); two campaign stars (10 points); and that totals 41 points. I've been recommended for the Bronze star and if that goes through I'll get five more points (Total 46). Not very many, is it? (Ha! Ha!) (Guess there are no points for liberating a prison full of walking, talking skeletons, or train cars and trenches full of corpses.) Ah well, I always did want to see China!

On V.E. day I was making a 540-mile trip after replacements for the Regiment. I did my little bit of celebrating the next night. About all we did was have all the company officers together and drink a couple of bottles of Champagne. (German stuff of course.) There was no wild celebrating cause everyone's thoughts turned toward the Pacific. So, no smooching here. I'm saving that for an all-American girl.

The picnic sounds wonderful honey, and if you'll accept my invitation, I promise we'll take in one whole day of swimming, eating, fishing, or whatever your little heart desires. Okay? Gotta run now "toots"! Be good, write soon, and keep punching.

Always love, Bob.

Margaret shared the last letter with Bea and asked for advice on how to respond.

"I was very clear in my last letter to him. We will simply be friends. I cannot have him coming home with the expectation that we could be anything more."

"Are you sure? Maybe you should take him up on that drink in Lincoln and just see where things go?"

"I truly hope that when I'm back in Lincoln I can focus on school without putting on an act for everyone that I'm more interested in men than my studies. I want a fresh start."

"If you want fresh, Bob's probably your guy. He's not holding back on that innuendo. Could be a fun, forget-about-Burke kind of weekend?" Bea waggled her eyebrows at her.

"My goodness Bea, you're sounding more and more like June every day. Could this have anything to do with the fact that you won the argument and Ted is going to be home in July, for good?"

"I suppose that could be part of it." Bea's smile as she, obviously, was going through quite the show in her mind, was somehow lascivious. "I wondered if having him gone for so long would make me forget about how much I love everything about him, but nope. I cannot wait for that man to step off the train."

Margaret chuckled. "I don't even want the details of what just went through your mind. That is definitely not my plan. Maybe I'll try a new tactic and stop writing back to Bob. That will teach him."

"What do you hear from Charles? Because I'm still holding out romantic hope that someone in all these men will capture your heart, your mind, and…" She raised an eyebrow again. "The ink you've wasted on men!"

"Think of all of the practice I've had writing! It's like I never left the paper."

It seemed somewhat inappropriate to be joking about other men after Burke's death, but she was not engaged to him; she was not a widow. He would forever cloud the memory of her time at the prison camp, but also, she occasionally found herself smiling through the tears when she thought of him and their brief affair.

Chapter Sixty-Seven

B̲ob obviously didn't let any time pass between writing a
letter and the v-mail, but the letter arrived a few weeks
later.

June 8, 1945 - Worgl, Austria
Dearest Margaret ---
Hi beautiful! How's my "dream girl" making out these days?
Still working hard, or have the PW's all gone home and left you
by yourself? I sure hope so anyway. I envy those guys no end.
Here I am, six thousand miles from home, and they are right
there with you. It just isn't fair.
Remember the picnic I asked you to go on? Well, it was im-
possible to have you, but the Capt. and I went on a hike and
a swimming picnic the other day. Course it was not like those
we use to have back in the states. How could it be without any
beautiful companions? Don't worry, we'll get our chance when
I come home, and you come down to see me. (How about it?)
We are not moving around as often now, but we never stay
in one place too long. This is a beautiful country over here and
has several lakes for swimming. I would like very much to come
back here on a visit someday. I'm getting a very nice tan and feel

better than I have for months. I'm down to around 180 lbs, now, which is less than I weighed at the University.

Nothing would give me more pleasure right now than to be able to take you shopping. In fact, I'd like to buy a lot of <u>civilian</u> clothes myself. Tommy Tucker and his orchestra sure would hit the spot over here, especially if there were some good American girls to dance with.

You and I can plan on a lot of dancing if and when I do get back, and if you do come down to see me. The important thing is will you come down to see me? I feel pretty sure that we will get home before going to the Pacific.

It is too bad they can't arrange for the sweethearts and wives of soldiers over here to visit. I think I should introduce a bill into Congress to that effect. How would you like a trip to Austria? (Ha! Ha!)

Speaking of pictures, which we weren't, but is as good a subject as any, how about sending me some more of those snaps of your lovely face? You know, you are pretty darn good-looking yourself, and very easy to look at. All joking aside though, you are <u>extremely</u> good-looking, and I would like some more pictures of you. Think you can take care of the matter for me?

There is really very little to write about, and I'm surprised that I could fill this much space, but I do try and write you at least twice a week, if not more. It will take a few days before they all start arriving, but I am writing them. I love to hear from you and am looking forward to really seeing you in person again.

Well, honey, that is about all for now. I'm getting a little sleepy now, and I want to write to my folks. Keep up the good work on the letters, and I'll do the same. Be sweet and write soon.

Always love, Bob.

The silent treatment wasn't going to work with Bob. Never did, never would.

Robert,

I'm curious. Did my message get lost in the mail? Or in translation? I guess I'm going to have to tell it to your face since you can't read (between the lines at least). So sure, I'm happy to come to Austria. Let me know what time the plane takes off.

Since we're just friends, there's no harm in sending photos. Of my dog. (Ha!)

Your dear <u>friend</u> — Margaret

Like it or not, they would always have banter in their communication, and she would always be happy to see his name on an envelope.

Chapter Sixty-Eight

I f people ever thought things could move quickly in the military, they would be sadly mistaken. Each day the discussion of the how, the when, and the where of the transfer of German prisoners out of the camp seemed to include new ideas, new processes, and new rules.

"It's like they're slow-playing things just to keep farm labor here for the summer." Margaret was suspect of the delays.

Bea's family benefited from the additional hands on their family farm. "Since our boys aren't back yet, we still need the help."

"Our boys aren't, most of them, prisoners. And the ones who survived being prisoners in those torture camps have been sent stateside for medical care." Margaret felt there had to be a better solution. Who would listen to a former Quartermaster assistant who is now a paper-pushing file clerk?

As the prisoners were preparing to leave, many of them were making gifts for the girls, some that even rivaled Rudi's dogs. There was a ship inside of a vinegar bottle made of matchsticks, string, and paper. Somehow the bottom was painted to look like the sea. There were portraits carved out of soap. Margaret was gifted a hand-carved letter opener. Many tried their hand at writing in English. So many of them longed to stay back in America.

Margaret was only working part-time, and, since the Feds couldn't figure out when everyone was leaving, she was given the afternoon off. She spent it catching up on the reading she knew she'd missed out on in her years away from school and writing to June and Charles. Life was starting to feel almost hopeful, a hope that felt tenuous. She was due to have dinner with her parents that night and planned to break the news that she'd be leaving in a few short weeks, right after Bea's wedding.

June,

For all that I know you are on a boat somewhere in the middle of the ocean and will get this when you arrive here in July. What good is the airfield just outside of town if it can't fly the future Dr. June Roth here to keep me company at the dinner I'm about to go to with my parents?

My resolve is firm, my countenance is strong, and you and I will be getting on that train on August 21st and heading back to school. I've spoken to the house mother (who sounds like just as much of a delight as ours from all those years ago!) and she has confirmed we will have a room together. I'm planning to cram as many classes in per quarter and stay through next summer so that I can make up for that lost time in 1942.

I picked up your dress for the wedding, and it's hanging in my closet with mine. Bea's wedding dress is in the middle. They are perfect. Untouched by war, straight out of the pages of a magazine. I don't want the middle one at all for quite some time.

Is that terrible? I think you might be the only person on this planet that truly understands ambition. You are my idol, my North Star, and the reason I know that I can make it through this dinner without throwing a slice of ham at Mother's head.

Counting the days. ~M

⎯⎯*ele*⎯⎯

Dinner that evening was, indeed, ham. Margaret liked to think it was the universe's way of sending June's strength to her.

"What are you hearing from your friends now that things are done in Europe?" Franklin liked having a personal connection to people on the front lines, and Margaret was sure that many mornings at the bank Franklin shared stories of her friends over a cup of coffee. He would have loved having the first-person connection to the war if she was in the press corps, but this was a good, close, second.

Margaret decided she'd skip right over Bob and dig into the conflict.

"June should be on her way home now, somewhere in the Atlantic on a ship tending to the sick and injured as they bring them back home and try to get them to hospitals near their families. She is hoping to get them settled in Omaha and then head back in time for Bea's wedding before she heads to med school in the fall."

"Oh, she's going straight back? Not spending any time here with her poor mother?" Rebecca would still have found something wrong if that had, indeed, been June's plan. "Isn't she still seeing that nice boy Milt from your class?"

"Mother, it's not all about boys and family for her. Or, since it's going to come up anyway, me. I am going back with her. The Dean of the college has confirmed my admission, the editor of the paper has confirmed I have a place on the staff, and I've already confirmed that June and I will be sharing a room at the sorority house." She realized that she had said that entire thought in one breath. "I have plenty of money to finish out school and am hopeful that you will not put up a fight."

Franklin looked at Rebecca with the shared glance that married couples seem to have that was somehow a full conversation complete with a fight and a resolution all in one moment.

"Your mother and I are thrilled that you're going back. And we are happy to pick up paying where we left off."

Chapter Sixty-Nine

The letter that arrived from Charles was in a larger envelope than normal and had a large circle of silk material with strings attached. The screen that he mentioned several letters back had arrived at her parents, but it wasn't just a simple small piece of silk. It was a package with four large grey silk panels with embroidered flowers and birds on the front attached to a rougher linen material on the back that, when pieced together, was a painting of Mount Fuji. She decided that it was too delicate to take back to school with her and she would leave it with her parents for safekeeping.

June 9, 1945, Okinawa

Dearest Margaret:

Just a few lines to say I'm fine. I've neglected you but for a good cause. I think I'm doing a good job but there are so darned many working to the opposite that I often feel a little bitter about the whole business.

I'm in Naka now and it's a mess. Just a mass of red tile rubble but it is a reasonably safe spot now. Margaret, read Time for May 18th— it is the whole story up to that time. My outfit, my new outfit, that is, took that Sugarloaf Hill and held it. I am now a Battalion Surgeon and have about 1000 men under my care. Right now, they need lots of it. I'm tired and much thinner. I hate this canned chow, but I feel fine and I'm glad I'm here where I'm able to help. I like my new duty better than the old.

It looks like it's about over here. We may have to go further for another tangle but there is a good chance we won't. This 6th Division has done a heroic job and it makes you proud to be a part of it, but we are tired and have lost so many friends. When I can give you some figures you will be deeply shocked at the cost. Our Battalion, in a spirited attack, drove the Japs from the last high ground on the Okinawa peninsula four days ago. The boys sure looked good going up that last hill. There are still caves to be blown shut because the little devils won't come out. We have sealed hundreds in these caves where they lived. I went into one which they had vacated.

There were accommodations for 100-175 men and food storage all under a hill. The rooms were large and connected by passageways, some of them had wooden decks. They had electricity but it was out when we got there. I did find a flag but nothing else. There were dozens of blankets, but they were so full of fleas I could not bring myself to carry them.

We are camped now where we stopped after our last push. My sick bay is in a ruined brewery on the west side of the Naka estuary. We have a good setup but no roof, so we hope it won't rain. A few yards away a water pipe comes out of the hill and from dawn till dusk the boys are crowded under it washing themselves. Water is a luxury. The other nite we killed a Jap a few feet from shower and each day we find a few nearby, many are surrendering.

We had fresh beef and apples yesterday and this morning fresh eggs. The second time in 80 days. This afternoon the cooks rigged up stoves and are making doughnuts. They are swell. I've eaten about 10. I'll have to watch out or I'll gain back that weight.

I am enclosing a chute from a flare. Thousands are used to illuminate the front lines at nite, They have saved hundreds of lives. Maybe you can use it for a head kerchief or something. You'll have to forgive the postage due. I'm out of stamps. I must close now. No ink.

Lovingly, Charles.

P.S. Using the last of my ink, and my courage, to ask for a photo. Do you have one I might have? The only one I have of you is that snap at the POW camp.

Margaret had wandered up the street to the bakery to get a donut and a cup of coffee to enjoy in solidarity with Charles as she drafted a response.

Charles,

Doughnuts and fireworks. Almost as good as pineapple trees and orchids? Thank you for the parachute. I have put it over a lamp in my reading corner. What a journey it, and you, have been on these last few weeks. We get cursory updates in the news. None of it sounds good but I don't need to tell you. I have read the Time magazine article about Sugarloaf. War is breathtaking in its brutality, and I cannot imagine how much death you saw and also know that you saved so many lives.

On a lighter note, Bea—I've mentioned her—is getting married in a few weeks, and the week after I'm heading back to

Lincoln. All this writing to you, talking of books, and your encouragement for my writing has inspired me.

I will always cherish the advice you gave me that day at the train station. Without you listening as I unburdened myself of the grief for Sam that I'd been carrying I would not have had the courage to call off my engagement the very next day. So, thank you. When you are home let's plan for a visit that's not cut short by the conductor shouting "All Aboard!"

I've sent some stamps, a book, and a photo. For all of my superstitions, I cannot seem to speed up the U.S. Military machine, so I guess our book club is still on.

With love ~ Margaret

She hoped that Charles would remain in her life for some time, but she knew that he would come home having seen more horrors than Harold ever did, and she was not the woman who could navigate his recovery.

Chapter Seventy

The end of July rolled around, and it sounded like Bob might make it home for Bea's wedding. He must have finally gotten the message that she was a friend first and only because that information came to her through the bridge club grapevine.

She was prepping for a busy month: wrapping up work, anticipating Bea's wedding, and getting things ready for the trip across the state back to school. She was brainstorming ideas for her goodbye article when the post arrived and another letter from Charles arrived. This was the first one in a Red Cross envelope and she was worried he was writing from a sick bay somewhere as a patient instead of a doctor. It had taken almost a month to arrive.

June 30, 1945 - Okinawa Japan (Red Cross Stationery)
Dearest Margaret,
The war on Okinawa is all over. This is the 91st day since we landed on Easter Sunday. I have been almost everywhere on the island. For three days now we have been "resting". In the Marine Corps this means only that we are not being fired upon and for the first time in over 100 days are eating from plates and mess

gear instead of tin cans. We do have showers and over the next hill is a movie so it's not so bad.

Our camp is on a hill in the midst of the last battlefield on Oroku peninsula overlooking the village of Oroku. The hill lies in a deep bowl surrounded by a high ridge and the lowland is green and fresh. Over on the right is Naha harbor. Behind me is ruined Shuri and costly Sugar Loaf Hill. The weather is ideal much like it is there and the sunsets are beautiful even surpassing those over Scotts Bluff. I'd rather see one of yours though. The countryside still shows the effects of battle. Most of the trees are burned and bare and the fields are littered with bulging fuel drums. It must have been a lovely place before the fracas.

After we secured the northern end, I came to MD on the 29th as Battalion Surgeon and the fun really started. Our first assignment was "Sugar Loaf Hill" an ugly pile of rubble already won and lost 4 times. For 2 ½ days our men fought like maniacs and scored a decisive victory taking positions which broke the back of the enemy lines making further progress down the island possible. We were then withdrawn and sat in the mud until time for the amphibious operation on Orokee peninsula.

That was a lulu. It was raining and we were cold and miserable and the mortar and artillery fire, almost as devastating as Sugar Loaf. We gradually moved to a place just across the estuary from Naha. From this spot we cleaned up the peninsula. I last wrote from there, the ruined brewery. You remember. A few days later we were assigned to a zone of action way down south. It turned out to be the cheapest phase of the operation estimated in human lives, that is.

Right now, I am sitting under a tent fly looking south across the ocean on my right is the East China Sea. In between are a few hundred yards of brush and trees burned brown by flame throwing tanks. There are still scattered Nips about, but they have not caused any serious trouble lately. Our patrols get a few every day. We killed 2 within a few yards of our aid station a few nites ago.

Some time I'll be able to fill in all the details and hope by then some of the bitter taste will have left the words. I have seen so much suffering and bravery, such fear and horror that I am as ready as anyone for a change. We have had no rain since we left Oroku but it is very warm for Okinawa. The 6th Division has done a wonderful job. We have taken 80% of the island and we are one of 6 divisions who fought here, but we paid the price.

We went into combat with 996 men and during the campaign 894 of them were evacuated as combat casualties. Not stomachaches but wounds. This included about one half of 150 dead. We had almost 100% replacements. Four of my 35 corpsmen killed and 22 wounded. Our division had over 14,000 casualties out of the 22,000 men. We, the 6th Division, took 80% of Okinawa but it was a high price we paid. People are wonderful though and most of the "scars" are pretty well covered up now. It's lucky we can forget. I'm surprised that one forgets or begins to forget so soon. Thank God it's over. I'd like to tell you lots of things but they'd sound a little heroic on paper so they will have to wait too.

Nine of my corpsmen are being decorated for conspicuous heroism. One Navy cross posthumously, two silver stars, and the rest bronze stars and commendations. All the others will receive the purple heart for wounds. Only 6 escaped without a scratch.

It looks like Denver will be crowded with our friends. As far as I'm concerned, it's the best place there is to live. I guess I have not told you that I have practically made up my mind about my specialty. I am going to go into neurology and neuropsychiatry. I can finish my training in about 3 years and make a little money to boot. I want to spend two years on the east coast probably Boston and the last in Denver. Denver can use a good psychiatrist. I am convinced that it is in this field of medicine that the greatest advances are to be made and I like it very much. There are so darn many people who have no actual disease but who still needs care and help. General Practitioners do not have the inclination nor the ability to take care of them. What do you think of it?

There are about eight characters offering suggestions as to what I should say in this letter, so it probably won't sound very smart. They saw your photo and have quite a bit of advice on what I should say. My apologies. None of what they're saying is fit to print.

We are hoping to leave here almost any time. The orders can't come too soon to suit us.

Sunday, I had to stand a watch this morning, so I missed church. For dinner we had canned meat stew, canned tomatoes, and beans. Yesterday one of the boys visited the Army's 96th and they were eating fried chicken and ice cream. We in the corps seem to get the short end. I am airing the musty smell out of my khakis in anticipation of some more comfortable day. We may even have them pressed a little later.

My C.O., who was quite subdued in combat, has begun to show his real self more and it was much better hidden. What a stinker he is, about 5'5" and as small as that in every respect. Our food is as a rule dull and monotonous. We have had Vienna sausages twice a day for the past 4 days and once each day for the 12 preceding days. The weather is unspeakably hot and damp, even the nites are warm and the red dust gets everywhere. Sing me not songs of a tropical isle I'll have the west if you please.

The book came yesterday and I'm going to start it tonight. Thank you so much for it and for taking the trouble to find it. I just finished "The World the Flesh and Father Smith", quite good, nothing extra.

Margaret the mail now is ready to shove off, so I'll close and write again very soon. Write when you can.

Lovingly, Charles.

Margaret was so grateful to read that her friend was going to take up the mantle of psychiatry. Maybe he could fix the issue from the inside with mental health and veterans. It seemed impossible that this was a new field. He seemed to have calmed his own mind with the plan in place to help calm others. Some of the articles she'd read about psychological trauma seemed to indicate that you would have to experience it yourself in order to treat it. That was Charles, through and through, finding a way to care for people even when he was struggling. She wished she could go back in time and wipe away all the things that boy at the train station would go on to see but hoped that all he saw would serve the purpose of helping others through their own trauma.

She had not told him about Harold's suicide. Maybe she would once he was stateside and they could see each other in person. If that ever was going to happen. It seemed like a conversation that needed to happen face-to-face, and she decided to leave it to fate. He'd seen and heard about enough death.

Dear Charles,

I'm so glad you're done. You're the last of my friends to close out their battles. I hope that means that you're headed back to the States soon to start the much-needed neuropsychiatry training that, in my opinion, every single soldier needs (and, if I'm honest...all of us.)

I wish I could send you real food, real showers, and a plane to bring you straight back to everyone who misses you here.

I hope to see you when you return. Maybe I'll plan a Long Beach trip for spring break.

May your final days of wartime be as peaceful as the Nebraska sunset I'm currently watching.

Love, your friend,

Margaret

Chapter Seventy-One

August 7, 1945

The entire front page of the paper screamed "U.S . DROPS ATOMIC BOMB," yet Japan refused to surrender. Margaret was heading to her parents for dinner that evening and to listen to the Truman address.

"We are now prepared to obliterate more rapidly and completely every productive enterprise the Japanese have above ground in any city. We shall destroy their docks, their factories, and their communications. Let there be no mistake; we shall completely destroy Japan's power to make war."

"Dad, how many civilians do you think they killed? The entire city just disappeared." Margaret envisioned a black hole in the planet where a bomb that was said to be the equivalent of 20,000 tons of TNT had been dropped from the sky. "I just heard from Charles, and he said they were leaving Okinawa for the final push."

"And you're sure you want to move back to a big city? Lord knows they might retaliate." He mother was fretting again. The reprieve had been short-lived.

"Rebecca, dear, I highly doubt that Lincoln, Nebraska, is on the Japanese target list. And, as Truman said, we have more and will just keep dropping them until there is no island left."

"Is that the right thing to do?" Margaret was uncomfortable with the idea of annihilating an entire island.

"Hopefully their leaders will come to their senses. As Truman said, we will win this war at whatever cost." He shook the paper to indicate that he was done talking for the evening.

"I guess I'm just happy it didn't happen next week on Bea's big day. How are those plans going? I should out to Bea's mom to see if she has all of the details under control. I had quite the list from your wedding that never happened. It might come in handy."

Margaret noticed her mother's restraint and appreciated that she did not use this opportunity to try and keep her home or get her married off. She rewarded her with some talk of wedding plans. "We're grateful that Ted had his points to come home. Milt is still going to be his best man even though he and June aren't together, and his friend Tim is due to stand with him as well, just to balance out the photo. That is, if the trains all show up on time."

"When does June arrive?"

"She's due in town on the same train and will stay with Bea and me while we attend the litany of bridal showers for Bea and every other soon-to-be-betrothed woman of this county. Our last day at the camp is tomorrow. June won't make the shower that the personnel office is throwing. Lucky girl. Anyhow, who knows how long until the last prisoner leaves, but I know I'm free."

Franklin lowered the paper, "Margaret, your mother and I are both proud of the work you did here. We know you didn't want to come home, and we're grateful that you did. We're not just proud of the work you did at the prison but the writing you did for the paper, too."

Margaret grinned. Franklin retreated behind his paper again.

Chapter Seventy-Two

August 8, 1945

The officers' mess hall was filled with crepe paper streamers and a few balloons. One of the prisoners who worked in the bakery turned out to be a pastry chef who was conscripted from Poland. Each of the women in the typing pool had used a portion of their sugar rations, and the head of the food service department threw in the rest to make a stunning cake.

Bea had taken to wearing as much white as possible to let everyone know that she was the bride-to-be. Margaret just sat back and smiled at her friend. Some women were absolutely made to be wives. Bea was one of those women.

There was very little war talk. The surreal nature of existing on a planet where atomic bombs can fall from the sky just days before you eat the lightest, fluffiest cake baked by a Polish prisoner of war was beyond explanation. Since the bombing couldn't be controlled, they might as well just enjoy the cake.

On the way out to their car with their boxes of things, having cleaned their desks out for the last time, Margaret noticed Rudi standing towards the back of the room with a small box in his hand.

"Just one second, Bea. I'll be right out." She crossed the mess hall. Rules had started to become a little more relaxed now that things were winding down.

"Margaret. I have one more hound for you." His English, though thick with a German accent, had improved greatly.

"Thank you. I have all of them on my bookshelves. They are beautiful. Should I open it here or at my house?" She was hopeful he understood.

"Your house is good." He nodded his head, almost in a slight bow, turned, and walked away.

What a difficult way to say goodbye to someone who she didn't know at all but who gave her the only physical reminders she had of the time she spent at the camp. Her longest conversation with him was when he handed her the milk when she broke Burke's cup. So much had happened since then.

She didn't wait until she got home but opened the small box in the car. In it was a perfectly carved rendition of Spike from the photo on her desk and a note folded into a tiny square so that it fit into the lid of the box.

Dear cousin Margaret,

At first, please excuse my poor English and try to understand my letter, for I wish to study this language.

Although I had something like a practice where I worked, I couldn't prove all of my English knowledges and for that reason would you mind pardoning me of my mistakes? I should like to ask you politely whether you might fulfill my desire. But it isn't my intention to get you in any unpleasantness.

Now another thing, can you remember when I handed over to you a bottle of milk? It was in our childhood. Now we are grown up and each of us lives in a different situation. That's my only memory which as I dare say is very unreliable.

For today I won't bother you any longer and wish you all the luck of the world.

May you be happy.

Your cousin, Rudi Stahl

"I'm going to miss this place." Bea had tears in her eyes. "Who misses a prison?"

"Makes sense to me. We felt like we were part of something here. We spent three years of our lives here. We're only 23 years old. We arrived as children, and now, at least one of us is almost an old married lady."

"It's not too late! We'll just grab the first soldier off the train and make him put on a suit."

"Oh Bea, you are worse than my mother."

With that, they drove through the gate for the last time.

Chapter Seventy-Three

August 10, 1945

Margaret was up early and went to get the paper to read it and hide it before Bea was awake. The news reports last night were all focused on the attack on Nagasaki. Margaret had gone and listened to the news in her car to protect Bea. Headlines like SECOND BOMB DROPS on the week of her wedding were giving Bea a case of the nerves. She was sure that Ted was going to be called back in a moment and she would never walk down the aisle.

Margaret was sure that Japan would surrender before June arrived that afternoon and they would add that to their list of things to celebrate. She was due to come in on the train with Ted, Milt, and Ted's friend Tim. Even though Milt and June had called it quits they had remained on friendly terms and the six of them were due to go to dinner that evening.

Her final column was in the paper, just a short goodbye, for now. She had already discussed the idea of mailing Jack a column weekly covering the university goings on.

It's Time to Go — Margaret Murphy, Gering Courier

If you had told this naïve young woman that when she headed off for her sophomore year of school at NU in 1941, that she would receive something more valuable than a degree in four years she would have thought you believed that she would be one of the many that were pressured to get their M.R.S. degree.

I nearly was one of those women that changed from a Miss to a Mrs. at the start of this war. That was what was expected of me and, what was expected of so many of us, men and women alike. The number of engagements in the winter of 1941 after Pearl Harbor was astounding. The number of bridal showers here in the summer of 1945 leaves those numbers in the dust. I imagine the baby showers in the next couple of years will be astronomical.

For this writer, it took going to prison to discover what was true and interesting and to realize that societal expectations might not be a fit for everyone. I think as a country we have all been through a trauma that we don't fully understand yet, and I worry that our generation will be one that just moves on and picks up on the marriage-and-family train right where we left off on that fateful day in December of 1941. I hope that we will take some time to reflect on all that we have gone through, even those of us stateside before we dive back into the way it always was.

Please indulge me this one last time as I reflect on just a few things I've learned during this war.

Love is somehow felt even deeper after death. The best re-minder that you're not in charge is the feeling of anxiety. Nothing is as heartwarming as a letter from a friend. Heroism and honor are not forcefields against trauma. Small communities provide incredible support. Life is nothing without friendship.

I must close this column with a thank you or two. Thank you to my parents who recognized that home might just have been the absolute right place to be for the war (though I did not want to be here, and I'm thrilled to go back to school). Thank you to Jack Ellison for giving me the room to continue writing. Thank you to the Army for hiring me as a Government Girl, I learned more behind the walls of a prison than I ever could have in a lecture hall, and I hope to tell these stories for years to come. Thank you to my dearest friends, Bea and June, for providing the love and humor that we've all needed to survive. To my pen pals Bob and Charles: I'm glad you survived this war. To Burke, I wish you could have.

Chapter Seventy-Four

A s the train pulled in, Bea and Margaret instinctively put their arms around each other.

"It seems like just yesterday, or ten years ago, that we were getting off this train after Japan bombed us. Seems appropriate that we bookend us bombing them with another train station." Margaret knew that once Ted stepped off that train that Bea was going to be, for all intents and purposes, married and out of her day-to-day life. "Let's go get your man."

Bea saw Ted step off the train three cars down and took off running. She zipped right past June, who had exited the train alongside the largest man Margaret had ever seen. Bea jumped into Ted's arms, and they entertained themselves while Margaret helped with the luggage.

"Since Ted's mouth is currently engaged," June smirked. "I will take the honor of introducing the man that will be walking down the aisle with me, Ted's friend from basic training and beyond, Timothy Theisen."

"You can call me Tiny." His voice was barely discernible over the noise of the train engines. Tiny was a monolith of a human who looked like a linebacker for a football team and had the quietest voice that she'd ever heard from a man.

"Tiny, it's a pleasure, I'm Margaret. June, where's Milt? Did you guys fight, and he got kicked off at North Platte?"

"He didn't make it to Omaha. He telegraphed that his discharge paperwork was held up somewhere, and it's not likely he'll be home in time."

"Let's let Ted break that news to her." She looked back at the couple that had not stopped embracing. "He'll probably come up for air sometime. I'm parked around the corner. Tiny, you look like you don't need help, but holler if you do." Tiny picked up the travel trunk with Ted's belongings, stacked the suitcases on top of it, and followed the girls to the car.

The wedding festivities were due to kick off the next day with the rehearsal, and Margaret, Bea, and June were spending a final night together as single women. Japan had surrendered a couple of days prior, and everything, barring the loss of a best man, was going off without a hitch.

"Now, who exactly am I going to be walking down the aisle with tomorrow?" There had been talk of swapping Tiny for the best man role and for he and Margaret to walk down the aisle, but June and Tiny had vetoed it. They had become friends and decided Margaret could walk next to a stranger. Besides, they wanted to see the look on the stranger's face when he saw Margaret, who deserved magazine covers but preferred bylines, on his arm. There were threats that Bob was going to make it home, but his discharge was delayed which was fine with

Margaret. The two of them walking down the aisle would give local folks something to wag their tongues about.

"My cousin Alice lives with her friend Sue in Cheyenne." Bea was grateful they found someone, she really didn't care who. "Sue grew up in Minatare, and Sue's brother was due to pass through town on his way home, so I sent Ted and Tiny to go pick him up. He was training to be a pilot in Florida but never got deployed, and with that second bomb drop, they just sent them all home. He's traveling with a uniform, so he'll do as well as anything."

"Imagine that something happened quickly in the military." Margaret was intimately aware of governmental inefficiency.

June interjected, "So, what's his name?"

"Bill something or other. He was a year behind us in school. I doubt you even know who he is. Not a lot of Minatare and Gering overlap. Those farm boys kept their distance."

"Let me get this straight: it's going to be your two best friends, a giant and a farmhand walking down the aisle. Your photos will be incredible." Margaret could just picture some country bumpkin next to her as they walked down the aisle.

June leaned into Bea. "What she means to say is that no one is going to look at any of us. We could have put a cardboard cutout of a scarecrow next to Margaret and everyone would still be staring at you. You're going to be the most beautiful bride, Bea." Bea leaned back into June. There was so little time left before their lives went in different directions once again.

Margaret felt nostalgic for the simpler times. "I've written a little something for you, well, for us, really since this is our last night with just the three of us." She handed them each a piece of paper with a typed missive. She knew if she read it aloud, she would lose her carefully curated composure so she didn't even try.

We are from a place where people are friends from kindergarten until old age. We are from a part of the country full of tumbleweeds, hills of sand with no ocean in sight, howling winds, tornadoes, and backyard gardens with tomatoes so juicy your mouth waters just to think of them. We are from somewhere where people who have never traveled beyond the county line will give you advice about who you can and cannot be.

We left this place together during a time of peace, of possibility, and with complete ignorance of what was to come. We have spent the infancy of our adulthood in service to a machine that is powered by conflict. We have survived that conflict by drawing not from our own individual fortitude but from the strength that only an unyielding, uncompromising friendship can allow.

We are now from a time of victory, of perseverance, of survival, and yes, of grief. For the rest of our lives, we will know that anything that is handed down to us, be it opportunity or strife, can be handled with each other by our sides. You, dear friends, are the loves of my life. May we celebrate it all—forever.

Handwritten at the bottom of Bea's page:

To my dearest Bea, I send you off into the adventure of marriage knowing that you will make the kindest wife and, someday, the most incredible mother, and that, potentially, years down the road, I might join you on that journey. Thank you for being my stalwart companion during our days back home behind the wire fence of Camp Scottsbluff. Because you were here, I never wrote to you to tell you just how much you mean to me and have for my whole life. I should have told you daily. I could not have survived these last months without you. It is because of you that I believe in the future possibility of love that might one day be as strong as the love I have for you and June. My heart, forever. ~ Margaret

At the bottom of June's page:

Here we go again. ~ M.

The End.

1. Staff, Editorial, ed. "No Thanks AFC." The Daily Nebraskan. December 4, 1941.

2. Radio Address, December 7, 1941 (Attack on Pearl Harbor): Eleanor Roosevelt Papers Project: The George Washington University https://erpapers.columbian.gwu.edu/radio-address-december-7-1941-attack-pearl-harbor

3. Higgins, Marguerite. "The Liberation of Dachau." New York Herald Tribune, May 1, 1945.

Acknowledgments

Without the collective support of my family and friends, I would not have been able to stay motivated for five years to keep trudging along on this project.

To my kids: real, fake, and step, who continue to be incredible supporters and who keep encouraging me to spend this empty nesting time creating new chapters that are focused on me.

To my parents: thanks for helping pay for my English Degree and continuing to make sure I have a safety net during the chaos.

To my friends and first readers: Paige, Anne, Elizabeth, Jana, and Jennifer, your feedback after the first draft helped me hone in on a story that I'm proud of.

To all of the friends that form my cheering section and have encouraged me to write a book for years.

To Katie Bradshaw and Kevin Brich who stepped in and provided editing services.

Thank you.

In the event that acknowledgments can be read on different planes of existence:

To my Grandmother: without your adventures (that you never talked about, but still tucked away in storage for someone to find) I wouldn't have discovered the inspiration for this story. I ask for grace for all the details I made up. I wish I could hear the real story.

To her friends: I wish I knew more about you.

To all the men that wrote the letters: Thank you for your service and for your frequent letters to that beautiful girl in western Nebraska.

To my Grandpa: Though you never knew why she picked you this project left no doubt in my mind on exactly why that was.

And, to my late husband: Though you were at times an absolute handful and a distraction, you encouraged me to sign up for classes and listened to all of the versions of the story as I was in the idea phase. Your time in the military influenced my trauma research and your death inspired me to grab life by the damn horns.

I wish you all could have lived to see my name on the cover of a book.

About Author

For over twenty years I've been a frequent blogger on life, love, and mental health.

Born and raised in Gering, Nebraska I grew up just a few blocks from my grandparents. I attended college at the University of Wyoming where I, initially, majored in education. When I realized I could race through in order to marry my college boyfriend I changed my major to English Lit. We moved to Denver, had two children in rapid succession, got divorced young, and I found myself as a single mom working running a work/life balance consulting firm, teaching piano, and eventually becoming a real estate agent.

Throughout that time I blogged about motherhood (getamom.blogspot.com) and then my adventures in single-mom dating (selfinflictedblinddating.blogspot.com). Friends kept telling me to write a book.

I remarried in 2013 to a military veteran with severe PTSD and addiction issues. In 2016 he had a breakdown, disappeared and, when he returned, went to rehab. This is only important because it caused me to work to develop hobbies outside of him, my career, or my children. When my youngest left for college in 2017 I took my first creative writing class.

On an empty-nester journey to visit my parents, and my elderly grandfather, I went through some of my late grandmother's things and discovered a packet of letters written to her from multiple men, none of which were my grandfather. In reading through the letters, I could feel the love each of these men had for that beautiful young woman but could also recognize their struggles with trauma, as I was married to a deeply damaged veteran. There was also one journal entry, in her handwriting, entitled *Behind the Wire*, which inspired me to start researching prisoner of war camps, WWII battles that these men were involved in, and developing a timeline for a historical fiction book based on these letters. I had no idea there were around 700 POW camps in the US during WWII housing German prisoners before starting this research.

I wrote, intermittently, until 2020 when I lost every bit of creativity in the pandemic. The novel, at 50,000 words, got put on the shelf. My husband and I moved to my childhood hometown in western Nebraska. Within 18 months my father had nine surgeries and was diagnosed with cancer, my husband started a new job, and my grandfather had two major surgeries and ultimately died on January 19th, 2022. My grandfather and my husband were best friends, and my husband suffered a manic breakdown and relapsed after his death. Eight weeks after Grandpa died, my husband killed himself.

It was in writing my husband's obituary that I finally broke through my writer's block. That obituary was shared hundreds of times by my friends and his former students. Journaling became my escape and I started blogging again. My blogs now are primarily about middle-aged widowhood, grief, mental health, and complex emotional trauma (and now book publishing). My creativity returned and, since I was on sabbatical from real estate, I decided to set a deadline for myself to finish the first draft and publish my debut novel.

I still live in that tiny community near the border of Nebraska and Wyoming with my big lug of a dog, Ivy. My parents live about 10 minutes from me. My kids live in Chicago and the DC area.

I am so grateful for you taking the time to read *Behind the Wire*. Please follow me at AndreaMyersAuthor.com, @myerswrites on Instagram and Twitter, or Andrea Myers – Author on Facebook to stay in touch on my works in development and in-person or virtual events.

Afterword

In time I may share the story of my Grandfather and why a "sugar tramp kid" won the race he didn't know he was in to marry the "small town girl with the Hollywood looks". For now, just know that most of the personal details in *Behind the Wire* were a complete product of my imagination. Grandmother was incredibly private. I've taken many liberties beyond just changing her name. Most of the letters are word-for-word of what these men wrote to her. I treasure those letters that were so obviously read, and reread, time and time again, and then tied up with ribbon and hidden in a storage trunk to be discovered in 2017.

Countless movies, newsreels, websites, and books contributed to my research of the various prisoner of war camps throughout America during WWII. Camp Scottsbluff was dismantled at the end of the war and I've worked to piece together details from those stories.

Please visit the entire bibliography of those resources on my website www.andreamyersauthor.com for more information and links to more information if you'd like to go on a more historical deep dive.

Book Club Discussion Ideas

1. What stories have you found hidden away that inspire questions that you wish you could go back and ask your grandparents?

2. How do you feel about the idea of utilizing prisoners of war across the U.S. during WWII knowing that the Germans treated our prisoners much differently?

3. Would you have been okay with a POW camp in your town? If there was a camp in your town (there were nearly 700 across the country) what are some of the legends you've heard about that time?

4. If your parents or grandparents served in the military how did they cope, or not, with the mental health challenges that come from war?

5. If a war started today, would you be tempted to bring your kids home from college?

Made in the USA
Columbia, SC
24 February 2023

12911726R00224